THE LAST SUPPER

Rosemary Shrager

THE LAST SUPPER

C

CONSTABLE

CONSTABLE

First published in Great Britain in 2022 by Constable

1 3 5 7 9 10 8 6 4 2

A CIP catalogue record for this book
is available from the British Library.

ISBN: 978-1-47213-535-3 (hardcover)
ISBN: 978-1-47213-534-6 (trade paperback)

Typeset by Hewer Text UK Ltd, Edinburgh
Printed and bound in Great Britain by Clays Ltd, Elcograf S.p.A.

Papers used by Constable are from well-managed
forests and other responsible sources.

Constable
An imprint of
Little, Brown Book Group
Carmelite House
50 Victoria Embankment
London EC4Y 0DZ

An Hachette UK Company
www.hachette.co.uk

www.littlebrown.co.uk

To my grand-daughter, Suki

Chapter One

The Chelwood Ghyll Harvest Fayre was the most important date in the autumn calendar – and not only for the
residents of the little village of Chelwood Ghyll. For the
Very Green Gardeners' Circle of nearby Godshill it was
the society event of the season; for the Allotment
Association of Rockbourne Abbey, it was the year's star
attraction; for the various rivals of the Langley Marsh
Vegetable League it was the chance to win victories that
could be savoured all through the long year. For one
week in October, villagers from across the regions flocked
into the old equestrian centre outside of Chelwood Ghyll
and filled it with stalls, tents and tables where they
proudly showed off the various pumpkins, marrows,
turnips and parsnips from their autumn gardens. There
were cakes built in staggering tiers, beetroots stacked in a
wild variety of rich, deep colours, kegs of cloudy apple
cider made from the local orchards, and so much more
besides. But the biggest prize of all, the prize for which
every kitchen gardener and allotment enthusiast
hungered, was the Chelwood Cup, awarded each year to
the fayre's biggest pumpkin.

And each year, the prize was awarded by none other
than Prudence Bulstrode herself.

The Chelwood Ghyll Harvest Association hadn't been able to believe their luck when Prudence Bulstrode strode into their lives. The idea that Prudence Bulstrode – who, for years, the villagers had watched weekly on the BBC, leading them through wholesome family recipes in her succession of starry television shows – might be moving to their village had caused something of a stir. Of course, it was widely known that Prudence's daughter and her family lived in the neighbouring village of Netley Pike – the Kitchen Garden Crowd there always put up a fierce display at the Harvest Fayre – but, even so, the idea of a *celebrity* in their own sleepy village felt like a shooting star touching down on the village green. Prudence, it was said, was leaving the starry world of television cookery behind for a simpler life. She was done with parties and award shows, done with the glamorous book launches and exhibitions that had so far characterised her life. But, the Chelwood Ghyll Harvest Association wagered, she wouldn't be able to resist partaking in country life. She might have turned her back on the money and fame that London had given her for so many years, but she surely couldn't have turned her back on the passions that had first driven her into that life – the passion for food, for recipes from near and far away, and the passion for *sharing* that knowledge with the world. Yes, Prudence Bulstrode would be quite an addition to the festivals and fayres Chelwood Ghyll was proud to host each season – and so she had turned out to be.

There she was now, surrounded in a half-moon by hundreds of excited villagers. She was standing on a decking area in the shelter of the Harvest Fayre's biggest marquee, about to show them all how to make her famous, iconic raspberry roulade.

Prudence Bulstrode was a magnificent woman. Practically perfect in every way, her husband used to say (diligently pretending that he hadn't stolen the line from an old copy of *Mary Poppins*). At sixty-five years old, she had the appearance of somebody fifteen years younger, with the same round cherubic features she'd had since being a girl, her face always adorned with the same pair of glitzy, aquamarine spectacles that had become her signature look in the days she used to grace the television screen. Her dress was as flamboyant a design as she'd worn on her most outlandish television show – *Prudence's Voyages*, which took her as far away as Indonesia and Azerbaijan, looking for interesting flavours – and her wrists and neckline were adorned with strings of bright plastic beads, which she had always counted her favourite jewellery.

The members of the Chelwood Ghyll Harvest Association had been right. Prudence had grown tired of the London circuit, but a little step back into the limelight, on occasions like this, could work wonders for the soul. She adjusted her spectacles, looked out at the crowd, and felt that old, familiar frisson of expectation and excitement rippling through her. The ingredients laid out before her, the sparkle of light off an electric whisk, the young enthusiasts in the front row, poised with their pencil tips over their notebooks – all of it made her remember why she'd first set foot in the world of cookery.

3

'Ladies and gentlemen,' she began, 'let me take you into my kitchen!'

The crowd cheered and laughed. Those were the very words with which she used to introduce her most famous series, *Prudence's Home Bakes*. She still liked to roll them out on occasion. It gave her – and, more importantly, her audience – a thrill.

'Later today, I'll have the honour – third year running! – of judging all of your fabulous pumpkins, turnips, beetroot . . . and, this year, even a marvellous collection of rutabaga from a secret garden in Netley Pike. Naughty Mr Arkwright over there managed to keep that a secret all year long! But right now, well, let's get down to business, shall we? This recipe, as some of you already know – indeed, most of you, I suspect, since I see so many familiar faces here – has been my loyal and trustworthy companion in life. In fact, my relationship with this recipe lasted longer than my marriage to my dear departed Nicholas – and may God rest his soul in peace. It was this recipe, as I recount at almost every after-dinner speech I've ever given, that first took me on to the television screens to begin a new, whirlwind life. Forty years ago, I was demonstrating this recipe at a little fair in Southend-on-Sea, when a producer happened across me and said: "Darling, I think I like the look of your face."' Prudence grinned; she was used to telling this legend, and it had, of course, been embellished across the years – but she didn't have to embellish the words or tone of that television producer, because he'd always been as camp as Christmas, and Prudence loved

4

him for it. 'Now, I can't promise that this recipe will change your life like it changed mine. But it's simple and beautiful and, if you get it right, you'll never be in want of a quick, easy dessert again. Ladies and gentlemen, my . . . raspberry roulade!'

White fluffy cake, raspberries rendered until they were almost becoming a fresh coulis, a layer of pure crystalline meringue (which was Prudence's signature) and more whipped cream than a saintly man could contend with – what wasn't to like about a recipe as easy and indulgent as this?

Prudence was cracking the first eggs into her mixing bowl with one hand and dazzling her faithful whisk with the other when everything changed.

From somewhere beyond the crowd of faces eagerly watching her, there came the guttering roar of an engine. Prudence looked up, eggs and whisk still in hand, just in time to hear the first scream. Suddenly, the crowd was no longer watching her. Suddenly it was scissoring apart – and there, rumbling through the gap they'd left behind (with, mercifully, nobody getting hurt), came a camper van.

It was a brightly coloured camper van, the colour of a peach with cyan window frames and bedecked in floral bunting as if it had rolled directly out of the Woodstock festival in 1969. The engines, which had fired so suddenly, died away just as quickly – but, by now, the camper was already rolling unstoppably forward, pointed straight at Prudence herself. Caught in its headlights – there was a fault in the electrics and, so long as the engine was running, they never turned off – Prudence brandished her whisk. It was all that she had.

She looked up. People were shouting her name, telling her to run – but she could not take her eyes off the camper van. It was the strangest thing.

There was nobody at the wheel.

At the last moment, some hidden camber in the ground turned the camper's front wheels. Arcing past Prudence, it ploughed on parallel to the stage, picking up speed as it rolled down the hill toward the equestrian centre itself. The crowd, now that they were in no immediate danger, turned as one to watch the camper van go. Twice more its wheels hit some bump in the earth and turned; twice more, the camper van careened at some wild, unstoppable angle on its uncharted journey to the bottom of the hill . . .

. . . where it crashed directly into the stalls where all of the fayre's pumpkins, turnips, squashes (and rutabaga) were waiting to be judged.

Mrs Moriarty, who had been running the Chelwood Ghyll Harvest Fayre tombola for sixty-four of her seventy-six years, had narrowly avoided being flattened by the camper van – but she had not narrowly avoided being splattered with the remains of a dozen prize marrows. Now she stood there, dripping with the marrow innards, with a look on her face plucked directly out of a 1970s folk-horror movie.

Prudence thought it had been a narrow escape – more narrow, even, than the time the television executive with the famous 'wandering hands' had made a beeline for her at the Kitchen Pride Awards, held each year in Covent Garden. She staggered out of the marquee and stood at the top of the incline, watching the rest of the fayre attendees rushing to the scene of the drama. She could already hear various howls of rage and consternation from the keen kitchen gardeners who had dedicated their year to cultivating those vegetables in the hope of winning a prize. Now, all of their dedication and hard work was spread across poor Mrs Moriarty's face.

Prudence would have smiled at the vegetable-ridden horror of it all, if only her heart hadn't been sinking.

There was a very particular reason why Prudence's heart was sinking at that moment.

The camper van that had come careening past, seemingly with no driver at the wheel, had an exceedingly memorable numberplate.

It read PRUBU 1 – and it belonged to her.

'Left your handbrake off, did you, Mrs Bulstrode?' came the voice of some figure cantering past.

Prudence looked up and was about to exclaim, 'I most certainly did not!' when she saw that the figure loping past was none other than Constable Mick Hardman – who, it seemed, was the most senior officer on the scene. It was just a shame that he didn't yet need to shave and, Prudence was quite certain, still had his mother lay out his clothes for him every morning.

'Come on, Mrs Bulstrode, there'll be questions to answer here.'

It pained Prudence to leave her raspberry roulade behind, but that was nothing compared to the pain going on at the bottom of the hill. Hurrying after the constable, she found the camper van crowded with all of the fayre's many attendees. Some of the entrants in the competition were vainly trying to salvage their pumpkins. Old Mr Chesterfield was down on his hands and knees, wrestling carrot tops out from under the camper's front wheel.

'Yes,' Constable Hardman began, dutifully taking notes, 'PRUBU 1. It's definitely yours, Mrs Bulstrode.'

Prudence thought Constable Hardman was a very diligent young man – but also a verifiable buffoon, because it didn't take a close inspection of the number-plate to identify this camper van as belonging to Prudence Bulstrode. The sign on the side of it read PRUDENCE BULSTRODE'S TRAVELLING KITCHEN in florid red letters, expertly (and expensively) painted by an old signwriter who plied his trade out of Downton, just up the road. Prudence hadn't meant to take up a second profession in her retirement; five years ago, she'd wanted nothing more than to leave the celebrity circuit behind and spend a long, happy retirement with her husband, Nicholas. But Nicholas had passed away a little more than three weeks after they moved into Chelwood Ghyll – and all those ideas Prudence had had about the future had been disabused in a moment. The camper had been her escape from all that. A re-invention, which was just what was needed to keep away the nagging little voice that told her she should return to what she knew – the whirlwind of London, the parties, the televisual life.

Now it stood there, its bumper creamed with smashed-up pumpkins, and all of Chelwood Ghyll baying around it like a pitchforked horde.

'Stand back, ladies, stand back!' declared Constable Hardman. 'I need to establish a perimeter! A *perimeter*, ladies. Yes, please, Mrs Whiteley, you too. This is now a crime scene, ladies, and I simply must have control. There may yet be a dangerous felon inside this camper van, and it's my task – as your appointed protector – to flush him out.'

Constable Hardman was so determined to drive back the horde of curious villagers that he didn't see what Prudence saw: a rake-thin seventeen-year-old girl, with raven-black hair (a raven-black scalp as well, because she was so careless with the hair dye) and an unmistakable drunken stagger, rolling out from underneath the camper van, picking herself up and scrambling off across the equestrian centre, back into the village. Prudence watched her go with a single raised eyebrow and the heaviest of hearts.

Constable Hardman was still establishing his perimeter when Prudence, sighing wearily and still staring after the vanishing girl, said, 'That's enough of this nonsense! *I'll* check the interior, Constable!' – and, before the over-zealous policeman could put up a fuss, she opened the camper's sliding door, established that precisely nobody was inside, and shut it again.

'The keys are still in the ignition,' said the constable, appearing at her side. 'Mrs Bulstrode, are you absolutely certain you didn't leave the handbrake off?'

The eyes of the village were on Prudence. She thought about it, thought about it again, and said, 'Constable, you're barking up the wrong tree, I'm afraid. It's obviously a case of teenage vandalism.'

'In Chelwood Ghyll?'

'Why, we have teenagers in Chelwood Ghyll, don't we?'

Constable Hardman snapped to attention. 'Then it's settled. I'm afraid, Mrs Bulstrode, I'll have to send for back-up. The police tow truck will have to come up from Lyndhurst.'

'Tow truck?' gasped Prudence. 'Why, it's only a bit of marrow, Constable. There's a little turnip stuck in the bumper, that's all. She'll drive out of here easily enough. I can have her scrubbed up in no time.'

'I dare say you can, Mrs Bulstrode,' said Constable Hardman with a new sobriety, 'but I'm afraid I couldn't possibly let it happen. This, here, is a crime scene, you see. There'll be *forensics* all over it. Fingerprints and blood samples. Tiny, microscopic bits of DNA. You wouldn't believe the traces a human body leaves behind. If I told you some of the things we learned at the academy . . .'

Prudence resisted the temptation to say, *Then you'd be able to tell me how to buckle my own shoes,* and simply groaned instead.

'I'm sorry, Mrs Bulstrode. There's really nothing I can do. Let's just let the forensic boys do what they need to do. I'm sure you can have your camper back in – well, six, seven weeks, I should think?' He looked around. 'Ladies, gentlemen, I'm afraid, this year, the fayre has come to a premature close. Would one of you be kind enough as to give Mrs Bulstrode, here, a ride back into the village?'

There were a good number of offers. David Goliath – whose name was made even more unfortunate by the fact that he was quite the most diminutive man Prudence had ever known – was only too eager to give Prudence a ride in his motorcycle and sidecar ('And perhaps we could drop in at the Fox for a spot of dinner too? You owe me a dinner date, as I remember'), but Prudence was determined to walk. It was only a couple of miles back to her house on the other side of Chelwood Ghyll, and it would give her some time to think.

It took the best part of the first mile for Prudence to stop being infuriated by the situation. It took her the best of the next mile for her to figure out that, as accidental as this afternoon's events might have been, she wasn't going to be able to forget them. No – she was going to have to do something about it. The question was *what*.

Prudence lived in a little bungalow on the edge of Chelwood Ghyll: two bedrooms, a cosy living room, a kitchen where her wonderful Aga pumped out heat all winter long, and the entirety of her garden given over to greenhouses and cold frames, trellises and wigwams of garden canes to grow her beloved sweet peas. It was all Prudence had ever wanted. She and Nicholas could have spent a very happy retirement here – Nicholas, who used to set crosswords for the Sunday papers, content with his puzzle books, and Prudence content to spend endless afternoons out in her kitchen garden. Alas, it was not to be – and, consequently, no matter how much she still

11

loved the fayres and festivals she attended, Prudence was used to coming home to an empty, dark house.

Not today, though.

Today, as she turned along the winding lane that led down to her garden, she saw that the lights were on in the living room. The garden gate had been left open, and the plumes of steam coming out of the vent on the side of the house told her that somebody had put the central heating on.

Well, thought Prudence as she stopped on the garden path, her bracelets jangling – an apology counted for *something*.

She opened the front door.

'Grandma!'

The same rake-thin, raven-haired girl who had scrambled out from underneath Prudence's camper van threw herself across the hallway and dangled her arms around Prudence's shoulders. Prudence wasn't immune to expressions of love from her eldest grandchild, and she might almost have forgiven her there and then, if only the smell of cheap alcohol on the girl's breath hadn't been quite so pungent. It was the alcohol that reminded her that this was not a misdemeanour to be forgotten about; it was a situation that had to be dealt with *now*. The problem was, it wasn't the first time something like this had happened. It wasn't even the fourth, fifth, sixth, seventh or eighth.

'Suki,' she said, 'oh Suki, you silly girl. What on earth am I going to do with you?'

Prudence's grand-daughter slipped backwards and said, 'I've made a pot of tea – mint from the garden, just as you like it. I've laid it out in the lounge, Grandma. And I've—'

'You've joy-ridden my camper van into a field full of pumpkins, and ended up with it impounded by the police.'

'Impounded, Grandma?' Suki hiccoughed in horror.

'Yes, well, I've seen brighter ladybirds than I have police constables in this village. That Hardman's a do-gooder to a fault – so desperate to do things by the book that he starts making up chapters and adding appendices himself. Anally retentive, I'd say. I knew enough eager young people pleasers like him in London. But it is what it is. The camper's gone for forensics. I dare-say I'll get it back if I kick up a fuss – but there's still the question of you, my dear.' Suki's body flagged. 'Come through, Suki. You said you'd made tea?'

She'd taken care to lay it out as well. Prudence's lounge looked more like a book-lined study than the regular cosy sitting room ordinarily associated with somebody of her age, and in its centre was an old wooden coffee table, one of the first wedding gifts she and Nicholas had received. On top of it, among the various wildflower books and garden glossaries Prudence had been perusing last night, was a china tea set, a bowl of brown sugar lumps, a strainer and a samovar of boiled water. Suki had dug out the short-bread too. Prudence was partial to a piece of shortbread.

'I'll pour. Sit down, Suki.'

So that was what Suki did.

After she had poured the teas, Prudence said, 'It's going to take more than a pot of fresh mint tea to sober you up, Suki. Wait there, I've just the thing.'

Among all the books on Prudence's shelves was a clothbound, tattered old tome called *Hedgerow Magic*. Following one of its well-thumbed recipes (Nicholas had been partial to a drink as well), Prudence mixed fennel seeds and turmeric, pulverised ginger root and dandelion from the garden and served Suki a concoction that, though it didn't taste bad, was quite the most unusual thing she'd ever sipped.

Then, flopping on to the sofa, Prudence said, 'Oh, Suki, what are we going to do with you? How many times have you turned up on my doorstep in this state? How many times have I helped you hide it from Ted and Rose?' Rose was Prudence's daughter, and Teddy her husband; he'd once played cricket for his county, and now coached at the local schools. Their ten-year-old son George was a promising batsman; Prudence often thought that, if only Suki had had a passion like that, she might have stayed out of trouble. 'Why did you take the camper, Suki? *My* camper.'

Prudence wasn't being unkind, but her exasperation was only too clear.

'It was Numbers who told me—'

'*Numbers?*'

'He's my friend, Grandma. The tall one. The ginger hair. The freckles. You've met him.'

'Ah, I think you mean Anthony.'

'We call him Numbers – he was doing a Mathematics degree, remember? He went up to Oxford.'

'And dropped out, as I remember.' Prudence paused. 'But he seemed such a sensible boy. Almost the only one

14

of your "friends" . . .' She was hesitant to use the word, because it seemed to Prudence that friends didn't ordinarily goad you into derailing your entire existence, '. . . who isn't smoking some funny cigarette or drinking down by the stream every night.'

'Oh, he didn't tell me to start the engine, Grandma. He told me I should go into your camper, just to sleep it off. Numbers is teetotal. A proper straight edge. He knew I'd had a tipple too many, so he thought I should crash out, just for a while.'

Prudence raised her knowing eyebrow. 'And . . .?'

'And I was going to, Grandma, honest I was. But your keys were in the ignition and I thought – well, I'd rather sleep in my own bed than in the back of your camper, lovely and comfortable as it is. So I thought – well, it isn't far home, is it? It's even closer if I drive. And, well . . . you know the rest.'

Suki slumped down on the sofa. Her shame was palpable. But it always was, thought Prudence.

'I didn't mean to cause a scene, Grandma. I promise I didn't. And I'm going to get myself straightened out – and if there's any damage, well, I'll pay for it. I don't know how, but I will. I'll clean your kitchen for a week. No, a month! I'll muck out your chickens and fox-proof the fences. I'll spit shine your shoes, Grandma. Just, *please*, *please* don't tell Mum and Dad. Just this once . . .'

She'd heard 'just this once' before.

'I don't know, Suki. I really don't. If I keep covering for you, then how are you ever going to—'

It was at that moment that the telephone rang – and Suki, seizing the opportunity to do something for her grandmother and prove just how much of a good girl she could be, leapt to her feet, tumbled across the lounge, and whipped the receiver to her ear. 'Bulstrode residence,' she said. 'Prudence's phone. How may I help you?'

Prudence watched with amused silence. She'd had plenty of assistants in her life – at the television shows, at the exhibitions, even, sometimes, on the private-chef requests she travelled to in her beloved camper – but few of them had shown the desperation to please that Suki was showing in this moment.

Few of them had gone as ghostly white as Suki went then. Few of them had had their jaws drop open, or turned to Prudence with a look of such surprise.

Moments later, Suki covered the mouthpiece and said to Prudence, 'Grandma, have you ever heard of a woman called Deirdre Shaw? A man here says she was an old friend of yours?'

Prudence had to stifle a laugh. She'd heard of Deirdre Shaw, all right. So had half of England! Deirdre Shaw was a darling of the cookery circuit. A doyenne of the foodie world. A darling of the establishment. She was the one who coined the phrase, 'you need to knead!' and 'the proof is in the proving' in her afternoon bakery show, *Right Said Bread!* It was Deirdre who'd beaten her to the pinch to co-host *The Big British Bake-a-Thon* just before she retired; that show had thrust Deirdre back into the limelight at exactly the same moment that Prudence herself exited the stage. Yes, half of the country knew who Deirdre Shaw was. But these young children today, they just didn't know their stars. If they weren't on YouTube or Instagram, with a jaunty theme tune and some stylish camera angles, jabbering into the camera as if they were God's gift, people didn't have any idea. It wasn't like it used to be – back when celebrity was something you *earned*, not something you *were*.

'Of course I have!' Prudence laughed. 'That's her, is it? What's she calling me for?'

'No Grandma,' said Suki, 'it isn't her at all.' Her face still white as a ghost. 'Grandma, I think you'd better take the phone. Deirdre Shaw – she's just dropped dead.'

Chapter Two

Prudence put the telephone down, her face now white as a ghost too.

It had only been half an hour since the telephone rang, but when she looked over her shoulder, she saw that, somewhere in the middle of the conversation, Suki's indiscretions had caught up with her. She was now lolling on the sofa in the bay window, the tasselled throw pulled down like a blanket, in a sleep so deep she might have been dead – if only it weren't for the suckling sounds she was making, her thumb planted firmly in her mouth. She was seventeen years old, but she'd been doing that since she was a baby.

Prudence paced.

She paced some more.

An autumnal dusk was settling over Chelwood Ghyll. Prudence could feel the chill. She resolved that another pot of tea was the only thing that would restore her – and, this time, she laced it with honey from the hive at the bottom of the garden. After news like this, she deserved a little pick-me-up. Nicholas would have mixed her one of his cocktails, but Prudence hadn't had a taste for them since he was gone. The honey, which was sweet with comfrey and borage, would have to do.

She had no doubt the obituaries would be in tomorrow's newspapers. Deirdre Shaw had been what they called a 'national treasure'. Children had grown up baking her jam tarts and Yule logs, then shown their own children how to make them. Her television shows had been fixtures in the country's calendar. She'd been the nation's grandmother. The kingdom's favourite aunt. There'd been thousands of bake sales named after her – and, one year, back in her pomp, the Deirdre Shaw Forever Bake-a-thon had dominated the school lives of ten thousand children all summer long, as schools across the nation came together to break a world record, baking fairy cakes to cure cancer. It hadn't worked, of course. Cancer wasn't cured by little fondants and French fancies. But it had captured the country's imagination, that was for sure. 'National treasure' was one of those terms most people awarded it didn't really deserve, but Deirdre Shaw had as good a claim as any. That was, if you ignored the whispers about her private life, the trail of ruined marriages she'd left behind her.

And now she was dead.

Nicholas's old study was set in a side room leading off the lounge. Prudence didn't often venture in there any more. She liked to leave it *just so*, which was exactly how Nicholas had liked it too. Sometimes, she thought she could still catch the whiff of his old aftershave in the air. She'd deliberately left his teacup on its coaster at the edge of his desk.

She'd deliberately not touched his computer too. Not that this was driven by the heartbreak of it. No, Prudence hadn't touched his computer because she couldn't stand the damn thing. All the tapping and beeping and whirring and boxes popping up with little 'notifications' all over the place. Prudence was glad that technology had happened – she'd be nothing if it wasn't for her electric egg whisk – but, if she had to answer a single 'email' again, it would all be too much.

Even so, she turned on the computer.

It was an ancient machine, so it took an aeon to start. Computers, it seemed, were like human bodies; they got slow and crotchety in their dotage as well. She was still sitting there, moving the little mouse thing about and trying to click on the 'browser' while a dozen other boxes popped up, when she sensed movement in the door – and looked up to see Suki standing there, half-zombified, with the tasselled throw still wrapped around her.

'Grandma?'

'Just in time, darling. Sit down here – you can start paying me back for all this trouble.'

Before she knew what she was doing, Suki had taken Prudence's place at the computer, opened up the web browser, and plugged the name 'Deirdre Shaw' into the search engine.

'There we go,' said Prudence, when one of the national newspapers' websites popped up. 'That's her. You wouldn't call her glamorous, of course, but Deirdre Shaw never was. She didn't need glamour, because she knew about hot cross buns.'

DEIRDRE DROPS DEAD!
A TWIST IN THE TALE OF
GREAT BRITAIN'S BEST LOVED BAKER

'Deirdre died doing the thing she loved most in the world –
rooting around in a kitchen garden,' says Harriet Bourdain-
Black, Deirdre's agent of forty-five years.

'That one,' said Prudence. 'Press on that one.'

'Press, Grandma?' Suki hovered the mouse over the headline. 'I think you mean . . . click?'

'Yes, well, clickety-click,' said Prudence. Lord, it was bad enough that these children stole your camper van and ruined your event without them lording it over you because they knew more about these little . . . widgets. 'Let's have a read of what it says.'

Deirdre Shaw, familiar to generations of television viewers from her wide and varied work across the BBC and ITV in the 1980s and 1990s – and to a new generation of viewers as the prize judge on Channel 4's *Big British Bake-a-Thon* – died suddenly this afternoon, her agent Harriet Bourdain-Black has confirmed. Shaw had accepted a private commission to cater a long weekend at Farleigh Manor, just outside the village of Nutwood St Knowle, and was reported to have been discovered in the manor's kitchen garden by the estate gamekeeper, Hubert Lowell, who has been with the estate since 1969. A local source is reported to have said, 'Mr Lowell's a rum chap. Gamekeepers are used to finding dead things. But you don't expect to find one of television's dearest stars, the nation's grandmother no less, face down in the rhubarb patch.

Something like that's got to sting. He won't have been expecting it.'

Although the local constabulary were called to Farleigh Manor, no foul play is suspected, and the local coroner is expected to formalise an announcement of death by natural causes this week. It is understood that Ms Shaw may have lain dead in the manor gardens for up to two hours before the alarm was raised. By the time emergency services attended the scene, she was already beyond resuscitation.

According to Shaw's agent, Deirdre had been suffering, for some time, with the effects of heart disease and an angina that doctors assured her was mild. 'Deirdre lived life at its fullest and has been taken from us too soon. I'm quite sure that she's up there in Heaven, right now, cooking up a storm for all of those who went before her.'

She is survived by a younger sister, Penelope, three ex-husbands, and three daughters.

Suki looked up. 'Dead in the rhubarb patch. But, Grandma, what's it got to do with you?'

Prudence returned to her sitting room and started browsing the shelves stuffed with books. After some time, she located one of the earliest Deirdre Shaws, *Big Fat Bakes,* and opened it to the colour prints in the centre. There was Deirdre's round, baby face staring back out. 'People used to make out like we were rivals,' said Prudence, casting her mind back in time. 'The truth was, there wasn't any hope of rivalry in it! Deirdre *always* had the edge on me. The camera loved her.'

Suki was still trembling – Prudence dreaded to think

what was still working its way through her bloodstream – when she too fingered the page. 'She's hardly Instagrammable, Grandma.'

Prudence, who had no idea what this meant, said, 'There was something about her, something the producers loved. Her ruddy red cheeks. Her North Country brogue. She just *had* it.'

'You had it too, Grandma.'

Prudence was quite certain Suki hadn't watched a single show of hers over the years, but she appreciated the kindness, nevertheless. 'Not like Deirdre. Oh, I could dazzle them with a kitchen knife and a cake breaker, but Deirdre was a part of the family. They felt like they could share their *secrets* with her. The truth is, Suki, I'd hardly have got to where I did without Deirdre – if she hadn't have turned down *Hey, Good Cookin'!* in 1985, I'd never have got my break. And, point of fact, you wouldn't even be alive.'

Suki screwed her eyes up. 'Grandma?'

'Well, I met your grandfather on set.' She paused, flicking through more pictures in a wistful manner. 'After that, I often got things Deirdre had turned down. It was half of my career – playing second fiddle to Deirdre Shaw. And now . . .'

'Now what?'

'Well,' said Prudence, and snapped the book shut, 'now they're at it again. Suki, I've been invited to take Deirdre's place at Farleigh Manor.'

Suki said, 'Oh.'

'Well, you didn't think it was just a courtesy call, did

you? Now, I wouldn't put it past my old agents to spin that sort of a line on me. "Pru," they'd say – "Pru, *now's* your chance! Deirdre's out of the picture – and you can shine! Imagine the work that's coming your way, Pru. Imagine the numbers!"' Prudence rolled her eyes in mock theatricality. 'That's what they're like in the celebrity world, you know. Some old dear doesn't have to be cold in the ground before they're squabbling over who's going to lap up what gets left behind. It's part of the reason I left London for Chelwood Ghyll in the first place.' Prudence realised she was rambling, and purposefully brought herself back on course. 'The man you spoke to on the phone was a gentleman named Rupert Prendergast. He's hosting a get together out at Farleigh Manor – a shooting weekend, I'm given to understand – and he'd hired Deirdre to give his guests the greatest banquet they've ever had.' Prudence smiled. She could quite imagine this Prendergast fellow – he obviously had riches (he'd have to be wealthy to hire Deirdre Shaw – now, *there* was a woman who knew the price of a loaf of bread), and he obviously had the desire to impress. He'd been caught quite on the hoof, and now he'd come knocking.

'How did they know to call you, Grandma?'

'I imagine there's a directory somewhere: if you can't get Deirdre Shaw, well, Prudence Bulstrode's your gal!' She paused. 'They want me there by lunchtime tomorrow – which means hitting the road with the dawn. This Farleigh Manor's up in the Cotswolds, and I'll need time to prep things too. Deirdre only got to serve one evening meal for them before she passed on, so I'll have to hit the ground running. Which rather brings us to the sticky matter of my camper van . . .'

Suki, whose face had already been pale, was suddenly green. The hangover was hitting her, it seemed, even while she was still under the influence of whatever cheap newsagent vodka she'd been chugging back.

'Grandma, I'm—'

Prudence clapped her hands, slipped the book back on its shelf, and declared, 'No more apologies! Apologies don't get the cake baked on time. Apologies don't season the salmon. It's rolling your sleeves up and getting your fingers dirty that gets things done.' She stopped. A playful smile was twitching in the corner of Prudence's lips, because the idea that had occurred to her the moment she put the phone down from Rupert Prendergast was about to come to fruition. 'Suki, what you did today crossed a new line – even for you. But I'm your grandmother and I love you – and I'm happy to keep the truth of the matter between us . . .'

Suki's greenness was suddenly fading. 'Oh, thank you Grandma!' she cried out, and hung herself around Prudence's neck.

'. . . *if* you do a little something for me,' Prudence concluded.

Now the reality of the situation seemed to sink in to Suki. She recoiled a little, considering Prudence with screwed-up eyes. Her grandmother was really too knowing and canny for her own good. You could get mixed up sometimes – you thought she was just pink peppercorn shortbread and raspberry roulades – but in Prudence Bulstrode there were hidden depths.

'First,' announced Prudence, 'is that you stop this reckless drinking, once and for all. You'll come to know, my girl, that one of the finest delights in life is a strawberry and banana daiquiri, or a Manhattan Mojito made with sprigs of chocolate mint – but, as for convenience-store vodka and Lightning Bolt cider, two pounds a bottle, you've had your last drink. Do you understand me?'

Suki looked green at the gills at the mere mention of the words. She nodded in agreement.

'And second,' Prudence went on, flourishing another finger, 'and most importantly, I'm going to need an assistant for a job like this. Now, I've had plenty of assistants in my time – some exemplary, and some who could no more wipe their own posteriors than they could make a simple remoulade. I daresay you'll be somewhere between the two – and, with as little time as we have, we'll just have to make it work. You'll keep your wits about you, do everything *precisely* as I ask – and you'll be grateful for the chance to prove yourself as diligent and trustworthy as I know you can be. Well, Suki, how does that sound?'

It sounded, thought Suki, like a whirlwind. And it looked, by the smile on Prudence's face and the light in her eyes, like a trap that had been sprung to pinpoint perfection.

'College doesn't start until Monday, does it?' said Prudence. 'Better to put the time to good use rather than waste it with these layabout friends of yours, wouldn't you say?' She didn't wait for Suki to reply before, warmly, she said, 'Get yourself home, Suki. I've got some phone calls to make – to try and excavate my camper. Get yourself in a long, hot bath. Sweat all this *silliness* out of you. And get a good meal inside you tonight. You're going to need some good ballast. I'll make sandwiches for the journey. I'll rustle up some angel cakes as well. Well, I had the baking itch today, and I didn't get to scratch it.' With an arm around Suki's shoulder, she guided her to the door. 'No dillying and no dallying, Suki. I'll be with you when the cockerel crows.'

Chapter Three

Farleigh Manor appeared through the trees.

It was exactly as Prudence had expected. She'd visited enough places like this in her television career – there was no better place for an out-of-studio shoot – and many more since she'd begun trading as 'Prudence Bulstrode's Travelling Kitchen', to have had a vivid idea of it in her mind, even as she drove into Netley Pike before dawn that morning to find Suki standing shivering on the doorstep, a suitcase at her side. Now, as the camper van rattled through the manor house's extensive grounds, she saw that she was right.

Not quite upper crust enough to qualify as true National Trust, Farleigh Manor nevertheless had that esteemed air about it. The manor house itself – a gorgeous nineteenth-century edifice crowned with brick turrets and a single fairy-tale tower – appeared above extensive lawns, peppered with the stubs of an old garden maze and a marble gazebo. The track leading up to it was lined with perfectly manicured banks of burgundy roses. As the camper van followed the zigzagging track, Prudence tried to pick out the brick archway leading into the manor house orchard, the low stone walls that surrounded its fabulous kitchen garden. Meanwhile, Suki's face was buried in the iPhone she kept in her lap, its white wire jacked into the camper van's dashboard.

'Says here it was built in 1806,' said Suki, 'but the last of the Farleighs died in the seventies. Now it's owned by . . .'

Prudence rolled her eyes. 'You'll learn more by looking up, dear.'

'I'm on Wikipedia, Grandma. It has its own page.'

'I daresay it does – but you don't learn what a lemon tastes like by reading, sweetheart. No, you sink your teeth in and scrunch up your eyes and suck up all that lemony—'

'Why would I want to suck a lemon, Grandma?'

Prudence could see that she wasn't quite penetrating Suki's seventeen-year-old mind. No matter – it was probably the after effects of all of yesterday's indulgences. She reached across and patted her grand-daughter on the knee. 'Put the phone away, darling.'

In that same moment, the phone gave an infuriating trill and started leaping about – too violently, Prudence decided – in Suki's lap. Suki was fumbling it up to read whatever message had just landed when Prudence repeated, more firmly, 'You don't need that silly thing, Suki. That's what this weekend is for. It's going to be me and you – grandmother and grand-daughter, and nothing but some good old-fashioned knife skills. Trust me – you'll come away from this weekend filled to the brim with all the new things you've learned. I'll have you slicing and dicing. You'll be plucking and deboning. I daresay you'll know a few things your mother doesn't know

– about choux and sugar and, if I have my way, a consommé or two. What is it with you young people and these . . . *things?*' She said the word like it was the most unutterable curse on the planet. 'You need to learn to *do*, my dear. These phones make you think there's a world out there you're missing out on. But what you need to see is there's a world right *here*, right in front of you – and that's what you're *really* missing.'

Suki handled her iPhone forlornly. The camper van had nearly reached the manor.

'It's only a message from Numbers, Grandma.'

'*Numbers?*' Prudence said, with horror.

'He's the good one, Grandma. Remember? It really wasn't his fault, what I did with the camper. He thinks this trip is a good idea too. Look – he's been digging up some information on Farleigh Manor for us. He's sent it over.'

'The less said about your "friend" Numbers the better, darling. Pop the phone away now. We're almost here.'

In front of Farleigh Manor was a great gravelled horse-shoe, where a bank of cars were lined up – and expensive ones at that; Prudence saw at least one Mercedes and what she was certain was a midlife-crisis level sports car sitting by the conservatory doors. By the time she'd found a spot for the camper van – it looked surreally out of place among the guest vehicles, but at least nobody would ever confuse this Rupert Prendergast's guests with the hired help – the front doors of the manor had opened and a lean, fidgety woman with the appearance of a shrew had appeared to welcome them. Prudence watched her anxiously waiting for them to disembark and fancied she'd been standing by the manor house windows all morning, fussing with the curtains and looking out for any signs of their arrival. Not one of the guests, then. This woman was clearly from the manor house staff – and, without Deirdre Shaw busying herself in the kitchen, the responsibility for the success of the weekend had fallen to her. Poor woman, thought Prudence with a smile she tried very hard to disguise, she obviously wasn't used to dramas like this. She should have worked in television. Cancellations, substitutions – and even the odd unexpected death – were practically par for the course in Prudence's old world.

As she unstrapped herself, she could see that Suki was still holding on to her phone – though at least she'd crammed it, along with her hand, into her jeans pocket.

'You can learn all we need to learn about Farleigh Manor from the manor itself, Suki. And, look, here's the staff to tell us everything else. The only thing we *really* need to know is what poor Deirdre had planned for the catering this weekend. We'll have to hit the ground running if we're to save it. A simple dinner tonight with whatever's in the larder. Then we can get thinking about tomorrow. We'll have to use all our guile if we're to make this a success. And . . .' Prudence paused, already stepping out of the van, 'I'd like to think we can improve on whatever poor Deirdre left behind, don't you?'

Possibly it was petty, thought Prudence, but she'd spent many long years playing second fiddle to Deirdre Shaw on the old circuit. Whatever the old bird had planned for the guests at Farleigh Manor, Prudence was sure she could add a little glamour to it. Deirdre didn't do glamour, but Prudence had never seen what was so bad about sprinkling a little *pizazz* over a dish.

The moment Prudence stepped out of the camper van, the shrew-like woman standing in the manor house doors scurried over, her arms flapping like a fledgling bird. Apparently this woman couldn't make up her mind what kind of flighty, panicking animal she was trying to be.

'Mrs Bulstrode?' she asked, in a breathy, anxiety-ridden voice. 'Oh, I don't know why I'm asking! Of course it's *you*. It just seems so frightful not to introduce oneself – and there you are, not needing any introduction at all. Mrs Bulstrode, Prudence – can I call you Pru? – I'm Genevieve Mathers. I'm the . . . housekeeper here. And I can't tell you how glad I am to see your face. Oh, you look just like you did on the television!'

It always surprised Prudence when people said this. Of course she looked the same as she did on the television. It was the same face.

'Mrs Mathers,' she said, 'we came as quickly as we could. This is Suki. She's going to be my kitchen prep for the weekend.'

'Yes, yes,' said Mrs Mathers, and now she had grabbed both Prudence and Suki by the hands and was shaking them effervescently, 'well, you'll need all the help you can get. It's been a dreadful business. A dreadful business! And here was I thinking that having the old Prendergast crowd back in the manor after all these years – and with

32

a famous chef running the show, no less – was going to be a doddle. Do you know, I even thought I might be able to put my feet up. But there's been none of that. None of that!' She stopped, but only because she'd been blathering so fiercely that she had to catch breath. 'But here you are,' she gasped, with such relief on her face that it quite contorted every feature. 'The cavalry have arrived. The saints have come marching in. Come on, I'll show you around.'

As Mrs Mathers turned to lead them within, Prudence and Suki shared a wry look.

'Baptism of fire,' Prudence grinned – and then they walked in.

The insides of Farleigh Manor were quite as exquisite as its outside surrounds. On the ground floor, the front of the house was dominated by a broad, sweeping drawing room with twin hearths, which looked out over the manor's extensive grounds. In the rear lay the billiards room – preserved since its nineteenth-century heyday – and the library (the last of the Farleighs, who had lived here childless, was said to have devoted his life to his studies, and filled the shelves here with a century of knowledge). There were two separate sitting rooms, one great dining hall, and a chamber that Mrs Mathers called 'the nook'. 'The Lord and Lady of the manor used to take turns to nap in here on an afternoon. It would have been such a great den for some children. But there haven't been children at Farleigh Manor ever since . . . oh, well, it's been almost one hundred and fifty years. Time marches on. I'll show you to the kitchens last – but first, your room . . .'

The manor house was replete with staircases, each of them leading to different wings of the building. The south-facing wing, which overlooked the kitchen gardens and old greenhouses, had traditionally been the servants' quarters, and consequently the rooms here were smaller than they were in the north-facing wing, where Rupert Prendergast and his coterie of guests were now staying. The two wings had once been completely distinct, but a refurbishment in the second half of the nineteenth century had connected them by another higgledy-piggledy staircase, which spiralled first on to an attic landing and then down again into the opposite wing. 'They did it for the nanny,' Mrs Mathers explained. 'The nursery was in the Farleighs' wing, but they couldn't possibly have the hired help sleeping among them – so they tucked her in here. It's where you'll be sleeping. Well, it's the biggest room in this part of the manor. You'll be quite comfortable here . . .'

Mrs Mathers opened a heavy oaken door and showed them through.

Prudence was quite sure she'd be comfortable here. She'd slept in a good number of hotels in her life, including downtrodden fleapits in Jakarta – where she'd gone to film a television special on the fabulous Spice Islands – and luxurious five-star resorts in the Maldives. The only thing, she'd discovered, that mattered was the quality of sleep – and the beds here looked comfortable enough. There were two of them, single cots with barely a sliver of floor space between them, and beyond them an arched window looking down over the greenhouse roofs. If this was the largest room in the old servants' quarters, Prudence thought, she'd hate to think where the chambermaids used to sleep. Probably the cupboards underneath the stairs.

The look on Suki's face was a picture. Like Prudence, she'd seen the two beds and, after a faltering silence, made the correct conclusion that, for the next few nights, she wouldn't only be working in the kitchen with her grandmother, but sleeping in the same room as her as well.

'I'll bring your bags up,' said Mrs Mathers, 'and then I can show you the kitchens. How does that sound?'

Prudence, who had seen all that she needed to see, said, 'I think, perhaps, the kitchens first. There's scarcely an hour before lunch . . .'

'Oh, you don't need to worry about that. The party's out on a shoot until mid-afternoon. They won't need feeding until dinner.'

'That,' said Prudence with a smart clap of the hands, 'is exactly my point. There's scarcely an hour before lunch . . . so, as any good cook would know, it's time to start thinking about dinner. Suki?'

Suki, who was still staring ashen-faced at the beds and wondering what *old lady snoring* might sound like, glanced furtively at a door that led into a cramped washroom and said, 'I think I might get cleaned up first, Grandma. I'm feeling a little . . .'

She didn't finish that sentence. Prudence was giving her a withering look so she added, 'I'll be down straight away, Grandma. I promise. You can count on me.'

But, as Prudence followed Mrs Mathers back out of the door, the two older women shared a conspiratorial look. *Not like in my day*, each seemed to be saying to the other.

And then they were off, back through the higgledy-piggledy house to set about their business.

Suki could have screamed. The washroom was tiny, and the basin tinier still, but there was a bathtub and she turned the taps on full blast – they guttered and choked before they started sputtering out hot water – and upended the fragrant salts from the counter, filling the air with a sweet pomegranate smell. A hot bath would calm her down. It would have to.

There was something else that would calm her down too. As she was waiting, she perched on the edge of the toilet and produced her iPhone, clutching it until it came back to life. No way was she spending a whole long weekend cut off from the world. Her grandmother could scold her all she wanted and talk about what it was like in the good old days, but Suki didn't think the good old days were cut out for much, really. You needed *connection* in this world.

She lifted her iPhone.

To get connection, you needed *a* connection – and her signal was miserably weak. She stood up, held the phone high, scurried out to the window and waved it about frantically, trying to get a stronger signal. But it was all to no avail. Eventually, accepting defeat, she sunk into the bath and, half subsumed by foam bubbles, scrolled through whatever had been on her phone in the first place.

That was when she saw the message from Numbers.

Suki, DARLING. Be good this weekend – and, if you can't be good, be SECRET. Remember to say Yes Chef, No Chef. Maximum respect in the kitchen, GORGEOUS. Been doing some digging and you won't believe the stories about Farleigh. Follow the link – and let me know if you see ghosts. Better sleep with the light on, GIRLFRIEND!

Well, that was enough to give Suki the shivers, even lounging up to her neck in a scalding hot bath as she was. She hardly wanted to click on the link Numbers had sent, but she had never been very good with temptation. In a roundabout fashion, that was exactly why she'd found herself shanghaied off to accompany her grandmother on one of her cooking missions. So she picked herself up, swished the bubbles away from her face, and followed the link.

Luckily the signal held out long enough for a Wikipedia entry for Farleigh Manor to open up. Numbers' link had taken her directly to a section entitled THE DEATH OF JANE SUTCLIFFE.

Jane Sutcliffe, born 1862, nr Salisbury, was first appointed nursemaid by the elder Farleighs in 1883, and took into her care the two Farleigh twins, Jack and Mary, who were at that time six years old. Three years later, on a bright summer's day in the August of 1886, Jane Sutcliffe planned a picnic for the two children at the banks of Hill Beck, the offshoot of the River Eye, which runs through the Farleigh estate. Soon after the picnic began, Jack Farleigh reappeared at the manor house and raised an alarm. Upon being escorted by Jack to the site of the picnic, the estate housekeeper discovered Miss Sutcliffe lying in the running waters of the beck. She was pronounced dead at the scene.

According to the Farleigh twins, Miss Sutcliffe had been encouraging them to paddle in the beck's waters when she slipped and hit her head – and the children, despite their efforts, had been unable to pull her out of the water in time. Yet the suspicions of a local constable soon raised doubts about this sequence of events and, some weeks later, a police detective from London's Scotland Yard was dispatched to investigate this parochial incident as a potential murder. Though a proper case was never established, it was widely reported in the press of the time that Jane Sutcliffe had inspired both the admiration of Lord Farleigh and the indignation of the Farleigh children – who were often rebuked by Sutcliffe and considered her a far more brutish nanny than those their parents had hitherto employed. Tabloid rumour quickly focused on the moment, two nights previously, that the children had been chastised and sent to bed without supper – and how this had prompted them to commit a most unusual murder, by pushing their nanny to her death in Hill Beck. However, detectives could not reliably establish the facts of the matter and charges were never filed. The Farleigh twins always maintained their innocence, and would maintain it for the rest of their lives.

The stigma of the accusations never left Jack and Mary Farleigh, who lived together at Farleigh Manor until their deaths, two months apart, in the autumn of 1971. Without any heirs to leave the manor house to, the Farleigh estate was acquired by a Zurich-based hedge fund and transformed into a country retreat, in which field it operates to this day.

The death of Jane Sutcliffe remains unsolved. For more information see . . .'

Suki flicked through her phone and dialled Numbers. When he did not pick up, she hammered out a message:

Thanks a billion. It's bad enough I have to learn about giblets this weekend. Now I have to think about ghosts.

Moments later, the phone buzzed back.

You never know, GORGEOUS. You might solve a murder or two this weekend. Ta-ta for now! XXX

Suki tossed the phone over the edge of the bath and sunk into the warm, loving bubbles.

Prudence enjoyed a kitchen like this. The masters of Farleigh Manor must have once enjoyed daily banquets because a kitchen of this size – populated with this many ranges, warming ovens and countertops where food could be prepared – could have been designed for nothing else. She waltzed through it, opening cupboards and rattling pans, breathing in the scent of the place, and turned back to Mrs Mathers, who had been hovering in the door.

'Well, time to get to work.'

She could feel the familiar buzz that always came at the start of a new job. The unfamiliarity of the kitchen always excited her. It was, she had once said – with barely a hint of a joke about it – like conquering her own personal Matterhorn. To get the best out of a kitchen she did not know, to read the runes and treat an alien oven with the respect it deserved, was a challenge she had come to relish after a long career on the road. But she had the feeling that this particular kitchen was going to be kind to her. It was bright and light, and there was so much space that she was quite sure Suki wasn't going to get under her feet.

'The larder's through here,' said Mrs Mathers, nervously leading her through the kitchen to a vast storage chamber at the end. 'The pheasants hanging up there –' a double brace of them were dangling, in death, from a hook, '– were shot on the first day of the shoot.

That would be the day before yesterday. If you want to know what she was going to do with them, her menu's up on the board. It's all her own concoction, of course, so I don't think Mr Prendergast would mind if you wanted to change things. The important thing is, Mr Prendergast makes a big point of the guests eating the birds they've shot themselves. It's a badge of honour. So you'll find them tagged with names. Well, it's a funny custom, but it's theirs. They've been doing it for years and years. It was the same every time they came, but this is the first they've been back in, well, eight years I should think.'

Prudence, who had been busy browsing the well-stocked shelves, looked up, at once, to see the paper that had been pinned to the wall. On it, in Deirdre Shaw's perfectly sculpted handwriting, was a full menu for all five days of the shooting 'weekend', beginning with last Wednesday when the party had arrived and ending on this upcoming Sunday night. Prudence could see the little ticks marked against the first day's meals:

11 a.m. Welcome brunch. Pork & leek sausage, sourdough toast, tomato and mustard chutneys
6 p.m. Dinner. Braised wood pigeon with cider apple sauce; dessert – raspberry roulade.

Prudence raised one quizzical eyebrow. Raspberry roulade? Well, it seemed as if Deirdre Shaw might have had a tiny little bit of envy for Prudence Bulstrode as

41

well ... Perhaps their rivalry hadn't been entirely one-sided.

She scanned the rest of the menu. It was classic Deirdre fare, if tarted up for her rarefied clientele. There was fresh sea bream with samphire; blackberry and bay leaf pavlova; even Deirdre's famous Scotch egg – which had been the talk of every newspaper in Great Britain twenty-five years ago. Those were simpler, better times, thought Prudence. You'd need to have baked a Scotch egg on board a satellite, then served it up in zero gravity to a coterie of reality TV stars to cause a ripple in today's cookery world.

Of course, she already knew that she had little desire to replicate Deirdre's menu in its entirety. It wasn't that there was anything wrong with it; it was that it belonged to Deirdre, and no other cook could hope to do it justice. You just couldn't, not if your heart wasn't in it. So, item by item, she took stock of the larder, allowing her subconscious to put together different combinations, to dream up different menus, to slide together different tastes and sensations until she lit upon something she liked.

Thinking on the hoof like this made her feel younger. It made her feel more alive.

'There's the garden, too,' said Prudence, as they came out of the larder. 'Herbs and winter vegetables and so forth?'

'Of course,' said Mrs Mathers. 'It's right this way.'

Back doors opened out into the kitchen garden, where the greenhouses were still full and, under banks of cold frames, chicory and endives, celery and the last of the summer tomatoes were in bright colour. A great pumpkin patch dominated one side of the garden, great balls of orange and deeper orange cascading on their vines from what appeared to be a huge compost heap. Through the brick archway, the trees of the orchard were still heavy with apples and pears and the last of the season's plums.

Prudence was about to step through into the orchard when, out of the corner of her eye, she saw a makeshift cross, built out of two pieces of fallen branch, hastily bound together in orange twine. A piece of fallen roof slate had been propped up against it, and on to it had been scratched the words 'DEIRDRE SHAW, IN LOVING MEMORY'. It looked, thought Prudence with some humour and some horror, like the grave a young child had made for a beloved pet. Even the handwriting looked juvenile.

'Mr Lowell put it up,' explained Mrs Mathers. 'He's our gamekeeper. Well, it's him who found her . . .'

Prudence realised where she was standing: among the stubs of rhubarb where Deirdre Shaw had clutched suddenly at her heart and fell to the earth.

'Well, apparently our Hubert was very fond of Deirdre Shaw. It cut him up, finding her like that as he did. You wouldn't think it to look at him, but our Mr Lowell's a sensitive soul. Apparently he always watched her shows, back in the day. Who'd have known? Mr Lowell's always been a pea-soup-from-a-can sort of fellow. You can't imagine him doing much cooking himself.'

There was something inordinately sad about standing here, in the very place where Deirdre had died. Prudence felt a little flutter of guilt at all the times they'd met, and then snubbed each other, at parties across the years. It got like that in the television world, of course. You couldn't stop it, not when there was so much money and so many egos floating around. But to be here now, in the very spot where it had happened, was humbling somehow. *There but for the grace of God go all of us*, thought Prudence.

'I can't think what she wanted with that rhubarb, though. She'd pulled it up, what was left of it, but it was months too long in the ground. Should have been had by August. It looked all woody and hard.'

Rhubarb, thought Prudence. And a little thought tickled in the back of her memory, something she couldn't quite pinpoint – but which she felt certain, in some inalienable way, was important somehow.

She had just got down and started to finger the ground where the rhubarb stubs still erupted from the ground when there came the sound of sudden commotion behind her – and, turning to look over her shoulder, she saw Suki (freshly bathed, and looking defiantly more human than she had in the last twenty-four hours) come stumbling out of the kitchen doors.

Of course, that wretched iPhone thing was in her hands.

'Grandma,' she said, 'you won't believe what Numbers sent me.'

'It'll have to wait, dear,' said Prudence, and in a trice she was back on her feet. The niggling thought about rhubarb faded away as she marched back across the garden, taking note of the carrot tops ready to be pulled and the crowns of celeriac up against the outer wall. 'We have a menu to prepare!'

Chapter Four

'Mrs Bulstrode, it's time.'

The afternoon had been a chaos of kitchen preparation as, together, Prudence and Suki took stock of every ingredient Deirdre Shaw had brought with her, cross-checked them against the recipes she'd devised and pinned up on the larder wall, and then started dreaming up recipes of their own. Deirdre, said Prudence, had always had rather old-fashioned taste, and perhaps that chimed well with the guests who'd hired her – but, as for Prudence, she fancied adding a little *pizazz*. 'I'm not all about the raspberry roulade,' she smirked at Suki, who – to her horror – had been set the task of itemising the herbs, spices and condiments in the kitchen cupboards. 'These old kitchens have been *lived* in, Suki!' Prudence thrilled. Her face was buried in the Frigidaire, where she'd found the carcass of a pheasant that must have been served the evening before Deirdre dropped dead, various stocks in glass jugs, and a wild mushroom and walnut pâté that Prudence knew, for a fact, had been made by Deirdre; it was one of her (very many) signatures.

Suki didn't give two hoots about whether the kitchen had been 'lived in' or not. Until now, Suki's only use for a kitchen had been somewhere to stop in at midnight, after a late-night party with her friends, to toast a couple of frozen potato waffles or grill one of those supermarket own-brand crispy pancakes she loved so much. She could have done with one of them right now, as it happened. The hangover she thought she'd slept off was back with a vengeance and she was quietly certain that the only reason Prudence had given her the condiments to sort through was because it was the only thing of which she was intellectually capable.

Prudence had her head buried in the fridge, the idea of a simple, aromatic consommé entering her head as she inspected what was left of the pheasant carcass, so she didn't hear when Mrs Mathers entered the kitchen. It was only when she called out a second time that she lifted herself, looked round, and saw Mrs Mathers standing there, her face displaying the same level of panic as a chicken upon realising a fox has just broken into the henhouse.

'They're *here*, Mrs Bulstrode. You'll just have to come. You'll have to introduce yourself. They'll want to know they're in good hands. The whole weekend's in ruins. Come on, come on! They're already pulling into the driveway.'

After Mrs Mathers scuttled off, Prudence gave Suki a wry look and clapped her on the shoulder. 'Lesson Number One,' she said, which made Suki screw up her eyes, because she was certain they were already on Lesson Number Seventy-Six, 'always please the lord of the manor. Come on – you better splash some cold water on your face first. You're starting to look a little peaky.'

Soon, Prudence – with Suki trailing behind her – was standing in front of the manor house. The October sun was hanging low in the sky and there was certainly a chill in the air but, aside from that, it was a crisp, still day. *Perfect for a shoot*, thought Prudence. And here the weekend guests came: two 4 x 4 Land Rovers had pulled into the great gravelled driveway, and out of them the guests were stepping.

Prudence was glad to see them. It was always good to get an eye on the people you were being paid to impress. That was why, across her career, she'd always preferred the buzz and intimacy of a live demonstration to the more clinical environment of a television studio. She had, perhaps, made a mistake in bringing Suki up from the kitchens, though. It wasn't strictly necessary to introduce an assistant to your clients – Suki might just as easily have been left doing prep work in the kitchen; it was only that Prudence didn't yet trust her with a knife and, as for preparing the wood pigeons hanging in the larder, well, *that* she would have to do herself. 'Stand up straight and look smart, Suki,' Prudence whispered out of the corner of her eye. 'Here they come.'

The first figure to step out of the Land Rovers was a tall hulk of a man who had the appearance of a bull in tweed breeks. By the general air of authority about him, Prudence took this to be Rupert Prendergast, the host of the weekend – and she was proven correct when the second man who stepped out, evidently the estate's elderly gamekeeper by the look of deference he gave every emerging member of the hunt, called him by his name. Rupert Prendergast was in his middle fifties, perhaps a decade younger than Prudence herself, and had the look of a man who considers all he surveys to be his own personal empire. Curls of thick brown hair were poking out from beneath his tweed cap, his face had the look of a Roman legionnaire, and his hands were as big as prize hams.

Soon, his wife Georgette – a striking, silver-haired beauty – was stepping out of the same Land Rover and ushering their son, Richard – who, at twenty-five years old, certainly favoured his mother's petite looks to his father's Alexander the Great tribute act – to follow after.

Mrs Mathers had scuttled up to Rupert Prendergast, even while the rest of the guests were disembarking. The gamekeeper – who Prudence remembered was named Lowell – had gone to the back of the first vehicle and produced the day's haul: a triple brace of plump partridges, a perfect addition to the larder. Prudence recalled a partridge recipe having appeared on Deirdre Shaw's menu for the shoot's penultimate evening. Deirdre would have served it pot roasted with red cabbage. But Prudence herself began to wonder about honey and thyme – or cinnamon pears. Yes, there were a lot of interesting things you could do with partridge.

'Mr Prendergast,' Mrs Mathers began. Prudence was bewildered to see her almost bowing down, as if they existed in some previous century – but, again, she remembered it was good to give the guests what they wanted. As long as you didn't believe in the deference yourself, it was perfectly OK. 'Might I introduce to you Mrs Prudence Bulstrode?'

Rupert Prendergast looked even more hulking as he came close. At nearly a foot and a half taller than Prudence, he had to reach down to shake her hand. Prudence felt the whip of it ricochet up her body.

'Yes, I remember the face,' he said. 'Used to be on the television, as I recall.'

Prudence said, 'A few times, Mr Prendergast,' quietly ignoring the fact that, hour by hour, she'd graced Great Britain's television screens a trifle more than Deirdre Shaw ever had.

'Well, we're very grateful for your stepping in at such short notice. A dreadful business about Mrs Shaw. One of this nation's finest treasures.'

'Of course, Mr Prendergast.'

'She cooked for us here once before, of course. That was back in her heyday – nearly twenty years ago, I shouldn't wonder. Well, we wanted to recapture a bit of those glory years – so I thought we'd get her out here again. It's just so damnably . . . unfortunate.' He shook his head. 'Well, let's keep our heads on. The weekend isn't ruined, and that's what matters. You'll be serving dinner tonight?'

There was a lot to process here – not least Mr Prendergast's defining of Deirdre's death as something 'unfortunate' and his relief that it hadn't ruined his weekend. But Prudence had dealt with moneyed people all her life. The world worked differently when you were wealthy. And if working in television had taught her anything, it was to know when she should bite her tongue and when she should say exactly what was in her mind. This time she said, 'Dinner at six p.m., Mr Prendergast, just like you ordered. You'll forgive us, of course, if it's a simpler kind of fare tonight. We have something marvellous planned for tomorrow and, of course, the day after that, your banquet night. We won't let you down.'

'I know that you won't,' said Mr Prendergast. Then he gave a wolfish grin and, sweeping around, made for the manor. 'Reputations depend on it, hey?' he laughed as he left.

Mrs Mathers didn't seem to have noticed Mr Prendergast's rude and dismissive manner. She just bowed again to him as he marched into the manor, his wife walking in his wake – with a kinder acknowledgement of Prudence – and their son marching behind her, looking sullen and with his gaze perpetually on the ground.

After the Prendergast family came the rest of the group. Mrs Mathers introduced them one by one. Terence Knight was ex-army and specialised in City securities, a friend of Rupert since their Eton days forty years before. Gray Williams was another old friend, part of the University of Oxford crowd, who was now housemaster at the very same school to which Rupert and Terence had gone.

'And allow me, last but not least, to introduce Mr and Mrs Maxwell Pendlebury,' said Mrs Mathers, acknowledging the final two guests to emerge from the Land

Rovers. 'Maxwell is, of course, the head of Countrywide Finance Systems. He built that company from the ground.' Prudence had known many mismatched couples in her lifetime, but few who looked as incompatible alongside each other as these. Mrs Pendlebury might not even have reached fifty years old, and had the look of somebody much younger – and all without the tell-tale signs of the little surgeries and personal improvements that Prudence had seen peppered across the television world across the years. Small and elfin, she had flowing black hair that hadn't yet faded to grey – and, in this, she was quite the opposite of her long, lanky beanpole of a husband. At twenty – perhaps even more – years older than his wife, Maxwell Pendlebury's face was an atlas of wrinkles and lines, and his hair a thinning silver nest on top of his head. His face, too, was set in what seemed a permanent expression of suspicion – and this, Prudence decided, had permanently lined him. He barely gave them a whisper of acknowledgement as he went by, walking with a cane (and an imperious air). Mrs Pendlebury stopped a moment, however, and shook Prudence's hand with her tiny, manicured own.

'I do always hate it when they call me Mrs *Maxwell* Pendlebury – as if I didn't have a name of my own. As if it isn't bad enough that, in the twenty-first century, we still take our husbands' surnames, we're even expected to shed our Christian names too.' She smiled. 'My name's Alice,' she said. 'It's lovely to meet you. I've enjoyed watching you over the years.'

Prudence wasn't too ashamed to admit that this pleased her enormously. It was the kind of thing you needed to hear, every once in a while.

'It was horrible what happened to poor Deirdre,' said Alice, 'but I couldn't be more pleased to have you aboard, Prudence. I just can't wait for our pheasants on our final night. Maxwell had to shoot mine, of course. The best I can do is wing a bird. I'm sure you have something incredible planned.'

Not quite yet, thought Prudence, relishing the challenge, *but I will*.

After Alice Pendlebury had followed her husband – who waited impatiently at the doors to the manor – Mrs Mathers gestured for the gamekeeper to join them, momentarily, on the drive.

'I've got to get back, duckie,' Hubert Lowell called out. He must have been close to seventy himself, and had the same kind of warm, ruddy appearance that Prudence had known in various gamekeepers over the years. It was that same 'lived-in' look that Prudence loved in her kitchens. Weather-beaten and lined with the signs of a life that had, well and truly, been loved.

There was a dog jumping about the gamekeeper too – a roan English setter which, by the look of it, had lived many long years at the gamekeeper's side.

'Hop up here now, Biscuit,' Lowell said, and the dog – wagging its body as well as its tail – scrambled up into the passenger side of the first Land Rover.

'Oh come on, Hubert – be a friend!' Mrs Mathers called out, with a cheery grin.

Lowell relented. Propping his shotgun up by the Land Rover's bumper, he tramped over – the poor man had developed a limp somewhere along the way, but that wasn't unusual of gamekeepers either – and doffed his cap at Prudence.

'Pleased to have you,' he said, nervously. 'Strange circumstances, of course, but you'll know all about them. I'm just glad that lot in there are going to get their dinners. I was worried I'd be being called on and, well, I'm not much of a cook. I fancy that lot in there wouldn't be too happy with beans out of a can.'

'Oh, I don't know,' grinned Prudence, 'baked beans on toast hasn't been forgotten in *my* house. Sometimes all you really want is a good can of beans. My Nicholas used to like to grill cheese on top.'

'Then he was a king among men, Mrs Bulstrode,' Lowell answered.

'Hubert here's been keeper of the grounds since – when was it, Hubert? Nineteen sixty-eight?'

'Hardly, ma'am,' said Lowell – and Prudence got the impression that this was some recurring joke between him and Mrs Mathers. 'Nineteen sixty-eight, I was only a bairn.' He turned back to Prudence. 'That was the first year I went on the shoots. My old man was gamekeeper here, and his old man before him. I don't have a son myself, so there the line ends – but, if I had one, I daresay he'd inherit the mantle, and the little cottage, too. Well, it's nice to keep some things traditional.'

Prudence couldn't agree more. It was another thing she liked about these old manor house kitchens.

'Were you the one who found Mrs Shaw?'

Prudence had quite forgotten Suki was standing behind her, until those words came blurting out. Inwardly, she cringed. *Yes*, she thought, *I should have left her in the kitchen.*

Hubert Lowell shifted, uncomfortably, from wellington boot to wellington boot.

'That's right, young ma'am. A terrible thing it was, too, to see somebody so loved lying face down in the rhubarb patch.'

Something niggled at the back of Prudence's head again. *Rhubarb* . . .

'I was just coming up to the house to get things sorted. Yesterday afternoon, it was. We'd gone shooting the day before, of course. First day for the guests. And I had some bits to organise for the partridges today. It was supposed to be clays yesterday, but, well, with all that happened, we had to call it off. It wouldn't have seemed right.'

'Well,' interjected Prudence, hoping she could smooth out the moment, 'I saw the little monument you put up, Mr Lowell. I knew Deirdre well, back in the day – and I know she'd have been very touched.' The truth was, Prudence didn't quite believe this at all; in her latter years, Deirdre had very much let the fame go to her head – she hardly ever wanted to deal with what she called the 'little people' any more, not even people like gamekeepers and butchers who shared her love of food. But you do not speak ill of the dead, and she was pleased to see that the thought gave Lowell some comfort.

'Just a terrible thing,' Mrs Mathers said, 'a death at Farleigh Manor – and a famous one at that!'

55

'Not the *only* famous death, of course,' chipped in Suki.

This time, Prudence was aghast. She wasn't sure if it was possible to smooth out another moment like this. 'Yes, well,' she said, 'we've much to be getting on with if we're to serve any kind of dinner this evening. Mr Lowell, it was a pleasure to meet you.'

'You ought to take the partridges, Mrs Bulstrode.'

Prudence took the bundle in her hands. The birds still had a trace of warmth to them. 'We'll do them proud,' she said. 'Might we send some over for you, Mr Lowell?'

Lowell had already turned to tramp back to his Land Rover, where the English setter Biscuit was happily lapping her big leathery tongue against the windows.

'Oh, don't mind me,' he said, 'I've got a can of beans in the cupboard.'

Then he was up into the Land Rover and – battling through the loving affection of Biscuit – he was gone up the track.

As they hurried back to the kitchens, Prudence threw Suki a scalding look and said, 'Why on earth did you say that?'

'Say what?'

'*Famous* deaths, Suki – my goodness!'

She'd told her all about the article Numbers had sent – and, it seemed to Prudence, that she'd told it with more than a little glee. Sensationalism, that was all it was – and, just like Facebook and Instagram and YouTube, it was a curse of the young. Everything had to be flashy. Everything had to be a 'moment'. Well, Prudence would be happy enough with good old-fashioned kitchen work. There was enough drama in Farleigh Manor without her and Suki stirring it up themselves.

'Oh Grandma, it's interesting, that's all,' Suki protested as, back in the kitchen, Prudence set about emptying the cupboards and fridge and lining up all their likely ingredients on the counter. 'You can't come to a place like this and *not* find it interesting, can you?'

'Interesting is all right,' said Prudence, debating the relative merits of redcurrant and cranberry preserve. 'It's *salacious* we have to avoid. Cooks must be unseen and unheard, Suki. Our dishes are the stars of the show. We ourselves must remain invisible.'

Suki snorted, 'That's why you were all over the TV, is it?'

'Well,' said Prudence, 'that, my dear, is quite a different thing. Television stardom and good private cheffing are two very different spheres.' She sighed. 'Suki, dear, these people – frightful as they probably seem to you – are here on holiday. You must have heard Mr Prendergast – they're here to relive their glory days, to get a good injection of nostalgia, to *enjoy* themselves. They've already had that disrupted once by poor Deirdre.' She flashed a look through the kitchen window and caught sight, again, of the spot where Deirdre had died. She thought, too, of Rupert Prendergast's dismissive manner – the death was trivial to him; it was the weekend that mattered. 'Do you really think they'll want reminding of some creepy incident that happened here one hundred and thirty years ago? Suki, dear, it's all dead and buried.'

'Just like Jane Sutcliffe,' sulked Suki.

Prudence heaved a great sigh.

'Don't you think it's strange, Grandma, that Deirdre Shaw just dropped down dead in the rhubarb? Just like Jane Sutcliffe dropped down dead, all those years ago?'

Prudence had lifted the pheasant carcass out of the fridge and placed it, defiantly, in a pot. There was still much goodness in this carcass. The thought of a lovely consommé returned to her – something light and bursting with flavour to begin the meal. Yes, she thought, that would be the *perfect* introduction.

'Your grandfather dropped down dead just as he was ready to start life again, Suki. My dear mother, your great-grandmother, dropped down dead in the middle of the Sunday crossword. A quite devilish one, I might add. It was Nicholas himself who set it. We always joked – it was "three down" that finished her off. It was just too damnably difficult.' She paused. 'The point is, my dear, that we all drop down dead one day.' Her eyes were inexorably drawn to the partridges, which she'd deposited on the opposite counter. They needed stringing up. 'Well, unless somebody kills us first, I suppose,' she said – and couldn't help, for a moment, picturing the dead birds staring at her with their small, glassy eyes.

To her credit, Suki worked hard in the kitchen. Prudence was glad to see it. The girl really could roll her sleeves up when she wanted – and, if she did keep nipping off to quietly sit in the corner, it was only to be expected. Suki's idea of a hard day's work was a couple of hours' study, followed by a seven-hour breather; work in any kitchen was so much more demanding than that.

Prudence was glad, too, that there wasn't another mention of Jane Sutcliffe and her unusual fate all afternoon. There was simply no time for it, with the task ahead of them. By 5 p.m., the consommé was simmering happily – it had perfect clarity, and the smells rising out of the pot were divine. Prudence tasted it here and there and decided that she could easily have drained the pot herself; but here she resisted, as all good cooks must.

As well as preparing the day's dinner, Prudence had started formulating thoughts for the days ahead. The pheasants could hang a day longer – they'd mature just a little, and the rich taste of them would deepen, so that the last-night banquet would be the finest meal of them all. Between now and then, there would be venison rolled in cocoa, with roasted autumn vegetables straight out of the garden, as well as partridge-and-pear puffs as a starter. And tonight, the simplest and most handsome of fares: the consommé would be followed by beetroots and radishes in a salad of green leaves, walnuts, and a dressing in which fresh orange juice and cayenne pepper were the stars. After that would come a handsome fish course, sea bream with a fiery chilli and lemongrass marinade. It was Prudence's nod toward modernity. The following two nights would be classic shooting-weekend dishes – venison and partridge and, finally, the pheasants as the star of the show. She'd have to dream up a way to liven them up, of course. Prudence wasn't a meat-and-gravy kind of girl, no matter how luscious the gravy – and certainly Rupert Prendergast and his ilk would be expecting more. Shooting-party traditionalists they might have been, but they were still City of Londoners, used to fine dining and expensive restaurants.

Six p.m. came around, and Prudence stood in the doors of the Farleigh Manor dining room. Mrs Mathers and her assistant Flick – a little older than Suki, Felicity 'Flick' Garrick had been hired by the Farleigh estate two seasons before – had done a fine job setting the table. It looked fit for kings and crown princes and lords of the realm. 'We'll take it from here, Mrs Bulstrode,' said Mrs Mathers, 'won't we Flick?'

The younger woman looked as if she'd served in this dining room many times before. 'I look forward to seeing it by the end of the night,' she grinned. 'There's a case of Veuve Clicquot just arrived at the tradesman's door – and that's on top of the Moët already on ice. They do like a drink, these London types.'

'Not one of you tell my grand-daughter,' said Prudence, and hurried back to the kitchens to start dishing up.

The consommé was the first to go out. Prudence didn't get to see how it went down – that was the lot of the private chef, never quite knowing what people were saying about their food – but, when the dishes were returned (all but one drained to the bottom), she had a good sense of where the evening was going. After that, out went the sea bream; and, after that, a baked gooseberry tart that, though it might not have been quite as adventurous as the rest of the menu, certainly seemed to do the trick by the increasing sounds of raucousness and laughter that were coming from upstairs. Prudence was canny enough not to put it down entirely to her menu (a critic would have called it 'hotch-potch'; Prudence preferred to think of it as 'fusion') because the champagne certainly helped the evening along – but laughter was always a good sign.

'Well,' she said, 'a job well done.' She came up from the oven, having made two grilled cheese sandwiches, oozing with Red Leicester and her special Marmite sauce. 'An indulgent pleasure, Suki.'

Suki liked the look of it much more than the delicate consommé and sea bream they'd sent upstairs.

'Hangover food,' she grinned. 'Thank you, Grandma.'

'Of course, you won't be needing hangover food this weekend – will you, dear?'

Suki's eyes drifted upwards. 'Not like Mr Prendergast and his friends, in any case . . .'

Suki might not have been drunk, but she certainly snored like one. Three times the sound of her snoring woke Prudence up – and it wasn't yet 2 a.m.

There had still been laughter echoing through the manor at 1 a.m., but now the world seemed deathly silent – all except for Suki. Prudence propped herself up in bed and took a drink from the peppermint tea she always kept at her bedside, no matter where she was staying. Cold peppermint tea was just the ticket for the dead of night. She was having a little discomfort in her stomach as well, and peppermint was always the thing to soothe it.

Suki's snoring sounded worse than ever now, so Prudence got out of bed, bustled across the room and – as she always did to poor Nicholas, back when he was keeping her awake into the smallest hours – she jostled Suki just *so*. The snoring would come back soon, but for a moment there was blessed silence.

Or there would have been, if Prudence hadn't heard urgent footsteps running down the hall.

Her instinct was to slope back to bed. What the guests were getting up to at this time of night was none of her business. Groups like this, she thought with a wry smile, were quite possibly hopping in and out of each other's beds. She'd seen and heard a lot of *that* during her time in the media world as well. Not that Prudence was a prude (no matter what her name suggested). What people got up to in their time was their own business. But quite how people of their generation had any space in their heads and hearts for *that* sort of thing was quite beyond her. Prudence herself would much rather go to bed with one of her recipe books and a nice tin of shortbread.

And she would have climbed back into bed for more shut-eye and peppermint tea, right now, if only she hadn't heard the groaning.

Somebody, out there, was in distress.

Uncertainly, Prudence crept to the door, opened it a fraction and peered out into the darkened passageway beyond. Houses as old as this always had their ghosts. There were always eyes glowering at you from some ancient portrait. There was always a floorboard creaking on a stair. Pipes rattled and things scurried in the skirting.

But this was not any of those sounds.

This was the sound of somebody staggering, up against a wall.

The sound of somebody guttering, somebody retching, somebody gasping and muttering oaths.

It was coming, Prudence thought, from the end of the old nursemaid's passageway, the one that led to the suites where the guests were sleeping.

So, in a sense – and if she was following the old 'upstairs, downstairs' code – it was none of her business.

But Prudence had never been a woman to ignore a cry of distress. It probably wasn't very *modern*, but it just wouldn't do.

So, with one last look back at a sleeping Suki – whose snoring was returning, resplendently, to the room – she stepped out of the bedroom and hurried toward whoever it was, out there, who needed her help.

Chapter Five

The old nursemaid's passageway was crooked and ill lit.
Prudence knew manor houses like this and she'd seen
such things before; their owners of yesteryear would
expend a fortune making certain that the areas their
guests visited were opulent beyond measure – but, when
it came to spending money on their servants' quarters,
the finances never stretched very far. As she palmed her
way along the passage, following the sounds of distress,
she felt, for a moment, as if she was in some crooked
fairground house, with floors that listed and zigzagging
walls. Not one of the portraits on the walls seemed to
hang evenly. Loose floorboards rolled beneath her feet.

The nursemaid's passage ended in three crooked stairs.
Somewhere beyond here were the suites where Rupert
Prendergast and his guests were sleeping – but, immediately on Prudence's left, light spilled out of a doorway
left fractionally ajar. She crept towards it.

The guttering groans were coming from the other side
of that door.

'Hello?' she ventured, timidly at first but with growing
volume. 'Hello, are you all right—'

Upon reaching the doorway, she heard one final retch.
That was the thing that made her feel certain she was

doing the right thing. She pushed the door further open, revealing a bathroom quite unlike the one she and Suki had been using further down the hall. This one was modern and luxurious compared to the rickety old wash-basin and tub in their room. A free-standing bath was set into marble surrounds, with faucets of gold filigree, and the room was walled with lavish mirrors in deep silver frames.

If it hadn't have been for the woman on her knees with her head in the toilet bowl, Prudence might even have been impressed.

She knew, at once, that it was Alice Pendlebury, the only guest who had deigned to stop and properly converse with them on their arrival that afternoon. Her shock of jet-black hair had been tied back, but now it hung in a cascade around her; evidently she'd given up in her attempts to keep it from tumbling into the toilet bowl. She retched again, and Prudence watched as her entire body started to convulse. By the acrid smell in the air, Prudence judged that she'd already brought up what-ever was inside her and was now just bringing up bile.

It had been a long time since Prudence was a hands-on mother, but she'd helped Suki through enough morn-ings of hungover sickness since moving to Chelwood Ghyll that her instincts took over. 'It's OK, Mrs Pendlebury,' she said, 'we'll get this sorted out. You do your job, and I'll do mine.'

In a moment, she was filling the porcelain sink with warm water; a moment later, she was unrolling towels from the storage cabinet, then unearthing a dressing gown which she draped around Alice's shoulders. The poor woman had started to tremor. That was the sickness leaving her body, Prudence was certain. Perhaps it meant the worst of it was over.

Finally, Alice lifted her head from the toilet bowl. Prudence had poured a glass of lukewarm water and this she pressed into her trembling hand.

'It's not for drinking, my dear. Your stomach won't like that. Just for wetting the lips – and for the taste of it. It will make you feel more human.'

Alice's face seemed to be conveying her gratitude, though her throat was so dry she couldn't croak out a word. She took the glass and sipped at it gently.

'Mrs Bulstrode,' she finally said, finding her voice, 'I didn't mean to make you—'

'Oh nonsense, dear,' said Prudence, soaking a small flannel in the warm water, wringing it half-dry and applying it, gently, to Alice's brow. 'I could hardly leave you in such a state. I'm no prude when it comes to these things. I don't have a squeamish bone in my body.' Professional cooks rarely did, thought Prudence. It came with the territory: all that gutting and deboning, the offal and giblets. You couldn't sauté a slice of calf's heart or prepare a bowl full of chicken gizzards without getting past a certain level of squeamishness. 'And, besides, you remember meeting my grand-daughter. I've nursed her through more than a few hangovers. In fact, were I to tell you—'

Alice's face had darkened. She looked up – glassy green eyes in her porcelain-doll face – and snapped, 'I'm not

66

hungover, you stupid woman. I haven't been hungover since I was twenty-seven years old.'

Prudence lifted the flannel from her head. She was good at keeping her composure. She'd had to be. She'd had the most frightful producers, back in the day.

'I'm sorry, dear. I rather thought that, with all the dancing and cheering we could hear last night—'

'I'm teetotal,' Alice snapped. She levered herself up from the toilet bowl and back to her feet. After a brisk scrub of her hands and forearms, she snatched a towel out of Prudence's hands and marched to the door. 'Rupert and the rest of them might have been making merry, but you can be damn sure I wasn't. I learnt my lesson with the demon drink many moons ago – all those damnable party weekends we used to come to here. If I'd have carried on that way, I wouldn't have made fifty-five, so I made sure I stopped. I've not so much as touched a drop since. Besides, I never needed alcohol to have a good time. It just got me into trouble.' She hesitated, a look of absolute scorn still on her face. 'I'm not sick because of alcohol, Mrs Bulstrode. *You* poisoned me, you stupid woman. I know what bloody food poisoning feels like. By God, it's ten times as intense as the worst morning sickness ever was.'

Then, without another word, she was off, into the darkness of the passageway and the guest suites beyond.

When Prudence returned to her own bedroom, Suki's snoring had returned with a vengeance. But it didn't matter. That wasn't what would keep Prudence awake – not any more. *Poison*, she thought. She'd never been accused of it before. In forty years of professional cookery, twenty-five years of it in front of television cameras, not once had she overlooked a bad shellfish, undercooked a sausage, or neglected to take into account the litany of allergies and intolerances that had come her way. You heard of professional cooks who didn't know one mushroom from another, but Prudence wasn't one of those. Nicholas used to joke that, if the end of the world was suddenly announced, he and Prudence wouldn't just survive, they'd positively *thrive* because she could make the most unappetising, unusual ingredients sing, and never put anybody in harm's way.

She looked at the sleeping Suki, whose snores were reaching titanic proportions. Quite probably they would begin registering on the Richter scale. It was, perhaps, foolish to bring somebody so untested – and so unused to anything in a kitchen except, perhaps, a microwave oven – on a job like this. But she was equally sure that Suki could have done nothing to imperil the cleanliness of the kitchen either. The poor girl had taken so long to sift through the spice racks and condiments that, in effect, Prudence had prepared dinner alone.

It was still several hours until the sun would rise upon Farleigh Manor. Prudence thought deeply and pondered through every last one of them.

'We won't be needing any breakfast, Mrs Bulstrode,' said Mrs Mathers, who had appeared in the kitchen doorway with her assistant Flick.

Prudence, who had been in the kitchen for an hour already, warming the range and preparing platters of baked sausage (heritage pork, from one of the local butcheries) and bacon, then chopping the ingredients for her very-own-recipe breakfast frittata, rose up from one of the warming ovens, her glasses steamed up so as to render her blind. After polishing them on a sleeve, she scrutinised Mrs Mathers.

'No breakfast?'

Suki, who had been chopping strawberries for the blender, stopped and looked around.

'I'm afraid not, Mrs Bulstrode. And I'll have to let you know about lunch as well. This weekend lurches from one disaster to another.'

Mrs Mathers wrung her hands anxiously. When she could say no more, Flick interjected, 'They were all up in the night. Didn't you hear them? Something in the wine, we think – they've all been sick, every last one of them. Except for Mr Prendergast, that is – but he has the constitution of an ox.'

'He could always drink more than the rest of them,' Mrs Mathers said, with a jitter. 'Silly fools, they think they're thirty years younger than they are.' She dropped her voice to a whisper. 'Money goes to the head, they say. They think it keeps them young. But they just can't drink their wine like they used to – and they drank as much, last night, as if they were twenty-five years old!' She heaved a deep sigh. 'I'm sorry, Mrs Bulstrode. But perhaps I can relieve you of some of those sausages?' They'd just come out of the oven, with dark brown skins and steaming with flavour. 'It would be a shame if they were to go to waste.' Mrs Mathers scurried across the kitchen, plucked a hot sausage from one of the baking pans, and tossed it from hand to hand as she scurried back. 'Flick, you could take some down to Mr Lowell. I should think he'd like that. Well, it's one of the perks of the job, isn't it, in a place like this? We underlings get the scraps the toffs leave behind!'

'Biscuit would enjoy some of this bacon,' said Flick, venturing across the kitchen to start filling a bowl.

Prudence had very little idea what to think. Not for the first time this morning, the waspish look in Alice Pendlebury's eyes came back to her, and those words, delivered with a barely contained fury: 'I'm teetotal!' She was still pondering them when she realised the silence had gone on for too long in the kitchen – and, pulling herself from the reverie, she said, 'Of course. Take what you must. Suki, dear, you'll go and collect the dishes from Mr Lowell after lunchtime. Hopefully, by then, we'll know what's what. Do you think they'll be wanting dinner tonight, Mrs Mathers?'

'Let's wait and see,' said Mrs Mathers, stealing another sausage and tucking into it like a child might do a toffee apple on Bonfire Night. 'By this rate, Mrs Bulstrode, you'll be able to charge a full fee for this weekend and scarcely cook a meal. Well, bye for now!'

Then, with a last flourish from Flick as she heaped up a plate for Hubert Lowell, they were gone.

'What was *that* all about?' asked Suki, ashen-faced.

'One moment, dear.'

Prudence turned on her heel. Suki recognised the decisiveness of that walk. It meant she'd had an *idea*. She watched as her grandmother marched into the walk-in larder and disappeared inside. Some time later – just when Suki was beginning to think that there was another mystery at Farleigh Manor, the Case of the Disappearing Grandma and the Locked Larder – she reappeared with three bottles of wine in her hand. These she placed on the kitchen counter and bent down to study their labels through her spectacles.

'Château de Fleur,' she read.

'Very fancy,' said Suki.

'You're missing the point, darling.' Prudence turned the bottle on the spot, then directed Suki's gaze to the label. 'Zero per cent by volume. This is the kind of champagne you ought to be drinking with this Numbers fellow of yours.'

'He's not my *fellow*, Grandma. I've tried to tell you. Numbers is—'

'Non-alcoholic, darling. Alice Pendlebury's a teetotaller.'

'So?'

Prudence shook her head, wearily. If Suki couldn't make that connection, there was little hope for her in a professional kitchen. Being a professional cook was as much about solving problems as it was creating recipes. You had to know which ingredients you might switch for which others; how to adjust a dish at a moment's notice to accommodate some peculiarity of taste or problem with digestion. You had to think on your feet and, above all, you had to be *observant*. So far, Suki had shown very few of these attributes.

'Alice Pendlebury was being violently sick last night. I know because I went to clean up after her. It didn't occur to me, until afterwards, that it was strange she was in the separate bathroom along the hall – because, of course, the guest suites all have en-suite facilities. It says so, right here in the manor house brochure.' Prudence walked to the laminated booklet hanging on a string from the wall. It had been one of the things niggling at her in the night and she'd checked it the moment they got up. 'Of course, *our* room has its own facilities, and we're the lowest people here – the hired help. It stands to reason that the Pendleburys had facilities of their own.'

Suki scarcely understood. 'So why wasn't Alice using hers?'

'Well, because her husband was, dear. Mr Pendlebury was being sick at precisely the same time. They *all* were. Alice staggered down the hall to use the facilities there. That's where I found her. Only,' she returned to the three bottles of Château de Fleur, 'there's a non-alcoholic cooking wine in the larder, too. I've used it myself – it's a good substitute. It would take an expert to tell the difference, once it's been cooked through.'

'Grandma, what are you talking about?'

'Alice Pendlebury isn't a drinker, dear. Oh, it sounds like she used to be. They hosted some debauched parties back in the day, by all accounts. I dread to think about the things that went on. But Alice gave all that up. These days, she doesn't touch a drop. So, you see, it wasn't too much merriment that made them sick last night at all.'

Suki was still. 'So what was it?' she finally asked.

Prudence shuffled the bottles of non-alcoholic champagne back into the larder, then returned to the kitchen window. It was a crisp, clear morning above Farleigh Manor. The sky was vast and blue and only a gentle wind disturbed the branches of the orchard beyond the kitchen garden. It would have been a good day for shooting, if only the guests had been fit for it.

Her eyes dropped down to the little cross Mr Lowell had placed on the rhubarb patch, and the place where Deirdre Shaw had died.

'*You* poisoned me, you stupid woman.'

Suki gasped. 'Grandma?'

Until that moment, Prudence hadn't known that she was speaking out loud. She came out of her vague, faraway thoughts and said, 'I daresay we won't be serving lunch, if lunch is wanted at all, until long into the afternoon, Suki. But we had better put that time to good use. If this was food poisoning, then I won't have it staining my reputation. Vomits and shakes and tremors all night long – a good cook can't tolerate that. We'll never get hired again. And, since we've suddenly got a spare day on our hands, let's make doubly certain it wasn't anything to do with us.'

Suki had a dreadful feeling about this. The feeling only intensified when she saw her grandmother get down to her knees, open up one of the cupboards beneath the sink, and pull out a glut of different bleaches, surface sprays, sponges, cloths and a single, unused mophead.

73

'Oh, Grandma,' she groaned.

'That's the spirit,' said Prudence. 'Well, you didn't think working in a kitchen was all syrup sponge pudding and Hasselback potatoes, did you? Get started, Suki. Use that whip-smart mind of yours to devise us a plan. Left to right, top to bottom, easiest to hardest – it's your choice. I'll be back in one moment.'

'Where are you going?' Suki was still contemplating the cleaning equipment with a face etched in horror.

'I need to make a phone call.'

In a flash, Suki was brandishing her iPhone. 'You can do it here, Grandma.'

But Prudence's face, upon contemplating the iPhone, had achieved quite the same level of horror as Suki's had been upon seeing the Antibacterial Lemon Cleanser (two parts bleach). 'You know I don't hold with those things, dear,' she said, and promptly left the kitchen.

There was a housekeeping office just inside the entrance hall and, by good fortune, Mrs Mathers and Flick had so much to attend to, stripping down a full set of beds and laundering the sheets, that Prudence was able to slip inside unseen. The fact was, as horrified by the thought of using Suki's iPhone as she had been, it was privacy that she wanted most of all. She closed the door behind her, took note of all of Mrs Mathers's notices – plastered to corkboards on the wall as if she was a harassed detective in the middle of some tele-vised murder mystery – and settled down at her desk. Quite possibly it was an intrusion, but Prudence didn't intend to be here long. All she needed was the number . . .

No doubt Suki would have told her to look it up on the computer whose lights were blinking at her from the corner, but Prudence didn't have the time – or the interest – to school herself in silly things like Google and Microsoft Edge. The telephone book was good enough for her – and Mrs Mathers was using one to prop up her printer. Prudence slid it out and carefully thumbed through the pages until she found the name of the local village, Nutwood St Knowle. From the picture postcards on the wall, it looked as quaint and dainty (*quainty*, Prudence thought with a smile) a place to live in as Chelwood Ghyll, with thatched roofs on all of its cottages and a vicarage ringed in flowerbeds that had won 'Best of the Cotswolds' three years running. By thumbing through the pages of the directory, Prudence was soon able to establish that, as well as six teahouses, a prize-winning bakery, an award for 'Best Independent Bookshop 2021', and an organic butchers that had once been visited by Prince William, it had a small police station, one of the county's oldest and finest. The number was right there in the book, so before she could begin to doubt herself, she dialled it.

It took two rings before somebody answered.

'Nutwood St Knowle Police Station,' a voice began, 'are you calling for an emergency?'

'No,' Prudence stuttered, 'not quite . . .'

'Well, that's a relief,' said the voice of a young man; there was a chirpiness to his tone that Prudence hadn't been expecting. 'There's only me here, and the car's in the garage, so if it was an emergency, I'd have had to borrow the one from next door. And Mr Jacobs is sick and tired of us scrounging lifts off him. We're the Thin Blue Line, after all. How can I help?'

Prudence's heart sank. Was it really only two days ago that she'd had that infernal conversation with Constable Mick Hardman, back in Chelwood Ghyll? If anything, this young man sounded several shades more useless. But at least, Prudence supposed, he seemed to *know* it. Better a fool who knows he's a fool than a fool so foolish to not even know.

'It's a rather delicate matter, I'm afraid,' she began. She wished that she'd thought to rehearse what she was going to say first. She had always been a great improviser – how she'd hated those dreadful autocues they'd made her read in her later television series! – but this was not like narrating the ingredients and method for a classic bread-and-butter pudding. She was quite certain she ought to tread carefully, even with an impish young policeman like this. 'My name's Prudence Bulstrode,' she went on, 'and I wondered if you might—'

'Prudence Bulstrode?' the young policeman chirruped. '*The* Prudence Bulstrode?'

Was there any other? Her mother and father had gifted her with two things that had lasted the whole of her life: the memories of warmth and comfort that always came with stepping into a kitchen; and a name that nobody else would imitate, even if they were paid.

'Indeed,' she replied.

'Oh, well, *my*, that's one for the diary tonight. My mum will be furious, *furious*, when I tell her who's called. She has all your books, Mrs Bulstrode. We used to make cakes out of *Cakey Bakey Milkshakey* when I was a nipper. She has *Suppertime Superstars* on the kitchen counter right now. Every Christmas, out comes *We Wish You a Merry Prumas*.'

Prudence shuddered. She'd fought against that particular title tooth and nail (on the basis that it was . . . rubbish), and lost out – as she sometimes did – to a particularly voracious and supercilious publisher.

'Well, that's wonderful to hear,' she said, 'but I've got a question and I'd really like some help—'

'Tell me,' the constable interrupted, 'what's the secret with that brandy-butter pavlova they used to sell in Sainsbury's?' It had been all the rage one Christmas: Prudence's face on every packet, gazing out of every supermarket fridge. 'We used to try and make it from the recipe in your book, but it never turned out the same.'

'Oh, oh, tricks of the trade!' Prudence chortled. Inside, she was squirming. She hadn't been prepared to put on her public face, not when she was digging up the kind of details she was about to ask for. The disparity made her feel deeply uncomfortable. 'Please, I hope you can help me.'

'Emergency, is it?'

'*I've already said it's not*,' said Prudence, this time through gritted teeth. 'It's about a dear old friend of mine. Deirdre Shaw. I'm sure you know what happened to her . . .'

The line went dead, for only a second.

'It was a terrible thing. She was one of Mum's favourites too. Not quite as favourite as you, Mrs Bulstrode, but she was up there, you know? You, and Mrs Shaw – and, you know, Delia and Nigella and all of the rest. She loved you all. The Holy Trinity.'

Prudence neglected to tell him that 'trinity' meant 'three' and resolved to carry on through this constable's inanity until she could finally get to the point.

'You see, I've been so dreadfully upset about my old friend's death. I keep thinking there's something I could have done – *anything* – that might have changed things. Oh, I always knew she wasn't in the rudest of health. Well, sometimes we cooks never are – too much of a good thing, I suppose . . .'

'Oh yes, Mrs Bulstrode. Just like that brandy-butter pavlova.'

She could almost hear him salivating down the receiver.

'I wondered if you could tell me – is there a coroner's report, yet? Is there going to be an inquest? I realise it's only been a very short time but I'd be keen to know.'

'Mrs Bulstrode, I'm so sorry for your loss. It's funny – we little people rarely think of what goes on behind the scenes, but I can imagine how very close you and Deirdre were. I'm picturing it right now: the two of you, cooking suppers for each other, the very closest of friends. But . . .' he paused, 'we'd only order a coroner's inquest if there were suspicious circumstances, Mrs Bulstrode. The sad fact is, Mrs Shaw simply died. It happens.'

'Indeed,' said Prudence, now only faintly masking her irritation – not that the constable seemed to notice. 'It happens to us all. But she was Deirdre, *my* Deirdre. The doctors must have said something.'

'Oh well, Mrs Bulstrode, I really oughtn't to go into details with you, of course. It's a private matter and I could get into a spot of—'

Prudence grimaced. 'I'll chat to your mother about the brandy-butter pavlova, if you'd like?'

She could feel the beams of positivity that came suddenly shooting down the telephone wire, bathing her in their resplendent light. 'Oh, well, Mrs Bulstrode, that *is* generous of you! And, yes, I can quite see why you'd want to know as much as you can about your dear, dear, *dear* friend. So let me tell you what I know. I hope that will help!' He took a deep breath. 'I was there, of course, when the ambulances arrived. She was quite dead, Mrs Bulstrode. Shocking as it is to say. Now, I know the obituaries have spoken about her heart disease and angina – that's a condition of the heart, by the way – and those conditions do feature on her death certificate. But the grisly truth is that she choked to death, Mrs Bulstrode.'

Prudence's own heart stopped. 'Deirdre . . . choked?' she whispered.

'The paramedics will tell you, it isn't unusual. They believe she had some sort of a fit, brought on by these conditions of hers. There was enough compost in her airways for the coroner to ascertain that she'd been alive when she fell into the rhubarb patch. She breathed it in, you see. And she must have breathed in too much

79

particulate – that's what they call it, *particulate* – because, it seems, that's what did for her. Oh, it's true that the heart kicked it off – and it was two hours until she was found by the estate gamekeeper, so there wasn't any saving her, and quite possibly the heart attack would have killed her too. I believe this sort of grisly detail doesn't make it to the obituaries, Mrs Bulstrode. It spares the loved ones, and nobody wants to think of a national treasure like Mrs Shaw leaving us in such an unhappy fashion.'

No, thought Prudence, trying not to roll her eyes. *Better that they imagine her floating off to heaven on a palanquin of fluffy, light Italian meringue.*

'Constable, are you *quite* certain there were no ... suspicious circumstances surrounding her death?'

The constable exhaled, long and slow. 'I'm sorry, Mrs Bulstrode. The certificate is right in front of me. *Death by natural causes.* Ugly, yes, but natural all the same. Poor Mrs Shaw. She was one of the angels, wasn't she?'

Prudence let the telephone receiver dangle in her hands.

Choked to death, she thought.

Rhubarb, she thought.

The chill was moving up her spine, spreading out through all the arteries and veins of her body. Prudence had a natural instinct that told her when a recipe didn't fit. If somebody told her to try cranberries with kippers, her sixth sense started tingling. One of these idiotic, but well-meaning, YouTube chefs had once tried to tell her that *grass* – common garden grass! – was a flavour that worked well in ice cream. Her senses had started tingling then. And her senses were tingling now. It might not have been a recipe, but something about this neither smelt nor tasted right.

There were footsteps outside the door. Prudence froze, her eyes darting around.

'Constable, I've got to go,' she said, her voice a low whisper. 'I'm afraid I'm—'

'But don't you want my mum's number?' the voice was buzzing down the line. 'What about the brandy-butter pavlova?'

The door opened up and, in alarm, Prudence dropped the telephone back on to the receiver.

In the doorway, there stood Flick Garrick.

'Oh,' she said, caught unawares. 'Oh, Mrs Bulstrode, it's . . . you.'

Prudence scrambled to her feet. Obviously, the telephone hadn't cut off properly because, ever so faintly, she could still hear a plaintive little voice bleating about brandy butter.

'I'm sorry, dear,' she blathered, 'I needed to make a call – and I wasn't quite sure where . . .'

But Flick didn't seem perturbed by this at all. 'I'm afraid I need to use the phone myself, Mrs Bulstrode. I was hoping Mrs Mathers was here. She must be . . .' She let the sentence falter, then squeezed past Prudence to pick up the receiver. When she put it to her ear, her eyes screwed up quizzically. 'Brandy butter?' she mouthed, in bewilderment, before hanging up, picking up the receiver again and dialling a number.

When Prudence saw the number she was dialling, her senses started tingling again.

9 . . .
9 . . .
9 . . .

'What happened?' she asked, breathlessly.

Flick looked up from the phone. 'It's Mr Williams. Gray Williams. I went to change his rooms, but he can't get out of bed. He was being sick all night, just like the others, but . . . it's different in him. He's paler. Everything's just the wrong colour. I need to get an—' She stopped as a voice erupted down the line. 'Yes, an ambulance please. Farleigh Manor – right away.'

Her eyes locked with Prudence Bulstrode's.

'Mr Prendergast says he's always been that way. That he could never take his drink like the rest of them. But I've seen drunk guests before, Mrs Bulstrode, and this isn't it. I know what Alice Pendlebury said to you, but . . . is it really food poisoning, Mrs Bulstrode?'

Prudence said, 'Food poisoning can be a brutal thing, of course. But . . .'

'But what?'

'But I don't know, Flick.'

Because, she thought, food poisoning would be accidental. Food poisoning would have been a one-off occasion, caused by whatever the guests had eaten last night. And if food poisoning was *all* it was, then how to make sense of Deirdre Shaw, dropped dead in the kitchen garden, two whole days ago? Deirdre Shaw – who, though they said it was her heart that had given out, had, in fact, choked to death right there in the rhubarb?

Prudence felt a terrible shiver.

No, she thought, she hadn't been summoned to Farleigh Manor to understudy in the aftermath of Deirdre's untimely, but perfectly natural death. She'd been summoned to understudy in the aftermath of a murder.

And now it was happening again.

Chapter Six

Prudence was standing on the doorstep, Mrs Mathers shifting anxiously from foot to foot at her side, when they saw the blue flashing light. At last, the ambulance was here.

'Inside, ladies, inside!' Mrs Mathers exclaimed, when the paramedics – two young women in their early thirties – stepped out on to the drive.

'Two visits in a week, Mrs Mathers,' said the first paramedic; Prudence took her to be the most senior, simply by her demeanour. 'It never rains but it pours.'

'Let's hope it's not like buses,' said the second paramedic, as together they rushed through the manor house doors.

The black humour of the medical profession had never startled Prudence, but it seemed to shock Mrs Mathers to her core. She had to take three deep breaths just to gather her wits. Then she scurried down the hall, zigzagging around them so that she could get ahead and lead the way.

Prudence followed.

The bedroom that Gray Williams was occupying was at the very end of the guest hall. As Mrs Mathers showed the paramedics inside, Prudence caught a glimpse through the door. There lay Mr Williams, curled up like a child beneath his covers. Evidently he'd tried to clean up after himself in the night, because the bedsheets had been stripped away and now he lay in a nest of naked eiderdown and bathroom towels.

'Is he going to be OK?' Mrs Mathers was bleating as the paramedics set about their work. 'Please tell me he's going to be OK?' She looked askance at where Prudence was standing in the hall. 'I'm not sure my ticker could take another death on my watch. I feel cursed, Mrs Bulstrode. Positively cursed!'

One of the paramedics stuck her head out of the door. 'Ladies,' she said, 'do we know what this man ingested?'

Mrs Mathers's face, which had the appearance of a shrew before an owl is about to strike, turned to Prudence for answers.

'I can give you a full menu, but it won't solve any mystery here. A light consommé, sea bream – a nice gooseberry tart . . .'

The paramedic smacked her lips; Mrs Mathers near fainted.

'It sounds like a dream dinner party.' She lowered her voice to add, 'By the way, Mrs Bulstrode, we *loved* you in *Pastries and Puddings*. We used to watch it every afternoon.' Her eyes darted back to Mrs Mathers. 'But what I was meaning was – has this man ingested any . . . substances?'

'Substances?' gasped Mrs Mathers. 'But I keep all my bleaches and polish and caustic soda under lock and key in the store cupboards . . .'

'Drugs, Mrs Mathers,' Prudence said, bold and plain. 'The young lady means drugs.'

The paramedic said, 'I do.'

The word only seemed to inspire yet more panic in Mrs Mathers. With her arms beating fiercely like the wings of a bird about to take off, she said, 'Well – I've never – *drugs* – real-life *drugs* in Farleigh Manor? Never – in my whole life have I – well – well . . .' The panic ebbed out of her. Then she said, softly and under her breath, 'I don't know.'

'Mrs Mathers,' the paramedic said, not unkindly, 'what your guests do in their own time and with their own bodies is every bit their business – and none of yours. Mr Williams here is old enough to know the risks. But we do *need* to know if he ingested anything untoward last night. It might save his life.'

Mrs Mathers froze. 'Is he going to . . .'

'He's depleted. It's possible he's already purged whatever was poisoning him. But we'll need to take him in for more tests. These things get in the bloodstream, and after that they wreak their damage. Bodies can be fragile things. Our liver, our kidneys, our hearts – they can only put up with so much abuse.'

'What should I do?' whispered Mrs Mathers.

'I need you to ask the party, and to impress upon them the importance of honesty. Can you do that?'

There was a hesitation while Mrs Mathers processed the words. Prudence was quite certain the woman was more likely to stagger back against the wall and seize her own failing heart than to do as she was asked.

86

She was about to declare that she'd do it herself when, suddenly – as if borne up by some sudden resolve she'd lacked only moments earlier – Mrs Mathers straightened her body, drew to her full height, declared 'I'll be straight back!' and scuttled off.

The paramedic watched her go and, with a final look at Prudence – 'It was the naked jam tarts we liked best – we've made them every summer since' – she returned to the room.

Prudence hung in the doorway as the paramedics ministered to Gray. At least the man was lucid. When they asked him if they needed a stretcher to get him to the ambulance, he declared, 'I might need some help, but I'm not gone yet' – and, bracing himself on the paramedics, swung one foot out of the bed.

When he started reeling, the lead paramedic said, 'On second thoughts, perhaps the chair *is* a better idea. We can confront the stairs when it comes to it. Stay here, Ruth. I'll be back in a jiffy.' Out in the corridor, she made eyes at Prudence. 'It's these rich folk. They forget that money doesn't stop you getting old. You spend your years stockpiling the shillings, but you can't stockpile your youth. I've seen it too often – middle-aged daredevils, thinking they've got the hearts of eighteen-year-olds. Then – BOOM . . . My bet's that there was a lot of *white powder* here last night, if you know what I mean.'

Prudence had seen a lot of *that* in her time in television as well.

She hurried down the hall, keeping pace with the paramedic. 'I hope you don't mind me asking, but I couldn't help overhearing when you first got here . . . You attended the manor when my old friend Deirdre was found as well?'

They'd reached the top of the sweeping staircase. The paramedic heaved a great sigh as Prudence followed her down it.

'Now *that* was a sorry story. Wasn't a thing we could do.' She paused. 'We used to make her jam tarts, too, but they were always a little too sickly sweet for my taste.'

'And Deirdre – they say it was her heart. But the village constable said . . .' Prudence didn't like to picture this part. 'He said she'd *choked*.'

'Well, I can't say until the post mortem – if there is one. All I can tell you, Mrs Bulstrode, is what I saw on the day. The poor old bird must have been digging for rhubarb when it happened. Quite out of season, of course – there were a couple of stalks that she'd uprooted, but they were horrible, woody things. Not nearly fine enough to feed this lot of posh toffs. She'd had her attack, right there on the patch. I suppose what they're saying is – she didn't die straight away. She keeled over, but she was still alive. Breathed in the dirt – that kind of thing. Death's a messy business, Mrs Bulstrode. You rarely come out of it in good condition.'

By now, they'd reached the manor doors.

'You'll have to excuse me, Mrs Bulstrode. We need to get on with this fast – get some fluids in the old boy. Fluids always help . . .'

Prudence waited for a moment, in a daze; then she retreated into the manor.

Voices were coming from the drawing room. Prudence would have walked directly past – returned, perhaps, to the sanctuary of the kitchens and a nice, calming pot of peppermint tea – had she not heard Mrs Mathers's stammering among those voices. She stopped, listened further. The raised voice – booming, in impenetrable indignation – was certainly Rupert Prendergast himself. She followed it from the top of the hall, reaching the frosted glass doors of the drawing room just as Prendergast exploded, 'Go and tell them then, you silly woman! What am I paying you for!?'

Prudence opened the door.

The rest of the shooting party lounged around the room in various states of repose. Alone among them, Rupert Prendergast looked as if he was ready and willing to launch into the day. His wife Georgette and son Richard remained dressed down; Georgette was even wearing her slippers. Maxwell Pendlebury looked half as sick as Gray Williams in the bedroom above; his elderly skin, already wrinkled and lined, had the pallor of some horror-movie wraith. Evidently, the night's privations had affected him even worse than his wife. At least Alice – with the help of a little make-up – looked purged of the evening's sickness. Prudence was put in mind of pictures she'd once seen of Florence Nightingale, ministering to the sick and wounded in the Crimea. There was, she detected, a certain unpleasant *tang* in the air.

'Oh, Mrs Bulstrode,' said Mrs Mathers, when Prudence appeared, 'Mr Prendergast insists there were no *substances* on the premises last night.'

'If Gray's stupid enough to be snorting up lines of powder like this is 1989 all over again, that's his own problem,' Rupert Prendergast casually announced, 'but I'm minded to think he has more sense than that. There were quite enough indulgences planned for this weekend without having to resort to that sort of thing. Besides, look at the rest of us – we'd have to have been snorting all night long, every last one of us. It would have been positively Bacchanalian. Get up there this instant, and tell those meddling doctors that it's food poisoning – pure and simple.'

It was at the mention of those two words that every eye in the room landed on Prudence.

'Indeed,' said Georgette, waspishly, 'I'm minded to agree. If Deirdre Shaw was here, this would never have happened. Yet, here we are, with some second-fiddle replacement – and every last one of us sick to the gizzards. It's quite ruined this weekend. It's ruined my poor Richard most of all!' Georgette turned and stroked at her son's brow, as if he was some needy toddler and not a twenty-five-year-old professional.

'Oh, Richard will buck up,' Rupert Prendergast interjected, 'won't you, boy? He has his father's constitution. A brisk morning walk, that's what we need – something to shake off the cobwebs. I'll call Lowell. See what he had planned for today. If we can't shoot, by heavens, we'll hike. I didn't pay good money for us to lounge around here all weekend, feeling sorry for ourselves.' He smirked. 'Trust Gray to be the one. The man never could handle a party. Does anyone remember New Year, '98?'

Prudence had remained steadfastly silent throughout, even though she broiled at the very suggestion that *she'd* done this. She was just opening her mouth to ask if she might be excused when she heard the paramedics huffing along the hallway behind her. The others in the party seemed to have heard it too. Soon they were on their feet, streaming out into the hallway to watch Gray being wheeled past.

Gray by name; grey by nature. Prudence felt her heart pull towards him as the paramedics rushed him onward – now with a mask over his face, and already with a cannula in the back of his arm into which a bag of fluids was being fed – towards the waiting ambulance.

At least he managed to lift his other arm to wave a feeble goodbye.

'Is anyone volunteering to accompany the patient?' asked the lead paramedic, when everybody was gathered in the manor house's entrance hall.

For a time, there was silence.

'Oh hang it!' announced Terence Knight – whose complexion hovered somewhere between 'ghostly' and 'pallid'. 'We can't leave the old boy to it. It's all right for you married chaps, but us bachelors have got to stick together . . .'

As Terence Knight hurried to the waiting ambulance, Rupert Prendergast grinned, '*Bachelors*, he says,' with a schoolboy smirk. Then he called out, 'Get back in time for dinner, Knight! Bring the old boy if his stomach can handle it.'

They watched as the ambulance pulled away.

'I don't know how you can be so blasé about it,' Georgette Prendergast said, with a sudden shiver. She put an arm around Richard. 'We've already had one death this weekend. But Deirdre Shaw was nothing to us. We've known Gray for years . . .'

'And we'll know him for years yet,' announced Rupert, with the authority of a military general. 'He's sick, not dying. He just needs pumping full of juice. He'll be back with us by dinner tonight, I shouldn't wonder.'

The rest of the party didn't look convinced, but Rupert's confidence was a mountain. They nodded meekly, even as the last lights of the ambulance vanished into the trees at the bottom of the estate.

The party was drifting away from where Prudence stood. She said, 'Will you be wanting dinner, Mr Prendergast?'

'Why, certainly!' the huge man boomed. 'And lunch, I should think. Some ballast inside of us – that's what we need. Something to feed our bodies and souls.'

Georgette Prendergast turned on her heel. 'Absolutely *not*!' she declared. 'Rupert, by God, how can you even *think* about dinner after last night? I won't eat another thing from this woman unless—'

'Steady on!' interjected Maxwell Pendlebury. 'You can't blame a cook when it isn't her kitchen. So the sea bream was off? Or maybe it wasn't? Some of that wine's been sitting in our cellars for a generation. Who's to say . . .'

Alice Pendlebury gave a polite cough. 'I fell sick too, Max.'

'Exactly,' Georgette Prendergast seethed. 'Look, Mrs Bulstrode, my boy's been more poorly than I can remember. I won't put it at your door – though there's plenty that would. I understand you've come to us in unusual and extenuating circumstances. I daresay a few corners had to be cut in that kitchen to serve us our supper on time. But I won't have my darling son –' Richard Prendergast looked so pale that he put up precisely no argument at his mother treating him like an over-indulged infant, '– eat another thing that comes out of that kitchen until every last one of its ingredients has been tossed out and replaced. Do you hear me?' She turned to her husband. 'Tell her, Rupert.'

Rupert Prendergast shrugged his enormous shoulders. 'You have a blank cheque, Mrs Bulstrode. Restock the larder. I dare say you'd find that preferable, in any case, to cooking with Mrs Shaw's ingredients?' He stopped. 'We'll take teas in the drawing room, if you please. Come on, come on! This weekend isn't finished yet!'

Not finished, thought Prudence, *but somebody is certainly trying to kill it off.*

She let that thought circle around her as she returned to the kitchens. At least, now, she had a mission on which to focus. Sometimes, you needed to switch the mind off. That was when the greatest leaps of imagination happened. There were times when she knew that one of her recipes was lacking something, but – no matter how hard she tried – she could never set it right. Then, when she grew furious enough to forget about the whole thing and went to potter in the kitchen or take a nice

93

perambulation around the village, the answer suddenly just sprung into her mind. Unbidden. Fully formed. This thing that was niggling at her now might be just the same.

The kitchen was empty.

She'd expected to find Suki busily decontaminating surfaces, but instead all she found was a note that read: *Gone to collect the breakfast dishes from Lowell – and to catch some autumn sun! Be back soon, Suki x*

She rolled her eyes. It was just like the girl, thought Prudence. One job at a time simply wasn't enough for the young.

She looked around the kitchen, stepped into the larder, opened up each cupboard in turn. It was a shame, in lots of ways, that all of it would have to go. But the wealthy got what the wealthy wanted. That was just the way of the world.

In the larder, her eyes were drawn suddenly to the menu Deirdre had pinned up, outlining every meal she had planned for the weekend. Prudence let her eyes roam over it. All classic Deirdre fare, she thought. It would have gone down well. But something was bothering her about it. Something was bothering her about *everything* – but this thing most of all.

Then it came to her. It wasn't the things she was looking at that were bothering her. It was the thing that wasn't there.

Rhubarb.

It didn't feature in a single recipe Deirdre had planned.

So why, then, had Deirdre been digging it up?

94

Rhubarb, rhubarb, rhubarb. It was at the centre of everything.

Suki was glad to be out of the kitchen. No doubt she'd pay for it later – perhaps find herself scrubbing the floors at midnight like a twenty-first-century Cinderella – but, for now, it was good to put being a kitchen assistant out of her mind.

The grounds of Farleigh Manor had seemed vast and wild when Prudence and Suki first rattled into them but, now that she walked through them, she realised there was order in the estate. The ring of gardens directly around the manor house itself was expertly tended – somebody had mown and edged all the lawns in anticipation of autumn – and all of the various trees and outbursts of shrubbery had been pruned at summer's end. It was only beyond that things felt wilder, as the lowland of the estate rose to meet the Cotswolds hills above. Here, the forested escarpments seemed dark and entangled, like the forests in fairy tales. Suki, who had spent many teenage nights tramping around the villages back home, had never minded forests much. Some of the old gang used to throw all-night parties in whatever woodland clearing they could find. Well, it was better than trashing some unlucky bugger's house – and, the further away from prying eyes, the better. So she was not unduly worried when the path she was following arced directly toward the woodland at the bottom of one of the hills. She was only fifteen minutes by foot from the manor. It was still, she thought wryly, civilisation – of a sort.

95

It was the same route along which she'd seen the gamekeeper, Hubert Lowell, take off when he left the manor house yesterday afternoon – so his cottage was surely somewhere on the other side of these trees. By rights she should have waited and asked someone for directions – but they'd all seemed so overwhelmed by the thought of some decrepit old idiot who'd drunk too much in the night that she hadn't wanted to bother them. She'd been worried she'd get roped into cleaning his dirty bed linen too.

Before it reached the woodland, the dirt track forked. One route led into the branches; the other dropped around the forest's edge. It was at this point that Suki's curiosity got the better of her. She tramped around the second fork, skirting the woodland in its shadow, until the track bent down – and she heard the babbling waters of a river turning somewhere below.

It wasn't much of a river. Not when she found it. 'River' was a generous description of what was effectively a small brook, replete with rocky stepping stones and a grassy knoll of an island in its centre. No doubt it conjoined, somewhere further along, with the River Eye, which marked the border of the Farleigh estate.

Suki's mind wheeled back to the information Numbers had sent through as they first approached the Farleigh grounds. She took out her iPhone. (God, but it was great to feel it in her hands – she had no idea what her grandmother hated about the things! They could make you feel as if you were connected with the world even in a place like this.) Her heart sank when she realised there was no reception – she just couldn't believe that places like this actually existed; there wasn't a phone mast for miles around – but at least the webpage Numbers had sent through was still open on her browser. THE DEATH OF JANE SUTCLIFFE. Suki felt a strange shiver at the words – and realised, there and then, that she was standing on the edge of Hill Beck, the same water course along which Jane Sutcliffe had brought the two Farleigh children for their picnic; the same water in which Jane Sutcliffe had perished.

She bent down and trailed her fingers in the ice-cold water.

She wasn't sure why the thought of a centuries-old murder tantalised her so much. She supposed it was the same reason people had been scandalised back in the day. The perennial fear of the unknown . . .

She was staring at her reflection, churned up by the water, when she heard the snap of a branch behind her. Breathlessly, she turned – but it was only a rabbit, darting hither and thither on the outskirts of the wood.

The moment had shaken her. She picked herself up, re-joined the path, and followed it back to the fork in the trail.

It was dark in the woodland. Sometimes, the autumnal sun shone through the branches, dappling the edge of the trail, but sometimes the trees crowded so closely that it blotted out the light. It was probably the idea of Jane Sutcliffe's improbable end that unnerved her, but she was grateful when she saw the light pooling up ahead and realised she had reached the copse's furthest edge. As she emerged, the smell of woodsmoke was strong in the

air. In a ring of stones, at the edge of a dry-stone wall –
beyond which sat a glum-looking little cottage, cloaked
in ivy and moss – the remains of a bonfire were breathing
their last. Suki had always liked bonfires. They reminded
her of those illicit woodland parties, or the mornings
after – when she and her friends had woken up, worse for
wear, and brewed tea over old barbecues and badly dug
firepits.

The difference was that *their* campfires had never had
the remains of charred carcases tumbling out of them.
Their campfires hadn't been crowned with a smoke-
blackened skull, nor been surrounded by a graveyard of
tiny bones.

Suki looked up, through the drifting smoke, and saw
that the door to the cottage was propped open.
Gamekeeper's business, she thought. *That's what happens
in a place like this.* Somebody had to manage the estate,
and all of the animals who inhabited it. To country folk,
death was just another part of life.

A wild barking erupted from the cottage doorway, and
out of it there burst a roan English setter. The dog was
already all over her, its tongue lapping and muddy paws
scrabbling, when she realised that this was not a fero-
cious attack but an outburst of canine adoration. She was
just about managing not to be completely bowled over
when a genial voice called out, 'Biscuit! Biscuit, get
down!' and she saw Hubert Lowell appear, in his tweed
jacket and flat cap, in the cottage doorway.

The dog immediately did what its master had
instructed, then flopped on to its back in the dirt with its

tail beating feverishly. Suki couldn't resist. She got down to her haunches and tickled her tummy.

'The daft bugger's gone soft in her old age,' Hubert Lowell said, plodding over to where they stood. 'And look at the state of you, she's got dirt all down you . . .'

'It's only a little mud,' said Suki.

Lowell arched his eyebrow. 'Aye, if only it *was* just mud. Here, come on in – you can sponge yourself down. You're the girl who's come for the dishes, are you? I have to say – every cloud has a silver lining. That lot up there might have drunk themselves silly last night, but there's always someone that profits. That was a nice round of bacon, and Biscuit and I shared so many sausages I shan't eat for a week.'

Suki followed Lowell inside – hesitantly, because Biscuit was now turning celebratory laps around her legs – and hovered in the doorway. Lowell's cottage was small and had the look of a lovingly tended hovel. The walls were crooked, the roof was low, the floorboards creaked with every step that was taken, and – apart from a small corner where an armchair was planted firmly in front of an old black-and-white TV – there was barely a spare inch of space. In the corner sat a tin sink and hotplate, beyond which a back door was draped in various overcoats, hats and scarves. A little bookcase was full of pot-boilers – and one peculiarly out of place copy of Deirdre Shaw's classic *Game Night: Plucking and Stuffing*. Suki remembered that Lowell had been a most improbable fan. Heaped around it were books so threadbare and old that Suki figured they were part of the manor's original fixtures and fittings.

'Here you go,' said Lowell, producing the crockery, which he'd placed carefully inside a cloth bag. 'My compliments to the chef.' He paused. 'They doing all right up there? It's never nice to see a party get sick like that. Though it makes my job easier, of course. It'll be a day off today.'

'They called an ambulance just now, for Mr Williams.'

Lowell hung his head. 'Did they indeed?'

'They seem old enough to know better,' Suki grinned. 'Are they all like that?'

'All?'

'All the toffs who come out here for their parties. Rich folk from London. I bet you've seen it all . . .'

'Well,' said Lowell, warming to the subject, 'I happen to remember the old times when Mr Prendergast used to bring his parties down here. Twice a summer, sometimes, and autumn for the shooting. They weren't the most popular lot in the village. Most times, the villagers here are pretty welcoming to outsiders. It brings the money into the area, you see. But Prendergast really knew how to rub people up the wrong way. He was always getting into some disagreement with a local landlord or one of the farmers. Got called a poacher once, when he strayed over the bounds of our licence. Yes, he knew how to raise hell when he was younger.'

'You were here back then?'

'Aye, ever since I was a boy, and there's no place else I'd rather be.'

Suki didn't know if she should say the next words that came to her tongue, but she could still feel the cold touch of Hill Beck as she'd trailed her fingers in the water, and she spluttered out, 'I suppose you get asked all the time, do you? About Jane Sutcliffe and those children?'

Lowell faltered before he said, 'Aye, sometimes . . .'

'A story like that is its own kind of ghost, isn't it?'

'What do you mean?'

'It hangs around,' said Suki, 'whether you like it or not.'

'Well, here's the thing I've learnt in all my years,' Lowell said. 'It's all just fashions. Stories come in and out, just like music and clothes and – whatever they're salivating over, right now, in London and Paris and New York. Some seasons people like a bit of murder. Some seasons they don't. Me? I don't care for all that Gothic stuff. The way I see it, if you go back far enough in time, there's been a murder on every street corner. It's all just stuff that's happened. Ancient history. I'm more inter- ested in what's happening right now. How my pheasants are doing. If the deer or the badgers or the foxes are getting too many.' Suki thought back to the bonfire sitting outside, the cascade of scorched woodland bodies. 'And if my Biscuit here is going to be able to walk off those sausages! Come on, girl!'

Lowell was too genial to say it out loud, but Suki sensed that this was her moment to leave. Thanking him for the dishes, she walked with him into the wood; then, when he and Biscuit followed some lesser track through the trees, she picked her way back to the manor.

By the time she got there, the ambulance had been and gone. Her grandmother was standing outside the open door of the camper, with a look that said her patience was being strained – but had not yet broken.

With a sinking feeling, Suki picked up the pace and hurried along the last length of track. 'I'm sorry, Grandma. I got the dishes . . .' She held them up, as if in triumph. Then she saw the look on her grandmother's face and paled. 'Has something happened? It's not . . . Mr Williams? Is he OK?'

'It's not Williams,' said Prudence, shaking her head. 'It's the Prendergasts. They've issued us an instruction.'

Suki furrowed her brow.

'Pop those dishes back in the kitchen, Suki,' said Prudence, and tossed her the kitchen-garden key. 'We're going for a ride.'

The village of Nutwood St Knowle sat a mere six miles beyond the edge of the Farleigh estate, announcing itself in a riot of autumnal colour as Prudence's camper van rattled past the welcome sign. Banks of burgundy roses grew at both sides of the road while, a little further into the village, the last of the season's sunflowers still stood, resplendent and tall.

It was nearly lunchtime and the village market was in full swing. Suki, who preferred to shop on the internet, thought that there was a time and a place for everything – and that the time for thriving village markets was probably 1956. But she knew better than to give voice to her opinions – because, suddenly, all the ill feeling Prudence had been harbouring since Farleigh had evaporated. It was the market stalls, ripe with produce, and the village shops, still picturesque and thriving, that had enlivened her.

'The very backbone of Britain!' Prudence was beaming as she perused a grocer's stall. 'There used to be a market like this in every corner of the land. Now you drive out of town to a car park and load up on tinned peaches and powdered potato. The world went mad, and nobody noticed. Look, Suki – an honest to goodness bookshop!'

There were, indeed, shops aplenty. Most of Nutwood St Knowle gathered around the village green, where the open-air market was a buzz of activity, and Prudence greedily took in the range of grocers, butchers, bakers (and even one or two candlestick-makers) with relish. Something about the chequered red-and-white awnings and cheery voices calling out prices made her feel forty years younger. She had quite forgotten what a joy it could be to spend an idle afternoon pottering in search of ingredients, instead of issuing some production runner with a list and dismissing them to the nearest supermarket.

They found one of the very few remaining parking spaces on the edge of the green, and stepped out into the bracing air. The sun might have been out, but there was a chill. 'The perfect weather,' Prudence announced, 'for a market outing. I wish we could spend all day here, Suki. Well, all *week*, actually. But there are at least five paying customers back there, and they'll want their dinner.' Prudence was a professional, which was the only reason she hadn't substituted 'paying customers' for 'snobs', 'knobs' or some more rarefied form of insult. The truth was, she was simmering with anger at them. No – *broiling*. Yes, she was broiling with the Prendergast party already. She just knew better than to let it show.

As they began perusing the shelves and crates of the nearest stall – replete with fine apples, berries, hazelnuts and a panoply of more exotic fare ('I dare say kiwano goes with a tender piece of sirloin – but I'll show them a breakfast they've never even dreamt of when I serve it with cream cheese and mint on toast . . .') – Suki said, 'Well, Grandma, at least they'll *know* we're not poisoning anybody this time.'

Prudence, who had been debating whether dragon fruit sorbet was too summery for this weekend, rolled her eyes and drifted on to a display of durians. 'Oh, Suki, I already *know* we weren't poisoning anyone. Yes,' she said to the market trader, 'six pomegranate, three guava, and toss in some lemons. You can never have enough lemon.' Then she looked back at Suki, knowingly. 'I've been working with food all of my life. For all of her gaucheness, so had Deirdre Shaw. I might not have trusted Deirdre not to steal a job from under my feet – or a gentleman, I might add, if my Nicholas hadn't been such a stalwart fellow – but I'd have trusted her with the cleanliness of a kitchen *with my life*. I'm one hundred per cent positive that there wasn't a spot of spoilage or corruption in that kitchen. Deirdre valued her celebrity enough to know the sorts of things that could derail it. And poisoning a household of paying guests would have made every gossip column in the country . . . *if* she were alive.'

Prudence collected her exotic fruit, asked the market trader for a bag of baking apples too, and drifted on to a baker's stall, where great whorls of challah sat alongside herb-encrusted focaccias, hard black loaves and fluffy white bloomers.

'What do you mean, Grandma?'

'Deirdre would no more cut a corner than I would, Suki. You didn't walk into *Ramsay's Kitchen Nightmares* yesterday. You walked into a well-ordered kitchen, with barely a spot of dirt to be seen.'

'So somebody cleaned it up,' said Suki. 'They had to. Otherwise, how did everyone get sick?'

'Wrong,' said Prudence, and decided on some simple loaves, with a big brioche in reserve; it wasn't fancy, but she had a recipe for an old-fashioned bread-and-butter pudding that might suit this occasion *just right*.

'Grandma, you're not making sense. We already know it wasn't the wine that made them sick – Alice Pendlebury didn't drink a drop. So what happened if they weren't poisoned?'

'Oh,' said Prudence – and hurried, this time, to the line forming outside the butcher's shop on the edge of the green, where plump speckled sausages hung on strings in the window and a line of fresh pheasants dangled from hooks, 'I didn't say they weren't poisoned, dear.'

'But—'

'I simply said it wasn't my cooking that did it.'

The line was moving glacially slowly. Evidently, the butcher was a popular fellow. Prudence could hear him talking about lamb shank through the open window. The best butchers always had a way with words. What was the saying? 'You sell the sizzle, not the sausage.'

'Grandma, what are you saying?'

Prudence looked to each side of them in the line. One lady had her headphones in, listening to Andrew Lloyd Webber by the sounds of it; on the other side, a couple in the first flush of real love were making goo-goo eyes at each other. Well, at least nobody was listening.

'Think clearly, Suki, dear. You'll have to learn to think clearly if you're going to work in my kitchen, so you may as well start now. Deirdre Shaw dropped dead in the rhubarb patch. Her heart, that's what they say. Well, what they say *might* be true, but it isn't the whole story – because the truth is she choked to death, after having dug up some sticks of woody rhubarb she didn't need for a single recipe on her list. Two nights later, the whole party at Farleigh Manor get a sickness – unexplainable, as I've made clear, because it *was not my cooking*. It seems, to me, that there are more pressing unanswered questions at Farleigh Manor than this business your chap Numbers got you all excited about from hundreds of years ago.'

They had almost reached the end of the queue. Ahead of them, an elderly gentleman emerged from the shop labouring under a ham hock twice the size of his head. Behind him, a little terrier gnawed delightedly on a trotter.

'Grandma . . . you don't possibly think Deirdre Shaw was . . . murdered?'

Prudence said, sagely, 'Deirdre Shaw had plenty of enemies, but they were in the cookery world, the publishing world, London and all its glitz. I happen to know one or two photographers who would gladly have planted Deirdre face down in that rhubarb patch.'

'But out here, Grandma? Murder, in a perfect place like Nutwood St Knowle?'

'Aha,' said Prudence, and slipped inside the butcher's shop, 'well, there you're making a grave error. You already know how darling little places like this can be the home of murder. Think, my dear, of your Jane Sutcliffe.'

'Who would want to do a thing like that? You're forgetting, Grandma – Deirdre didn't know anybody out here.'

'That's not quite true. Remember – our Deirdre cooked for Mr Prendergast's party once before. This wasn't her first time at Farleigh.' She looked up, into the ruddy, beaming face of a butcher who fitted his role so well she had no doubt he was actually called Butch. *Butch the Butcher's Boy*, she thought. 'Two brace of pheasants,' she said, 'and six Cumberland whorls. I'll need one kilo of back bacon – unsmoked – and some of that terrine you have in the window. Oh – and two-and-a-half kilos of chuck, twelve of those rabbit legs on the counter, and two dozen eggs.'

'A dinner party, is it?' the butcher winked. Only then did he seem to recognise his customer. 'Why, Prudence Bulstrode! As I live and breathe! This lot's on the house,' he beamed, 'just give us a mention next time you're doing an interview, eh?'

'I won't hear of it,' said Prudence – and, reaching into her purse, produced a wad of banknotes which she handed over. 'I'll pay any price.' Then she, too, beamed. 'Well, it's not my money I'm spending, you see ... so chalk it up, as much as you like.'

Outside, laden down with fruit and vegetables, breads and meat, fresh eggs, fresh milk, and a full larder of tinned pulses, seasonings and oils, Prudence and Suki wove their way back towards the camper.

'Grandma, those people we're cooking for – you think one of them wanted Deirdre Shaw dead?'

Prudence opened the camper and began to load her up. 'I'm saying something doesn't add up. It's like when you're not paying attention, you add salt instead of sugar to your tea. At first, it seems everything's perfectly normal. Then you taste it. Well, this tastes *off*, sweetheart.'

'So what are you going to do?'

Prudence swung into the driver's seat and told Suki to buckle up. 'I don't know. *Yet.*'

The camper turned a full circle around the village green, Prudence winding down the window to soak up, one last time, the perfection of Nutwood St Knowle, with its thatched rooftops and buzzing market.

They were waiting at the lights at the end of the green when, all at once, Suki opened the camper door, clattered across the road and through the door of another shop. Prudence just had time to shout out, 'Suki, my goodness!' before a horn started tooting behind her. Begrudgingly, she heaved the camper to the side of the road to let a farm vehicle trundle past.

It was the bookshop door that Suki had tumbled through. Beneath its striped awning, the display in the window read LOCAL INTEREST in bright blue letters. A bell tinkled whenever the door opened or closed.

Suki wasn't gone long. Prudence was daydreaming about rhubarb – *again* – when the bookshop door opened up and her grand-daughter re-emerged, to clamber back into the camper. In her hands was a paperback book.

'Look,' she said.

Prudence read the title:

THE BODY IN THE BECK
A History of the Farleigh Manor Murder
by Katie Winterdale

'Listen to this,' Suki said, and read from the blurb as Prudence drew the camper away. 'A summer's day, 1886. Jane Sutcliffe, for three years the well-regarded nanny to Jack and Mary Farleigh, takes the children for a riverside picnic from which she will never return. But was it a mistake – or was it murder? In this illuminating study, Katie Winterdale untangles the true story behind a notorious case and, in doing so, shines a spotlight on a sordid century.'

Prudence gave her a look. 'It sounds like a tabloid.'

'It's very well-regarded, Grandma. It has a quote from *Woman's Own*. And, well, you did say we're going to be murder detectives this weekend, not *just* the hired help . . .'

From the corner of her eye, Prudence saw that Suki was smiling. But Prudence wasn't smiling at all. She was

109

thinking about the centuries, and how one so often reflected another. She was thinking about human beings, with all their faults and flaws – and how, from one century to the next, they never really seemed to change. And she was thinking of two dead women, both found in the grounds of Farleigh Manor – separated by the centuries, but united all the same.

She was still thinking of this, trying to ignore Suki as she prattled on about the sensationalist things she was reading in her book, when the camper van cruised back into the grounds of Farleigh Manor – and there stood Mrs Mathers, flapping her arms around as she stood by the door.

'Mrs Bulstrode, there you are!' she cried, hurtling to the camper door before Prudence had even disembarked.

'Whatever's the matter?' asked Prudence.

'It's the kitchens,' Mrs Mathers exclaimed. 'Mrs Bulstrode, I think you'd better see for yourself!'

Chapter Seven

The shattered glass was everywhere.

Prudence and Suki stood in the kitchen doorway, the stairs behind them climbing to the manor's central hall and the drawing room where the guests had earlier been gathered. 'But they went out not long after you,' Mrs Mathers explained. 'Mr Prendergast rallied them up for it – well, those who could stand it. A bracing walk to shake off the cobwebs.' So nobody heard the smashing of the backdoor glass. No one had heard the tramping of boots or the slamming of cupboard doors as whoever this was brazened their way inside, directly from the kitchen gardens, and tore the place apart.

'Flick and I were still in the guest suites. I'm afraid Mr Williams has made quite a mess of his room, so we had rather a lot of work to do. I only saw it myself half an hour ago . . .'

Prudence ventured into the kitchen. A messier thief there could not have been. Half the cupboards still hung open, with one door hanging off its hinges as if having suffered some violent onslaught. The toaster, kettle and free-standing grill were all gone, as was the iPad from its holder on the wall. (Well, thought Prudence, a kitchen really *wasn't* the place for anything as fancy as that anyway.) The fridge, when she looked in it, had been denuded – and, in the larder, the boxes of wine, even Alice Pendlebury's non-alcoholic Château de Fleur, were all gone. So were the three-dozen eggs and birds left hanging from the weekend's first shoot.

'The mixer!' Suki exclaimed, pointing to the place on the counter where a state-of-the-art KitchenAid once stood.

'It's worse than that, dear,' said Mrs Mathers. She elbowed past Prudence, who had gravitated to the garden door and the shattered glass trampled into the doormat there. Then she opened one of the drawers. Inside lay nothing: not a fork, nor a table spoon. 'Some of these things have been with the manor since the very beginning. They're practically heirlooms. There are silver teaspoons missing. All the fine china.' She directed her gaze to a glass cabinet on the far wall, whose doors had been smashed and shelves stripped bare. 'It was planned, wasn't it? Somebody was watching the house. They had to be. They waited until you'd gone into town, Mrs Bulstrode, and then until the guests took their leave . . . Mrs Bulstrode?'

Prudence was only very vaguely listening at all. For some time now, she'd been crouched at the doormat, lifting the bigger pieces of glass out of the doormat threads, then running her finger around the muddy impressions left there. She was only startled from her reverie when Mrs Mathers repeated, in a panicked voice, 'Mrs Bulstrode?'

'Yes, dear?' She looked up.

'It was some of the locals. It isn't the first break-in we've had – though it's been a while. Time was when people turned poacher to steal from the Farleigh Estate. Now they just turn burglar instead.'

'Well, dear, that's the modern world for you. There's not much money in honest poaching any more. No,' said Prudence, 'better to steal the fine china. Except . . .' Her eyes fixed, again, on the muddy impressions at the garden door. Then she lifted them to the larder. 'Why steal three-dozen eggs? And a double brace of pheasants? The irony is, Mrs Mathers, that they could have had it all for free – we were about to toss almost everything in here on to the compost heap.' She paused. 'Did you call the police?'

Mrs Mathers nodded, fervently. 'He's cycling out here now.'

'*Cycling?*'

'That nice young constable from Nutwood St Knowle.'

Prudence decided it was better not to comment on this. She only hoped the young man had his cycling proficiency certificate.

'And you said Mr Prendergast took the whole party out?'

'Oh no,' Mrs Mathers replied, 'not quite. He tried to, of course. He was quite adamant about it. But Richard wasn't feeling up to it. There was a row about that, as you can imagine. Mr Prendergast thinks his son ought to be made of sterner stuff – like he isn't living up to the family name, and all because he doesn't drink and debauch like they used to, back in the day. Well, after that, Alice

113

decided *she'd* stay too – just to keep Richard company, you know? Well, *that* caused an almighty upset. Alice's husband Maxwell has always been a jealous sort.'

Suki snorted, 'You would be when you're as old as him and Alice is as young and beautiful as . . .'

'Suki, dear,' interjected Prudence, sternly, 'these are our clients.'

Suki groaned. 'I'm only saying what you're thinking too, Grandma.'

'It's OK, Mrs Bulstrode,' said Mrs Mathers, 'it won't go any further. I'd be lying if I said Flick and I haven't given in – often – to that kind of gossip ourselves. It's a strange thing, people flitting in and out of lives like this, but we get it a lot here. It's like catching up on a soap opera you haven't seen in years. But Alice was always a wild one. Until she married Maxwell, she had a *reputation* – can I say it like that? – for falling in love with somebody new every summer. And if they lasted until Christmas, well, he was a lucky man indeed. Mr Pendlebury remembers that. It spooks him sometimes.'

'I've known men like it,' said Prudence. 'He thinks he owns her.'

'The funny thing is, I'd say Alice is quite the sort of woman who *wants* to be owned.'

'How so?' asked Prudence.

At this, Suki found the courage to interject again, 'Well, you don't marry somebody like Maxwell Pendlebury for his good looks, Grandma . . .'

So, thought Prudence: *three of them out on their walk; Richard and Alice sequestered somewhere inside.* She let her

114

eyes roam all around the kitchen again. One thing was for certain – unless that constable showed significantly more wit than he had on the telephone earlier, he wasn't going to find much of any value here. Country houses were being burgled all the time. They were easy marks: big, largely empty, and in the middle of nowhere. A few silver teaspoons could be fenced without much effort. And all of the fancy kitchen equipment and gadgetry would be easy enough to shift, unnoticed, on one of those internet marketplaces Prudence barely took time to understand.

'Maybe we should speak to Richard and Alice?' she ventured. 'Well, Mrs Mathers, I'd like to start some kitchen prep – but if this fine young constable is coming to cast his eagle eye over the incident . . .'

Mrs Mathers nodded. 'They're in the music room,' she said. 'Alice wanted to play the old records. I'll show you in, Mrs Bulstrode.'

Prudence was following Mrs Mathers through the door when Suki piped up, 'Grandma . . .'

'I'll be back shortly, Suki.'

'No, Grandma, it's . . .'

Prudence turned. She saw that Suki had been drawn to the broken glass in the kitchen-garden door. Her face was creased in confusion.

'I don't understand,' Suki said.

'Well, isn't it obvious?' Mrs Mathers put in. 'This brigand smashed his way in.'

Suki touched the door handle. She lifted it up and down. Then she gave Prudence a certain kind of look

– and Prudence's eyes opened in realisation. 'Oh,' she said, and hurried back over.

Moments later, Prudence too was fingering the door handle ('But what about fingerprints?' Mrs Mathers was fretting), then sliding her finger up and down the frame.

'The door wasn't locked,' Prudence whispered. 'Well, what are we to think? That he smashed the glass on his way in, reached through and took the key, then unlocked it?'

'No, Grandma,' Suki said – and then, with her face flushing red, she added, 'because I didn't lock the door.'

Prudence's mind flashed back in time, reeling back through the hours until she was standing by the camper, waiting to head out to Nutwood St Knowle. In her mind's eye, she saw Suki hurrying forward along the path, the breakfast bowls in her hand. She saw herself tossing Suki the kitchen-garden key, then waiting as she slipped inside to leave the bowls on the counter – which was (she saw, looking up) exactly where they remained.

'You didn't lock the door?' Prudence asked.

Suki fished in her own pocket and brought out her fingers, dangling the key.

'I came back through the kitchen-garden door to put down the breakfast plates. But you were just waiting by the camper. I suppose I didn't want to keep you waiting.'

Prudence stared. She felt certain there was an answer in this, if only she could see it. There were more questions, too, but between them there was the shape of some solution. It was like a half-remembered dream – she couldn't quite tell just what it was, or what had happened, but she knew it was tantalisingly out of reach.

'All the more reason, I think, to speak with Richard and Alice.' She turned on the spot. 'Lead on, Mrs Mathers.'

The music room was Farleigh Manor's second parlour. Smaller, and less frequented, than the drawing room, it had a benevolent, cosy air about it – conjured up, no doubt, by the great fire that was eternally flickering in the hearth, and all the portraits of the old masters of the manor, the Farleigh family, which stretched back as far as 1802. An exquisite record collection, covering all of the early twentieth-century greats, had been compiled by one of the earlier Farleighs and was provided for the guests to use. Consequently, as Mrs Mathers led Prudence and Suki through the doors, they could hear the strains of one of the big swing bands from the inter-war years filling the air: Tommy Dorsey or Benny Goodman.

Prudence hadn't expected to find Richard Prendergast and Alice Pendlebury dancing – but that was what they were doing. There was precious little space on the thick, carpeted floor for the couple to move freely – but, in front of the fire, Richard had taken Alice into hold and they were performing a simple box step up and down the hearth. Prudence's first impression was that Richard was as uncomfortable as a prude asked to model at a life drawing class. It was certainly Alice who'd been taking the lead. She'd arranged Richard's hands and arms in perfect formation and her laughter was in perfect opposition to Richard's tortured concentration. The poor boy

(Prudence, too, thought of him as a boy, even though he was twenty-five years old) seemed both grateful and deeply humiliated by Prudence and Mrs Mathers's sudden arrival. He wriggled out of Alice's arms and snatched a glass of some effervescent orange fizz – no doubt a soluble vitamin drink – from the mantel.

'Sir, madam,' said Mrs Mathers, her eyes rolling around, looking anywhere except at the guests, 'I'm afraid we've had to call the police.'

Richard spluttered on his effervescent vitamin solution. Alice's face was a startled mask. 'The police?' she asked. 'We're only dancing.'

'There's been a break-in,' Prudence intervened. When she clasped Mrs Mathers by the shoulder, the housekeeper visibly calmed down. She was, thought Prudence, like a child who doesn't know whether they've done wrong. 'While we were on our supplies trip into Nutwood St Knowle, somebody broke into the kitchens and ransacked the place.'

'The iPad's gone,' Mrs Mathers blurted out.

'Among many other things,' said Prudence, who was most perplexed at the importance everybody seemed to place on the missing technology. Technology could be replaced. Manor house heirlooms could not. And what use was an iPad in a kitchen anyway? 'There's a smashed window down there, and much more besides. It wasn't an opportunistic job. Somebody was watching the manor. They knew we'd gone out and that the kitchen would be empty. And they knew the shooting party had gone for a walk as well.'

'Not all of us,' said Richard, glumly. His face had blanched and he sank into one of the burgundy armchairs. 'I'm still shivering.'

Alice, at least, seemed to have purged the poison from her body. Compared to how she'd looked in the night, she seemed positively resplendent. 'Ransacked the kitchen? While *we* were sitting here?'

Prudence's eyes fell on the record player – a vintage cabinet that looked to have originated sometime in the middle of the last century. To Prudence, it wasn't dissimilar to a unit her father used to have – and that would have placed it somewhere around 1960. 'I suppose you didn't hear anything?'

Alice said, 'Not a thing. I'm afraid I've taken it upon myself to teach young Richard, here, a thing or two about the classics. Can you believe the boy never learnt how to dance?'

Richard gave a weak shrug. 'My father sent me to boxing lessons at the age of six, but he wouldn't have dreamed of me dancing.'

'As a matter of fact,' said Alice, with a smile, 'I think he'd lose his mind if he thought Richard was dancing, even today. It almost makes it *illicit*, doesn't it? To dance when nobody's watching.'

At first, Prudence was surprised that Alice hadn't batted an eyelid at the idea of the kitchen being ransacked; it was only when she reminded herself that this was not *their* house, that they were merely rich interlopers flitting through for a weekend, that her ambivalence started to make sense. Even so – Deirdre Shaw dead, Gray Williams laid up in a hospital bed, and now *this*. The fact she was the only one who seemed to give it a passing thought was beginning to grate on her.

'Who do you suppose it was?' asked Richard, glumly.

Well, at least the younger man seemed to have noticed.

'I was rather hoping you might have heard something.'

Richard and Alice shared a look. 'The music,' Richard shrugged.

'And the *dancing*,' Alice smiled.

Richard looked suddenly green – and, right there and then, Prudence was quite sure there had been something other than dancing going on in this room. She wasn't quite certain whether the younger man knew it (he was so green around the gills that a romantic liaison seemed quite off the cards), but Alice had certainly been enjoying herself. Well, Richard *was* a good-looking young man. There was little doubt about that. What he seemed to lack in get-up-and-go (and constitution) was more than made up for by the matinee idol good looks, his proud jawline and velvety-chocolate eyes. And, if what Mrs Mathers had said about Alice's reputation – back in the wild, hedonistic days – was true, it was not such a leap of imagination to think she'd enjoyed cajoling some attention out of him while nobody was watching.

'My father might have heard something,' Richard said.

Prudence breathed in. 'I thought Mr Prendergast rallied the others out for a walk?'

'He did,' Richard shrugged, 'but he stepped back in a little while later.' He became aware Alice was staring at him quizzically and said, 'It was when I took myself off to the ... little boy's room,' he coughed. Evidently Richard was still throwing up from the night before. 'He was coming back down the guest stairs, with his Miroku.'

Prudence made a gesture, as if asking him to elaborate.

'It's his prize gun,' Richard explained. 'Sporting grade five. My mother had it especially engraved. I suppose he came back because he fancied a shoot after all . . .'

'Without Mr Lowell?' gasped Mrs Mathers.

It was, Prudence knew, a cardinal sin of game-shooting weekends: you did not go rogue. The gamekeeper was king out on the estate. He was the one who briefed the 'guns' – the weekend's shooters; he was the one who chose the sites and spotted the birds; it was his dogs who accompanied the expeditions and recovered the kills; it was he who put together the team of beaters to drive the birds out into the open. You did not go out alone – not even if you were as rich and powerful as Rupert Prendergast.

So what was he doing?

'You'd have to ask him,' said Richard. 'But, I suppose, if he'd heard somebody breaking into the house – well, he's hardly likely to have ignored it, is he?'

Prudence was about to press him further – what *exactly* was Rupert doing back here? – when the music room door inched open and Flick Garrick poked her head in.

'Sorry to disturb, Mrs Mathers. Constable Littleton's here. He's waiting for you in the kitchen.'

*　　*　　*

Prudence was right. The constable looked less like an insightful, experienced detective than he did a twelve-year-old playing dress-up for 'What I Want to Be When I Grow Up Day' at school. He wasn't even wearing uniform – 'I'm afraid it just makes me sweat, and I've had to cycle a long way without any lunch' – as he paraded around the kitchen, making diligent notes in his spiralbound notebook.

Prudence wasn't sure if it was just plain bad luck, or if every constable in Great Britain had come from the same kindergarten. The older she got, the younger these fresh-faced young scamps seemed to get.

Either that, or the police had simply dispatched their least important officer for a job that nobody wanted.

'Three – dozen – eggs,' he wrote in his notebook, finishing off with a big tick. 'Four freshly shot pheasants. One – case – Château – de – Fleur . . .' He looked up, tossing his floppy brown hair (he must have visited a salon) out of his eyes. 'Oh, it's rather like making a shopping list, isn't it?'

Prudence hung her head. 'Constable Littleton, there's something you ought to see.' And she took him to the garden door, where she explained about the broken glass and the fact that the door had already been unlocked.

'So what you're saying is . . . it wasn't actually a break in at all?'

'Well, no,' said Prudence, who could sense another nonsensical argument coming. 'Somebody *did* break these windows. Somebody *did* come in.'

'Aha,' he said, making another elaborate note, 'but it

122

wasn't, in the truest sense of the words, a *forced entry*. This might change everything.'

'Really?' asked Alice Pendlebury – who, with Richard, was hovering on the other side of the kitchen.

'Well, quite. *Forced entry* is a very serious business.'

Prudence was tempted to be forceful with the scribbling constable herself – but she'd dealt with so many ineffective television runners and production assistants across the years, well-meaning young fools who didn't know one end of a kitchen whisk from another, that she'd had to come up with tactics for dealing with them. As her mother had always said: you catch more flies with sugar than vinegar. Consequently, she put an arm around him, angled herself so she could see the scribble rapidly filling his notebook pages and said, 'The way I see it, Constable, is there are two possibilities. Either our man didn't try the door handle – in which case he was a pretty useless burglar, because it's the first thing you or I would have done – and broke the window straight away. Or . . .'

'Or he crept in some other way and had to break the window to get out!' the constable exclaimed.

There was so much obviously wrong with this theory that Prudence didn't know where to begin. But she was uncertain whether or not she ought to voice the real thought that had been brewing in her mind ever since Suki brought her attention to that door handle.

Prudence distinctly remembered a rival television chef – a short-lived star, one of the hip young things who'd come up on Instagram and YouTube, banging on about 'street food' and 'fusion' as if these were things they'd only just thought of. He'd been an amiable young man – just a little useless. And when, at a show where Prudence was also demonstrating, he'd made a botch of his signature recipe, a thirty-minute tagine (the juxtaposition of those words was ridiculous – it had made Prudence so cross!), he'd somehow got away with it by pretending the mess he'd made was actually a completely new recipe, one he'd been dying to share for ages. It worked, too; hip young things often got away with nonsense like this. But the story was bouncing around Prudence's head right now – how easily you could make one thing look like another, if only you had the imagination.

'Consider this, Constable,' she said. 'Our man – or woman, of course; we mustn't make assumptions – comes to the garden door. By chance, they find it open. In they come, and into their sack go all the silver teaspoons and fine china . . .'

'And the iPad,' said Mrs Mathers, miserably.

'Now, our chap – or *chapess* – could just stroll back out the way he came. Why not? The door's wide open. As a matter of fact, he doesn't even need to rough up the kitchen that much. It *could* be a silent burglary. If he was careful, you mightn't even notice, at first, that anything's gone – not until you open the drawers or want the silver teapot.'

'Or the KitchenAid,' Mrs Mathers opined.

'So the question is . . . *why*? Why all the mess? Why all the wreckage? And . . .' Prudence directed everyone's eyes back to the shattered glass in the door, 'why smash a door on your way *out* of the place you're robbing? Why not just slide on out?'

Constable Littleton licked the top of his pencil in deliberation. Then, when the silence had gone on a moment too long, he asked, 'Well, why?'

'Why else,' said Prudence, 'unless you only *wanted* it to *look* like a burglary? Why else, unless it's like one of those dreadful gastronomic experiments – making a dessert that looks like a fried egg, or a cake that looks exactly like a tramp's smelly old boot. Or—'

'Green ketchup!' Constable Littleton exclaimed, as if he'd just this minute unmasked a murderer. Then he thought a moment and said, 'Mrs Bulstrode, I'm not quite sure I understand.'

'He did one thing, Constable, but he wanted it to look like another.'

'Mrs Bulstrode – you're not meaning to suggest this *wasn't* a burglary?'

Prudence shrugged. At least the constable had half his wits about him, because this was half what she was trying to say.

'It's got "burglary" written all over it. By God, I've got a list one, two, *three* pages long of all the things taken.'

'Theatre, Constable. Like in a fine-dining restaurant. They'll bring your dessert to the table in wreathes of pine-needle smoke, or set fire to it right in front of you, just to give the evening a little *pizazz*. But, when you get down to the eating, it's still just a tiramisu.'

By the way the constable's face lit up, Prudence could tell he liked tiramisu.

'Constable, there's no earthly reason why our man smashed through this door. He didn't do it to get in, and he didn't do it to get out. There was simply no need. I'd hazard a guess there was no need to take half of the things in here either. Three-dozen eggs? Three jars of pecorino peppers? A few pheasants, hanging on their hooks? Constable, please – it's all just stage dressing. He didn't come for those things – at least, not *all* of them.'

'Then what *did* he come for?'

'The hidden ingredient,' Prudence mused. Her eyes flashed around the room, landing on every spot where something was missing. 'There *was* something he wanted in this kitchen, but if he crept in and took just that, well, it would be like hanging a big sign over the top of it saying, "LOOK THIS WAY." So he came, he snatched what he wanted . . . and then he hid what he'd done, by taking everything else. By filling his swag bag with pheasants and silver teaspoons. By smashing the door to make us think this was a hit-and-run, pure and simple.'

Constable Littleton was still licking the top of his pencil, trying to make sense of it. 'It's a theory,' he said, 'but what did he want? What could possibly have been in this kitchen that was so important?'

For a time, there was silence. Then, with an air of revelation, Suki piped up, 'The iPad, Mrs Mathers . . .'

Mrs Mathers clutched her chest, as if prophesying a heart attack.

'What was on it?' Suki asked.

'Just . . . recipes,' Mrs Mathers said. 'It was filled with cookbooks.'

126

Prudence shuddered. Her last publishers had wanted to make special electronic editions of her cookbooks too – and, of course, this being the twenty-first century, she was obliged to let them. But she would never understand the appeal. Cookbooks were things to be treasured. Things to be loved. Prudence had cookbooks that her mother had owned before her – and even one that her great-grandmother had owned, its margins filled with the spidery handwriting of centuries gone by, the recipes amended to account for particular tastes and the sweet tooth that ran in her family line. Cookbooks became stained and splattered with the love of all those who had thumbed through their pages, leaving little traces of themselves behind. An e-book might have been *conveni-ent*, but it could never be the same.

'And videos,' Mrs Mathers added.

'Videos?' asked Prudence, suddenly intrigued.

'You know, instructional things – how to make a sponge cake, how to debone a rabbit, that sort of thing.'

Prudence looked at Suki. 'Can an iPad *make* videos, Suki?'

Suki, pleased to have her own area of expertise for once, nodded. 'It can do almost anything, Grandma.'

'Mrs Mathers,' Prudence began, with a fresh urgency in her voice, 'did Deirdre Shaw use that iPad?'

'Deirdre?' Mrs Mathers blinked. 'Why, I suppose so, yes. Well, *yes*, I know she did – because she was just so delighted that all of her own books were loaded on to the thing. Yes, she found that quite exciting, I can tell you!' She paused. 'But why are you asking about Deirdre?'

Prudence was still. It was better, she thought, not to blurt out the thoughts that were starting to form in her mind: how somebody had come to this kitchen, seeking to eliminate what scraps of evidence they'd left behind; how, prompted perhaps by the poisoning of last night, they'd rushed back here to knot off any loose ends. How whoever had killed Deirdre Shaw was still here, among them.

She was trying to make sense of it all when Suki said, quite unprompted, 'Because something's wrong here. Something's dreadfully wrong. That wasn't food poisoning last night. And Deirdre Shaw didn't drop dead by accident. My grandmother thinks she's been murdered.'

Silence.

There was silence in the kitchen.

Mrs Mathers grappled with the wall, as if to keep balance.

Richard Prendergast's eyes turned as large as saucers.

And Alice Pendlebury looked like she'd just stumbled in on some liaison so salacious that it was going to be the talk of society for all the seasons to come.

'Murder?' Alice Pendlebury snorted – and Prudence, who was making despairing eyes at Suki, heard the laughter in her voice. 'Oh, Mrs Bulstrode, you can't be serious? *Murder?*'

'How else do you explain everything that's going on?' Suki interjected. She could feel Prudence's quelling eyes all over her, and her cheeks had already flushed red, but she'd come too far to stop now. It needed to be said. 'Deirdre Shaw, and last night's poison . . . and the mess in this kitchen, right now. There's something rotten here. My grandma can't be the only one to see it.'

'See what?' came a baritone voice from the kitchen-garden door.

Prudence turned round. There, peering down at the shattered glass from the other side, was Rupert Prendergast. Maxwell Pendlebury and Georgette stood on either side of him, their faces twisted in confusion as they tried to ascertain what was going on.

'Perhaps *I* can explain,' announced Constable Littleton, opening the broken door to permit the newcomers through. 'Sir, I'm a representative of the county police, attending from Nutwood St Knowle. We received a report of a break-in at the property. It seems some valuable items have been taken, by parties unknown – but rest assured that—'

'Darling!' Alice Pendlebury called out – and, for a moment, Prudence wasn't sure whether she was addressing Rupert or her husband at his side. 'It's the most confounding thing. It turns out that Mrs Bulstrode, here, isn't just a private chef at all. She's an amateur *sleuth*, darling,' she laughed, emphasising the preposterousness of the idea. 'And she thinks that one of us has murdered Deirdre Shaw!'

Chapter Eight

'You wanted to see me, Mr Prendergast.'

Supper had been served – a light crab-meat salad, follow by braised rabbit legs and a fresh radish garnish – and Prudence had already dismissed Suki, so that she could have some quiet time in the kitchen, when Flick Garrick came to tell her that Mr Prendergast requested her appearance. Now she stood in the manor house library, Rupert Prendergast sitting behind an antiquarian desk like a captain dressing down some junior officer. His face was scored in deep lines of vexation as he looked her up and down. All around him, the Farleighs' extensive library was kept in exquisite condition, while, on the desk in front of Mr Prendergast himself, a thick visitors' log spoke of all the manor house's guests since the last of the Farleighs passed away.

'Was dinner to the party's satisfaction?' Prudence asked; it was only an illusion of deference though – she knew she was not here for a critique of her cooking, because every element of the dish had been prepared to perfection.

'Supper was superlative, Mrs Bulstrode – but I'm afraid the conversation of the evening was anything but. This evening, my guests – those who are left – and I ought to have been turning back the years, recounting stories from times gone by. That, Mrs Bulstrode, is what this weekend was for – I'm sure you know the feeling; I'm sure you have glory years of your own. Old stories, tall tales, near misses, lost loves – the whole gauntlet of life. We played much of it out in this very mansion.' He stopped. 'But do you know what we've been speaking about instead?'

Prudence considered Rupert Prendergast carefully. He was staring at her along the line of his striking, Roman nose, and his eyes had a look that could have curdled cream. She got a fleeting feeling of what it must have been like to have faced the man in some boardroom in the City of London. His hands were curled into fists on the table in front of him; they were an ogre's hands, with fingernails chopped so short that the forefinger of his left hand showed traces of blood.

'I can make a guess, Mr Prendergast.'

'Murder,' said Rupert.

'Murder,' repeated Prudence.

It was now that Rupert Prendergast stood. At more than a head taller than Prudence, it wasn't just his hands that gave her the impression of him being an ogre.

'I hired you, Mrs Bulstrode, because of your star quality as a chef. I didn't realise, until this evening, that your real star quality is how much of an attention grabber you are. I'm quite sure I would never have got this level of *conceitedness* from Mrs Shaw, may God rest her soul. Now, *there* was a national treasure. *There* was somebody who got to the top of her profession without having to concoct fabulations just to get some attention. Mrs Bulstrode, *really*! All I wanted from you is your obvious talents in the kitchen – and it's only those obvious talents that are stopping me from sending you away from Farleigh Manor with a flea in your ear, and a ninety per cent deduction in pay, this minute! My guests deserve *service*. They don't need to get swept up into a faded television personality's codswallop murder mystery. Now, there's one day left of my reunion weekend – and I want it to go smoothly. Do you understand?'

Prudence had long ago learned how to bite her tongue – well, nobody liked a snappy, waspish celebrity; the media training teams soon beat it out of you – but, right now, the only thing that stopped her from immediately snapping back, declaring that she and Suki would be leaving the manor house immediately and that they could jolly well cook tomorrow evening's 'banquet' themselves, was the image of Deirdre Shaw, with her face planted down in the rhubarb patch. Because, if Prudence left the manor house tonight, then Deirdre's death would forever be an accident. If Prudence left the manor house tonight, then whoever killed Deirdre Shaw would continue to live their lives without penalty. If Prudence left the manor tonight then another murder at Farleigh Manor would go unexplained. And, no matter what clashes she'd had with Deirdre across their careers, she didn't intend to let that happen.

So she quietly said, 'I understand, Mr Prendergast.'

'Well, see that you do. No more dramas, Mrs Bulstrode. And I shall look forward to my pheasant tomorrow immensely.'

Prudence was still simmering with fury when she stopped in the library doors, looked back and said, 'On the matter of the kitchen, Mr Prendergast . . .'

'Local hoodlums!' he snapped. 'The country's full of them.'

'I don't suppose you heard anything, then? Richard said you came back to the manor after you'd set out for your walk?'

Rupert Prendergast purpled. He shook his head – and Prudence wondered, for a moment, if she'd pushed him too far; she was like a terrier dog, nipping at his heels – and, if she did it one too many times, he'd simply kick her away.

'I came back to get my gun, Mrs Bulstrode. It's a goddamn shooting weekend. And *no*, I didn't hear a thing. But I'm quite sure you can get by without all those expensive gadgets. We'll be dining on pheasant tomorrow night – it's just a damn shame it's not the pheasants we shot. It's a tradition – to eat our own kills. But needs must. Pheasant, Mrs Bulstrode, and make it delectable!'

Prudence had to take a walk in the grounds to calm herself. She lingered, for a time, in the kitchen garden. Only when she was quite certain of herself did she retire to the staff quarters, where Suki was tucked up in bed, her nose firmly buried in her new book.

'You won't believe all of this, Grandma. There were a hundred different theories about what happened here, back in 1886. The London newspapers were *obsessed* with it. Actually, they only really stopped writing about it

133

when 1888 came along – and you know what happened in 1888, Grandma . . .'

Prudence wracked her brain. '*Mrs A. B. Marshall's Cookery Book* was published. They called her the Queen of Ices. The very first recipe for an edible ice-cream cone . . .'

'Jack the Ripper, Grandma!'

'Good Lord, Suki, put that book down!'

Prudence had felt a terrible shudder. She stepped into the bathroom, changed quickly into her nightclothes and came back into the sleeping area, scrubbing her teeth. For somebody with such a sweet tooth, she'd scarcely had a filling across her lifetime; she knew how to take good care of her teeth.

'There was one detective, an amateur one, you know – kind of like a Sherlock Holmes – who said it was the father. All an elaborate set-up. He'd been sleeping with Jane Sutcliffe and needed to get rid of her quickly – only she started blackmailing him, you see, and he thought it would be easy if he just framed the children for it. *Nobody*, he thought, could ever condemn the children. And then there was an Investigative Society, came down out of Manchester – just a group of old busybodies, really, with too much time on their hands – but *they* said it was a haunting. Supernatural stuff. Death visits on his black horse . . . or was it white? I can't quite remember.'

Suki started turning the pages feverishly, while Prudence slipped back into the bathroom to put down her toothbrush.

When she returned, Suki blathered on, 'But the author, this Katie Winterdale, she doesn't hold much truck with any of these theories. *She* has one of her own. You see, the Farleigh children, Jack and Mary, *they* always said that Jane Sutcliffe tripped and drowned. They didn't change that story until the day they died, right here in the manor. Nineteen seventy-one. As far as I can tell, they used to sleep where the guest suites are now. Mr and Mrs Prendergast are in what I think was Jack's old room. Anyway, Jane Sutcliffe was a beautiful young woman but, by all the local accounts, she was a bit of a monster as well. She had a history of punishing the children. That's why suspicion fell on them on the first place. She just *hated* how inquisitive they were. Children should be seen and not heard – she was one of those types . . . Jack just loved his wildlife, his plants and his animals, so he was always turning up covered in filth, or she'd find frogs and toads in boxes under his bed. She punished him for that regularly. And Mary, well, she was a bit of a dreamer. She'd constantly be writing these stories about the fairies she insisted lived in the grounds of the manor. The Farleigh Fairies – you can imagine them being classics, like *The Water Babies* perhaps, if history hadn't turned out quite so dark! Well, Jane Sutcliffe didn't approve of this either. It says here that the maid of the manor had found Mary Farleigh sobbing in the library, three days before Jane died, and all because Jane Sutcliffe ripped the stories she'd been writing to shreds . . .'

Prudence remembered a particularly brutish book editor ripping *her* writing to shreds early in her career, when she'd been writing the introduction to *A Countrywoman's Kitchen*. That was the sort of thing that truly could compel one towards murder.

'Anyway,' Suki went on, 'if you follow everything she's saying, you do start to think the children really did get away with murder.'

'They'd have to be very lucky,' Prudence said. She had gravitated back to the window and was looking down upon the kitchen garden. 'Two children, to overpower their nanny and drown her in the river – all without getting wet?'

Suki said, 'Ah, but they *were* wet, you see. Mary had soaking ankle socks. She said she'd gone into the river to try and pull Miss Sutcliffe out – while Jack ran to get help . . .' She paused. 'Do you ever think a *place* can be haunted? I don't mean with real ghosts. I mean with bad luck, or bad feeling. Like bad things might be happening at Farleigh Manor *just because*?'

The net curtains fluttered around Prudence's face. 'I don't believe in ghosts and ghouls – but there's something happening here, Suki. Something I can't explain.' She turned. 'Who would *want* to kill Deirdre Shaw? *Here*, I mean. She hasn't seen these people in twenty years – and, even then, she was only their chef.'

'Maybe somebody's been waiting twenty years, Grandma. You've got to be mad to murder, don't you? Maybe twenty years is nothing to them.'

'Rupert Prendergast warned me off.'

Suki exhaled.

'He said he'd send us away, this instant, if I didn't stop poking my nose around in it. But what I can't decide is

– was he *really* warning me off, or was he just being the conceited kind of fellow who won't even let a thing like murder ruin his weekend?'

'I suppose we can rule out Richard,' said Suki, with a shrug. 'He'd barely have been a boy when the group last hired Deirdre Shaw.'

'Mmm,' said Prudence, who refused to rule out a thing. 'Well, let's not forget that Jack and Mary Farleigh were children too. It didn't stop murder dogging them throughout their lives. No, Suki, there's something we're not seeing. Like beetroot in a chocolate cake – it's the centre of everything, you just don't know it's there. If it's a murder, there has to be a motive. We need to know what that is. What, beyond mere cookery, bound Deirdre Shaw to somebody in this manor? What tied her so powerfully to somebody here that they brought her here to kill her?'

Suki dropped the book into her lap, and it seemed to Prudence, for the first time, that her grand-daughter was afraid.

'I suppose I could call Deirdre's agent,' said Prudence, 'ask her a few questions of my own. But I'd be stirring up a hornet's nest. If only there was some other way . . .'

Suki looked up. 'Grandma,' she declared, 'I know just the person to ask.'

Anthony Neville Watson – who preferred to go by the nom-de-guerre 'Numbers' for some of his less legal activities – was delighted when his iPhone buzzed and the face of his absolute *darling* Suki lit up in the corner of his room. He'd been missing her enormously since her grandmother shanghaied her off to some far-flung corner of the realm – his Suki was a positive princess, hardly kitchen skivvy material! – and worse still was the fact that the old prune seemed to have requisitioned her iPhone as well. Under normal circumstances, Suki was hardly ever away from the thing – she and Numbers would speak all day on WhatsApp, Messenger or FaceTime – but apparently for this forced trip out to Farleigh Manor, communication was NOT ALLOWED. It was tantamount to a human rights abuse. Numbers was quite certain they tried cases like this at The Hague.

He was ready to announce all of this when he picked up the phone and, in the glow of the multiple laptop computer screens open in his bedroom, said, 'Suki Penrose! DARLING!'

'Numbers,' Suki whispered, 'I need some help.'

'I need some help too,' Numbers replied. He looked at his reflection in one of the laptop computer screens. Devilishly handsome, of course – if you thought that having a round face, a generous helping of freckles and spectacles was handsome. His red hair perched on top of his head in an extravagant quiff. He'd have looked quite debonair (even if he did say so himself) if he hadn't been crashed out in his pyjamas all day long. His mother – with whom Numbers still lived, having dropped out of his studies – had spent half the day telling him to get dressed, and suggested that perhaps today was the day he finally got his arse in gear and went to find a job; Numbers just didn't have the heart to tell her that lounging around in his pyjamas all day, watching the laptop screens, *was* his job. He'd made more money this month by hustling online poker than any of his old classmates – the ones who'd actually finished their degrees and joined the graduate training schemes in London – had in the last year. Now, he crept to his bedroom door and peeked out. 'She's lurking. She has her new boyfriend round. Oh, Suki, DARLING, he's positively ghastly. Even worse than the last one. *Even* worse than my father. Can you believe, they wanted me to go *out* tonight? Well, where would I go, Suki, when you're not here?' He hesitated. 'You're coming home soon, Suki, aren't you? Well, aren't you?'

'Numbers, there's something going on out here. You remember what I told you? About Deirdre Shaw?'

'Ah, the Death by Chocolate!'

'Numbers, I'm being serious!'

Suki didn't often admonish Numbers – ordinarily she hung from his arm and corpsed at almost everything he said – so, by the tone in her voice, Numbers knew something was wrong.

'What is it, princess?'

'Mrs Shaw was murdered, Numbers. I'm serious. Poisoned, we think, right here in the manor. And ever since we got here, *things* have been going on. Just this afternoon, while we were in Nutwood St Knowle, somebody broke into the kitchens. They took everything. My grandma thinks they came back to clean up after themselves, but . . .' She realised she was babbling and faltered. 'Can you do some digging for us, Numbers? We're trying to find a connection. Anything that ties Deirdre Shaw to

139

the guests here this weekend. There has to be something that binds them together. If she was murdered, she was murdered for a reason. My grandmother's calling it the "secret ingredient".'

'Suki, DARLING, I absolutely *told you* you'd end up solving a murder this weekend. I just thought it would be an ancient one. The coldest of cold cases.'

'Yes, well . . .' Suki was about to launch into another spiel about Jack and Mary Farleigh and the suspicious demise of Jane Sutcliffe when she caught herself and said, 'Let me give you a list of their names, Numbers. Deirdre Shaw met them once before – about twenty years ago, when they hired her to cook at Farleigh. But there just *has* to be something between then and now that explains everything away. Do what you can, won't you? Anything at all?'

'Your wish is my command, princess. If it's available, I'll find it. You name it – tax affairs, births, divorces, salacious City gossip . . . it's all out there waiting if you know where to look.'

'Numbers,' Suki said, 'you're a dream.'

'A dream*boat*, Suki. I'm a dream*boat*.'

'That too,' she said, and blew kisses into the phone as she signed off.

The Sunday morning breakfast comprised of the plump, fat heritage sausages from the butcher's in Nutwood St Knowle, along with tiny bruschetta topped in kiwano pips, cream cheese and mint. 'Even breakfasts deserve desserts,' said Prudence as Flick Garrick hustled up and down the kitchen stairs, getting ready to serve. 'I just hope this satisfies them. The lunch bags are already packed. Ham rolls, a nice piece of fruitcake each, some cheese and biscuits. That should see them through.'

'Yes,' said Flick, who'd already gathered the lunch packs Prudence had put together for the final day's shoot. 'Well, at least it will keep them out from the house and under our feet for the day. Are you all prepared, Mrs Bulstrode?'

Prudence looked across the kitchen. Suki was hard at work scrubbing the breakfast pans before they went into the dishwasher, and after that there was much slicing and dicing to be done. Preparation, Prudence had tried to impress upon her, was key. At 6 p.m. tonight, when the party gathered for their big end-of-weekend banquet, everything had to be perfect. The problem was there were a hundred other thoughts tumbling through her mind now, ones that had very little to do with the range of ingredients in the kitchen around her. Right now, she found she could hardly keep the image of the banquet she needed to prepare in her head. It just dissolved into pictures of Deirdre Shaw, frantically digging up rhubarb before she dropped dead; the spectral image of some dark-cowled intruder creeping in through the kitchen door, then smashing the glass to make it seem like a random attack.

At least the kitchen looked more ordered than it had yesterday afternoon. Before supper, Hubert Lowell had arrived – with Biscuit bouncing in tow – to board up the broken window, and Prudence and Suki had themselves set about scrubbing down the surfaces, tidying and disinfecting everything the interlopers might have touched. Constable Littleton had announced the local constabulary would be making enquiries in the usual places – there was a particular drinking spot in Nutwood St Knowle, he said, where ne'er-do-wells were known to gather – but Prudence held out little hope that they'd find anything. There wouldn't be some shadowy man in the corner of an old country boozer, seeking to sell silver teaspoons or a kitchen iPad – because it hadn't been any old burglar who broke in. It didn't matter what Rupert Prendergast said, nor how much Constable Littleton objected. Prudence knew, in her bones, that something was wrong. She couldn't get it out of her mind.

Which was a problem when you had at least five hungry – and opinionated – souls to feed.

Still, there were all sorts of things you could do with a pheasant. On arriving at Farleigh Manor, Prudence had entertained the idea of providing the party with something they hadn't tasted before – a wild Keralan curry, heavy with cardamom and coriander, or pheasant à l'orange with apricots and figs, something to bring a bit of unseasonal glamour into the traditional shooting weekend. But she supposed the thing, now, was to keep it simple and traditional; at least, by doing that, she risked less of Rupert Prendergast's wrath. She'd pot roast them with a healthy helping of brine to make sure the meat was tender and the skin delectably crisp. She'd shred the meat from one bird, roasted earlier in the day, to make savoury bonbons (she envisaged folding

142

miniature pheasant samosas for a starter, but quickly decided against it), and sit breasts upon celeriac rostis, all served with a parsnip puree, winter greens and an indulgent mushroom sauce. For dessert, she wanted to go a little more extravagant; if the kiwano toasts were met favourably at breakfast, she'd go to the dragon fruit for dinner – but, if they were not, she'd resort to a rich, spiced bread-and-butter pudding. Classic English fare. Rupert Prendergast couldn't find fault with that. The guests wouldn't be able to eat pheasants shot by their own hand this evening – those pheasants were no doubt hanging in the larder of whoever smashed their way through the kitchen yesterday afternoon – but Prudence had always found that, if a meal was tasty enough, most of a guest's other complaints fell by the wayside. So she knew what she had to do.

After breakfast, the guests assembled in front of the manor house. From the kitchen-garden door, Prudence watched as Rupert, Georgette and Richard Prendergast, and Alice and Maxwell Pendlebury, climbed into the waiting Land Rovers – Hubert Lowell and his head beater at the wheel of each – and rolled off across the estate. A cold October wind was blowing, and the smell of woodsmoke filled the air.

'Pheasants again,' said Prudence when she came back into the kitchen. 'Mr Prendergast thinks it would be a waste of a weekend not to kill and eat your own bird, so they'll take their kills home with them. I'd like to see them home cook anything as well as we'll do tonight though, Suki.'

Suki, who had finished with the breakfast pans and was gathering a list of ingredients from her grandmother's list, said, 'I don't know how you can think about it, Grandma, not when—'

Prudence lifted a finger to hush her. 'A good cook can have her head in three, four, five recipes at once, Suki.'

She marched across the kitchen, making for the inner doors.

'What's that supposed to mean?' Suki called.

'It means – I can think about more than one thing at once, my dear!'

There was still time before the preparation had to begin in earnest. In one hour, she'd get the first pheasant into the oven; once it had been roasted to perfection, she could shred its meat for the bonbons and rostis. Until then, it wouldn't matter if Prudence wasn't *quite* in the kitchen. Suki could manage the slicing and dicing. It didn't take an expert to scrub celeriac down.

And Prudence had spotted something yesterday that she simply had to see again.

At least she knew she wouldn't be disturbed. With the guests having vacated the manor for the day and Mrs Mathers entrenched in her duties, cleaning their suites, she didn't miss a beat as she crept into the library where, yesterday evening, Rupert Prendergast had given her such a stern dressing down. Now that she was here again, she realised how *ridiculous* that had been. Once upon a time, Prudence Bulstrode had been the Head Girl at St Marianne's School for Girls; she didn't get 'told off' back then, and she certainly didn't get 'told off' as a sixty-five-year-old woman. She'd wipe the smile off his face, she thought, if it was the last thing she did. It would be the perfect *aperitif*.

The library sat alongside the manor house drawing room, a perfect reflection of that much cosier chamber. Here the alcoves were filled with shelves that stretched from the floor to the ceiling, and on each of those shelves were lined up a multitude of hardback books. Prudence's eyes picked out copies of Dickens and Wilkie Collins as she looked up and down; threadbare Gothic romances and books of common verse, the shelves punctuated by household editions of the Bible, as well as instruction manuals for raising good children, old dictionaries, and three whole shelves devoted to the hills, forests and wild-life of the Cotswolds. Prudence supposed there was a fortune in first editions waiting in this room – but she wasn't interested in any of that, not now. She looked, instead, at the visitors' book that was on the desk where Rupert Prendergast had been sitting the night before. She checked that she was alone, one last time, and then hurried down to sit beside it.

The visitors' log was thick and heavy. She opened it at its first page, and saw that the very first inscription was dated 2 June 1974.

Delighted to be Farleigh Manor's first ever paying guest! What a time was had. Excellent service. Very comfortable. Loved the trifle. Maggie and Michael Green xxx.

That chimed, thought Prudence, with what she already knew: Farleigh Manor hadn't fallen out of the hands of the family until the twins, Jack and Mary, perished in 1971. Three years later – enough for all the legal wrangling to be worked through and for the consortium who acquired the manor to dust it down and spruce it up – it had opened to paying guests.

The first decade yielded nothing interesting – or, at least, nothing that immediately set the cogs in Prudence's mind whirring; there were plenty of comments about the manor's trifle, which (according to the Beaumonts from 1979 and the Richardsons of 1981) seemed to involve an incalculable amount of sherry. According to various comments (and one or two replies scribbled in the margins), the manor had, in those days, employed a resident chef by the name of Fortescue, who excelled at cooking both game and party-pleasing desserts. It would, Prudence reflected, have been a good gig for a working cook.

She found what she was looking for in the tattered pages marked 1985 – because it was here that she first lit upon the name 'Rupert Prendergast'. Summer 1985: Prendergast & Party. They described their stay here as 'Full of memories, full of wine, we'll come again!' and that was that.

Come again they did. They were here in October 1985 for the shooting, and again for two weeks across the summer of 1986. Every year – with only one or two seasons missed – the party returned to sample the delights of Farleigh Manor. She was watching the formation of a tradition, she thought, and was grateful when, after a few years, the Prendergast party's other guests started signing the visitors' book individually – as if it was important to them that they each, not just Rupert, leave some lasting memory behind. Gray Williams had written, 'Shot my first buck – proud moment!' in the autumn of 1993; in 1994, Georgette Prendergast had written, 'Apologies for my husband's naked nocturnal forays!', to which Rupert had appended the message, 'No apologies needed – your thanks will be enough.' In 1999, a woman named Alice Frith had written, 'Found the love of my life!' and Maxwell Pendlebury – appearing for the first time in the book – had, underneath this, written, 'Excellent supper'. Well, thought Prudence, there were all sorts of different kinds of flirting. It might not have been the most auspicious start to a love story – but it was where you ended up that mattered, not where you started.

Frith, thought Prudence. It was a shame when women felt as if they had to take their husband's name; she clearly recalled the conversation when she'd first met Alice. Prudence, of course, had never had to confront the idea – Nicholas had always understood that her name was half of her livelihood, and there had never been any suggestion that she ought to change it. Alice did not seem the sort who would have wanted to change her name either. And yet, somewhere between the year 1999, when she'd seemingly met Maxwell Pendlebury, and 2003, when the name 'Alice Pendlebury' started appearing in the record instead, she'd got married and done just that.

147

Prudence screwed up her eyes.

She flicked back through the pages.

The name 'Alice Frith' appeared several times between 1999 and 2003. It was there every summer, when the Prendergast party – now including Terence Knight, and occasionally one or two other hangers on – descended. But it was there throughout the year as well. Odd weekends, off-season weeks, times when the manor seemed to have few other guests. In the Christmas of 2001, the whole Frith family seemed to have taken the manor and hosted celebrations here. Alice Frith, it seemed, hadn't just fallen in love at Farleigh Manor; she'd fallen in love *with* the manor itself, and come back at almost every opportunity, even without her other friends.

No matter, thought Prudence – with a sly look at the door, because she'd become certain that there was movement somewhere on the other side, the soft tap of footsteps tramping up and down the entrance hall. A place like Farleigh Manor had hosted hundreds of parties over the years. Prudence had her mind fixed on just one. She knew, from what both Mrs Mathers and Rupert Prendergast himself had said, that Deirdre Shaw had cooked for them in their heyday, twenty years before. That made it sometime in the summer or autumn of 2002. She flicked through the pages until she found the right dates.

A great time was had by all. Seventeen years at Farleigh! Monumental scenes, and monumental cooking by the one and only Deirdre Shaw. Pheasant perfection. I'll remember this weekend always – Georgette Prendergast

A culinary triumph to round off a stellar shooting weekend. Props to Mr Lowell and his beaters for his excellent expeditions – Gray Williams.

My love affair with Farleigh Manor continues! Love Alice xxx

Late nights, red wine, sunset over the manor – here's to the best companions with whom a man was ever blessed. PS Apologies for the drawing room carpet – Rupert P

There were other names scribbling messages here. A man called Hunter Fields. Another who had simply signed his name 'Stag' – and must have been the sort of man who thought he owned his wife, because he'd appended her name to his too: 'Stag and Sarah'. By the looks of things, Deirdre had cooked for around twelve people the last time she attended Farleigh Manor.

Prudence flicked further on. There had been Prendergast parties since then, but the very last one had been eight years ago; after that, it seemed, the Prendergasts hadn't returned to Farleigh until only a few days past.

She closed the book. None of it helped. She was no closer to knowing what had happened that weekend; what connected Deirdre to one of the party so closely that they had plotted to kill her.

She was hanging her head when she sensed movement at the library doors. Quickly looking up, she saw a familiar figure peeping his head around the door.

'Mr Knight?'

Terence Knight, last seen rushing into an ambulance with Gray Williams, looked less ghostly than when Prudence had last set eyes upon him. He'd got a change of clothes from somewhere as well – he even looked smart, in a sports jacket and jeans; and there was, at least, some colour in his cheeks. He must have bathed in after-shave because his floral scent had preceded him into the room. Lean and blond, he was, in many ways, the polar opposite to his old friend Rupert. And it was after Rupert that he now asked.

'Mrs Bulstrode, I'm sorry – I didn't mean to disturb you. I'm guessing Rupert and the rest are out on a shoot?'

Prudence nodded. She didn't know why, but she felt compelled to hide the fact that she'd been snooping in the visitors' book, so she stood up, stepped in front of the desk and said, 'I'm afraid they are, Mr Knight. But tell me – is Mr Williams OK?'

'Fit as a fiddle,' said Terence. 'Well, perhaps not the fittest fiddle. He's slightly out of tune – if you see what I mean. As a matter of fact, he's up in the drawing room right now.' He paused. 'If the rest are out on a shoot, I don't suppose . . . is there any chance of some lunch? Something light, just to see us to supper? Of course, you must have so much prep to do. I'll wager Rupert's been rather demanding about the banquet tonight.'

Prudence was only relieved that Gray Williams hadn't succumbed to whatever sickness had run through them that night. 'I'll bring something straight away, Mr Knight – something you can graze on across the day.'

A short time later, after preparing a tray of finger sandwiches, cold sausages, fresh fruit and pickles, Prudence was pouring tea in the drawing room while Terence Knight paced up and down, and Gray Williams reclined on the sofa. He may have looked more hearty than he'd done two days before, but there was still something beaten-up about him; something, Prudence thought, that was in retreat. Even so, he was grateful to see her.

'Mrs Bulstrode,' he croaked, 'I wanted to say – I owe you no ill will. My constitution has never been what it might have been. I'm sure that whatever didn't agree with me, it was nothing to do with your fine cooking.'

Indeed not, thought Prudence, but she decided not to pursue it further. 'I'm afraid they're just simple pâté,' she said, indicating the sandwiches. 'We've rather a lot going on downstairs.'

'I'll wager,' said Terence Knight. 'Rupert had high hopes for this banquet. He's been talking it up since summer. He was quite pleased with having snapped up Mrs Shaw again. Mrs Bulstrode, I'm sure there have been *comments* – but don't take them to heart. We're glad you're here.'

'Well,' said Prudence, sensing an opening, 'I *did* wonder about that.' Prudence remembered the summer, ten years before, when she'd spent Monday, Wednesday and Friday afternoons on a certain daytime television show, first doing the cookery segments – and, on one memorable occasion, filling in for the show's main presenter (a lovable dimwit by the name of Emmett Brogue) when he was taken ill. Interviewing the show's

151

guests – a reality TV star, a young girl who wanted to be a dog, a magician with a penchant for terrible card tricks – had been an enjoyable affair, but she'd always found that the best interviews came when you asked a kind of 'sideways' question, approaching a familiar topic from some unexpected angle. You always got a more telling answer if you had an unusual approach. 'Well, as you know, I always *loved* Deirdre. One of my idols, in fact. She's the reason I took to cookery in the first place!' It made Prudence feel quite ill to say it, but at least it seemed to get them on side. 'And I wondered – why Deirdre? Well, apart from the fact that she was *fabulous*, of course – and God rest her soul. But why did Mr Prendergast hire Deirdre then, and why now? There are probably more glamorous chefs he could have hired these days. Did somebody have some personal connection to Deirdre, perhaps? Did they stay in touch with her over the years?'

It was fortunate, thought Prudence, that neither Terence nor Gray had been here to hear talk of murder. Perhaps, without those thoughts hanging over them, she might get some answers.

'Well, there's glamorous and there's *feted*,' said Gray Williams from the couch where he was lying back and nibbling at a finger sandwich. 'I know Deirdre was a big hit when she cooked for us the last time. I think Rupert merely wanted to conjure up the feeling of yesteryear. But, of course, they'd become good friends after the first time. Deirdre and Rupert, I mean.'

'Oh yes?'

'I believe she cooked for him on several occasions, privately. Georgette was furious about it. She fancies herself a dab hand in a kitchen herself. But Deirdre did some dinner-party catering for them – oh, five or six times, I'd say. Georgette put her foot down in the end. *My kitchen, my rules.* Well, I'm sure you know that feeling, Mrs Bulstrode.'

She did indeed.

'So Georgette had Deirdre dismissed?'

'You'd have to ask Georgette for the details of it, Mrs Bulstrode. But Georgette's a strong lady. She doesn't like to feel threatened. And Deirdre mightn't have been the most glamorous lady, but she had talent and she had fame, and, if I remember correctly, she had a habit of jettisoning one husband for another. I'm sure Georgette didn't only feel threatened in the kitchen, if you know what I mean.'

A thousand mental notes started scribbling themselves down inside Prudence's mind. She said, 'It sounds as if Deirdre had almost become a personal friend to Mr Prendergast. But then ...' *Questions, questions,* she thought, and tried to remember all those chat-show techniques she'd learned from the researchers: how to segue one subject into another. 'There must have been lots of personal connections made here, back in the day. Didn't Alice meet Maxwell, right here in the manor?'

'Oh yes,' croaked Gray. 'He'd been hunting her for years before she gave in.'

'Not only that,' said Terence. 'Gray and I met here as well.'

'Oh yes?'

'I've always thought Rupert brought us here for that very purpose,' said Gray, 'but Terence thinks I'm an old fool.'

'I just can't imagine Rupert playing matchmaker to two old fruits, darling.'

'We were young, once.'

'Gray and I are – how shall we say this? – bachelors in name only, Mrs Bulstrode. We've been together for nearly twenty years.'

'So it's a couples' weekend,' said Prudence. 'Did you two ever come back to the manor without the rest of the party? I couldn't help noticing, in the visitors' book, that Mrs Pendlebury seems to have made the place a bit of a playground.'

'Yes, well, Alice always was a law unto herself!' Terence laughed. 'Quite, quite wild in her youth. The apple of everyone's eye.'

'Oh, especially Rupert,' said Gray.

'Especially!' Terence scoffed. 'We're being terribly indiscreet, Mrs Bulstrode – but make sure you don't sit Alice near Rupert at the banquet tonight. Georgette would not like that one bit. It would be a recipe for . . . Well, we've already had one recipe for disaster this week-end. It probably wouldn't do to have another.'

Recipe for disaster, thought Prudence as she took her leave. Another food-poisoning joke, she supposed. But the poison in this manor wasn't to do with food. It was to do with people and the secrets between them.

At least she now knew that Rupert and Deirdre's association had lasted longer than one weekend twenty years ago. At least she now knew that there had been enmity between Georgette and Deirdre. And at least she now knew that, no matter how nostalgic and united in fond memories the Prendergast party might have seemed, there was bitterness and envy broiling between them.

The question was: how had any of it resulted in the death of Deirdre Shaw? What was it Deirdre had done to trap her in these people's envies and deceits?

Why Deirdre?

And why *now*?

Quietly brooding on all these thoughts, she tramped back down to the kitchen.

In six hours' time, the banquet would begin.

Chapter Nine

After two hours of slicing and dicing, Suki had endured quite enough of working in the kitchen. It hardly seemed fair that, while she was sobbing over the onions and painstakingly grating potatoes (what was wrong with good old-fashioned oven chips?) for the rostis, her grandmother was up in the manor house gossiping with the guests. So, when lunchtime approached – and the only time she'd seen her grandmother was when she'd sashayed through to put together a couple of lunch plates for Gray Williams and Terence Knight in the drawing room above – she picked herself up, scurried out of the kitchen and retired to her room.

It was, after all, a Sunday. Sunday was the Day of Rest – and Suki had always taken this commandment particularly seriously, sleeping half the day away back home. Today, however, Suki had no designs on snatching a well-earned hour of sleep before she was shanghaied back to service in the kitchen. The moment she stole back into the room she shared with her grandmother, she unearthed her copy of *The Body in the Beck* and lost herself in its pages.

She wasn't sure what appealed to her most about the story – whether it was the tawdry sensationalism of all the newspaper reporting (whoever said that tabloid journalism was a modern phenomenon?), or the unnerving black-and-white images of the characters at the heart of the grisly narrative – pictures that brought the story of Jane Sutcliffe's murder to painful life. Perhaps it was only the feeling that she was walking in the same halls where Jane Sutcliffe had once walked; that, only this morning, she had popped her head into the library where Mary Farleigh had secretly scribbled her Farleigh Fairies into the margins of manifold old books, and been severely reprimanded by Jane Sutcliffe when her crime was discovered.

Suki had almost reached the halfway point in the book, a chapter devoted to a visit Jane Sutcliffe's estranged sister Meredith had made to the manor after the news of her death, and came at last to the full-colour plate section in the centre of the edition. She had already flicked through these images before – the colourised portrait of Jack and Mary, standing with Jane on the eve of some expedition was particularly haunting – but the image that drew her eye now was a police sketch, made that fateful summer, that showed the mansion grounds as if from a bird's-eye view. On the opposite page was a more recent bird's-eye view of the mansion, this one a photograph taken by drone, upon which were marked all the ways the manor house had changed in the intervening years. Suki pored over both images, trying to imagine the manor as it had once been – but it wasn't until her eyes lit upon a little corner that had been walled-off, separated from the orchard behind the kitchen garden, that she felt a lurching in her chest.

Some moments later, Suki was crossing the kitchen and barrelling through the boarded-up back door, over the kitchen garden, past the rhubarb patch where Deirdre Shaw had met her unfortunate end, and under the old brick arch that led into the manor's small orchard. Through a succession of apple and plum trees, their leaves turning slowly to the russets and reds of autumn, she stumbled onward – until, at last, she came to the walled-off section that had not been there in 1886. Beyond it, untended and covered in thistles, nettles and more, two simple gravestones rose out of the earth.

Suki felt the chill of discovery rippling up her spine. She dared step between the graves, brushing back the thistles with the flat of the book so that she could read the inscriptions on the stones. The first read 'JACK FARLEIGH 12 September 1877 – 19 September 1971'; the second, 'MARY FARLEIGH 12 September 1877 – 21 November 1971'.

Long lives, thought Suki – and was surprised to discover that her overriding feeling, on seeing these graves, was one of sadness. The Farleigh twins had lived for all but nine years of their lives under the scrutiny and suspicion of murder; one summer's afternoon, that had blighted the next eighty-five years of their lives. According to the caption beneath the image in the book, their parents had followed the Farleigh tradition of being buried in the churchyard at Nutwood St Knowle. But theirs was to be the last generation afforded that honour. Jack and Mary, pariahs for the long decades of their lives, had been buried in the only place they ever knew – the manor where they had lived out their lives as murderous recluses.

It seemed to Suki, then, that – whether or not they truly had killed Jane Sutcliffe – it was a tragic story.

But nor could she ignore the frisson she felt whenever she thought about it. It was, she supposed, safer than thinking about Deirdre Shaw and the rhubarb patch; safer to think about a murder more than a century in the past than to imagine you were cooking for a killer right now.

She turned to the next page in the colour plate section: an artist's depiction of the entirety of the manor house grounds in 1886. The map, beautifully rendered in pastel shades, showed a pair of dotted lines to mark the routes originally taken, first as Jane Sutcliffe led the children down to the river for their picnic, and then the route Jack Farleigh had taken as he cantered back to the manor to raise the alarm. The alarm for a murder he himself had committed – if all the various reportage was to be believed.

Soon, Suki found herself following the same path.

It wasn't difficult to follow the dotted line across the manor grounds. Much had changed in the intervening decades, but the contours of the land remained the same and, in truth, it was not so very far from the manor to the riverside. Neither was it so very different from the route she had taken before on her way to pick up the plates from Mr Lowell's cottage. Scarcely twenty minutes later, Suki was emerging from a wooded lane to discover the burbling waters of Hill Beck somewhere below her.

She fancied she could even hear the faster-moving waters of the River Eye somewhere beyond it – though perhaps that was only her imagination, for when she got close to the beck's edge, she could see the way its waters broke and diverted around a multitude of stepping stones, creating miniature rapids and whirlpools where fallen leaves eddied and gyred.

So, she thought, she was back here, back where it had happened. She dared to come close to the water's edge, looking at the annotations on the map as she came. If she was right, *this* was the depression – in the shadow of an ancient willow tree, which had been but young at the time – where the picnic blanket had been spread out; and these were the very rocks on which Jane Sutcliffe was said to have slipped and fallen. Standing at the water's edge, it was difficult to imagine that a grown person had drowned here. The waters seemed so playful, almost inviting, somehow.

'Hello?'

Suki froze. So lost had she been in thoughts of the ancient past that, at first, she thought she was imagining the voice. Only when it came again, and she looked over her shoulder, did she see Flick Garrick approaching along the same path she had just followed. Startled, she almost lost grasp on the book she was holding, narrowly saving it from falling into the beck.

'Flick,' she said, as the young woman approached. 'You startled me. I didn't think—'

Two sharp gunshots rang out, startling her again. By instinct, Suki staggered back and would have stumbled into the beck's frigid waters if only Flick hadn't reached out and grabbed her by the hand.

'They've found the pheasants then,' Flick said. 'Not that there's any sport in it – not really. These woods are filled with pheasants Mr Lowell's released from his pens. The stupid birds hardly know how to fend for themselves. They practically walk into the guns. All you have to do is track them to the supplementary feed sheds, beat them out of the underbrush, and drop them out of the sky. I can't see the appeal of it myself, but plenty do.'

Suki was still cringing as she picked her way up from the bank of the beck. 'Are we likely to get hit?'

'They're shooting up and in the opposite direction. It's quite safe. I come down this way most afternoons. Well, otherwise it's spending all my breaks with Mrs Mathers, gossiping about the guests – and there's been *quite enough* of that this weekend.'

'Oh yes?'

'Well, with what happened to Mrs Shaw and every-thing. Something *always* happens when the Prendergast party arrives. That's what Mrs Mathers said. Some falling out or drunken row – or somebody's husband touching somebody else's wife. You could write a book about them. But I need to get out of there, every now and then. You can't spend your life living out other people's dramas.' Flick paused. 'But haven't you got the big banquet to be worrying about? They'll be expecting something big. It's bound to get raucous. They've got another delivery of wine coming in from Nutwood this afternoon. Mr

Prendergast had us place it especially. You won't believe the amount he's just spent.'

Suki was about to reply that the banquet was her grandmother's preserve – Suki was just here to skivvy around – when something caught her eye above Flick's shoulder, some dark shape moving on the edge of the woodland that rose up the escarpment, leading away from the beck. It took Suki some moments, Flick's voice droning away in the background, before she realised that the shape was a dog, weaving in odd zigzags out of the trees and down towards the water. It took her some moments more before she realised that it was a dog she'd seen several times before – Biscuit, the roan English setter who ordinarily bound along at the side of Hubert Lowell.

'Flick,' Suki said, with mounting urgency, 'Flick, look . . .'

Flick turned just in time to see Biscuit teetering towards the water. Suki had never seen a dog looking like that before; its eyes were misted and moist, and around its lolling tongue there erupted plumes of frothing spittle and long green strands that she could only take for some concoction of spittle and bile. The dog was trembling, up and down its spine, moving raggedly and disordered, with the coordination of a drunk.

But some remnant of light remained in Biscuit's eyes. Some element of recognition. The dog locked eyes with Flick and, suddenly, the tremors working in the back half of its body had turned to the wagging of its tail. It limped towards Flick, head low as if grovelling.

Then it fell on to its forelegs and face, and rolled over at their feet.

'Biscuit?' Flick ventured. Dropping to her knees, she stroked the dog's fur; all around its muzzle was wet and glistening. 'Biscuit, what happened?'

'She's hurt,' said Suki, scrabbling down to the dog's side. Then, running her hands over the raggedly breathing dog's flanks, she said, 'Maybe she was shot? But I can't find any wound . . .'

'Water,' said Flick, with mounting urgency. 'Quickly, bring her some water!'

Suki scrambled to the bank of the beck, cupped her hands to the frigid, flowing water and hurried back up the slope. By the time she reached Biscuit, most of the water had filtered through her fingers – but what little remained, she lifted to the dog's snout. Biscuit's tongue lolled miserably, trying to lap up the water; then she hung her head once again.

Flick's eyes were flashing urgently around. 'My mobile phone,' she said, 'it's in my back pocket. Can you reach it?'

She'd pulled the tormented Biscuit up on to her lap, so it was left to Suki to reach into Flick's back pocket and produce her mobile phone. There wasn't much reception, but one bar flickered on the phone's home screen. Flick dialled a number and lifted it to her ear. Moments later, she uttered, 'He isn't picking up. Look, Suki, we're closer to Mr Lowell's cottage here than we are the manor. We have to get her back there. Here, take this.' She pressed the phone into Suki's hands. 'I'll carry Biscuit. You keep dialling Mr Lowell. He'll have to meet us there.'

Up through the woodland they came, under the very same branches from which Biscuit had emerged. It was dark in here, the air close and moist, and the woodland path that Biscuit had followed kept petering into nothingness, then erupting again through stands of bramble and bracken. Flick, who was cradling the labouring Biscuit in her arms, led the way – while Suki's eyes kept flashing at the phone. When there came a gap in the trees and the reception returned, she dialled for Lowell again; but either the reception was too fragmented or Lowell was too deeply engaged in the shoot to realise his phone was ringing. They hurried on, in breathless silence and anticipation, through dark forest grove and clearings of dappled sunlight.

Some way further along, Flick burst through the trees into a clearing where the earth seemed to have been scorched black, as if it was the site of some bonfire from the season past. Inside a ring of stones, the stumps of old trees were charred black as the night, and around it the earth was heavy with charcoal and ash.

'Check the phone,' said Flick.

There was reception. Suki hit redial and listened as, on the opposite end, Lowell's phone began to ring. As it tolled in her ear, she looked around the desolate clearing. Lowell's handiwork, she supposed. Gamekeepers had to do all sorts of things to manage their estates, and no doubt burning back the underbrush to encourage new life was part of it. Probably it was just the natural order of things that some of the woodland wildlife fell prey to the technique; as Suki gazed around, willing Lowell to pick up, she saw the charred remains of some woodland rabbit on the edge of the clearing and, beside it, the feathery mess of some carrion crow that had dropped dead at its side. Nature, she thought, could be a beautiful thing – but it could be cruel and bitter as well. There was death in this woodland. She only hoped it was not hanging, with its tongue lolling out, in Flick Garrick's arms.

'Yes?' came Lowell's voice.

'Mr Lowell!' Suki stammered. 'It's Suki, from the kitchens. I'm – I'm here with Flick. Mr Lowell, something dreadful's happening. We found Biscuit, in the woodland. She's—'

'She's what?' the gruff voice, now tinged in panic, crackled down the line.

'She's . . . sick, Mr Lowell.' She didn't know how else to describe it. 'We're taking her back to your cottage. We're not –' she looked up at Flick, who mouthed a word back, '– ten minutes away.'

'Phone me when you get there,' grunted Lowell – and Suki fancied she could feel both terror and heartache in his voice. 'Hang this lot out here! I'm on my way.'

The door to Lowell's cottage was locked, but Flick directed Suki to ferret under one of the flowerpots by the door – and, moments later, they were crashing into the cluttered little front room, laying Biscuit down in her basket in front of the hearth.

'Is she still living?' Suki breathed.

Flick was on her knees at Biscuit's side, running her hands up and down her flanks. 'She's breathing,' she said, 'but it's not right. It's just not—' Before Flick could go on, a telephone started trilling in the corner of the room. 'Pick it up, Suki. It might be Mr Lowell.'

The phone was on a table by Lowell's armchair, buried beneath newspapers, magazines, old tobacco pouches and packets of seeds. As Suki unearthed it, her eyes took in the shelf hidden in the alcove behind it. Strange, but the copy of Deirdre Shaw's *Game Night: Plucking and Stuffing* she'd seen on the bookcase the last time she was here had been stuffed on to the shelf, as if hidden away from prying eyes. A painful memory, Suki supposed, after Lowell had stumbled across the rhubarb patch. Crammed on top of it was a bundle of *Country Life* magazines – Suki was startled to see that the top edition featured a picture of Farleigh Manor itself, and the headline read ON THE FARLEIGH ESTATE WITH THE LATE, GREAT HARRY LOWELL – battered copies of Agatha Christie's *The Mysterious Affair at Styles*, *Horticulture for Beginners* and *So You're Going to Be a Parent* with half its cover torn off. Suki guessed that Lowell's reading matter consisted almost entirely of books that the guests left behind.

On the fifth ring, Suki snatched up the receiver.

'Is she alive?' barked Lowell, down the line.

Suki stammered, 'Y-yes. We've got her in her basket.'

'Tell me everything.'

Suki barely knew where to begin. 'She's still trembling. She's . . . vomited, somewhere in the woodland, she told him. Her eyes have lost all focus. Her breathing, so ragged. 'She's just lying there now. It's like she's—'

'Not given up,' said Lowell. 'Not yet. That dog's been poisoned – I'd stake my life on it. Now, listen here, and listen very carefully – I'm still fifteen minutes away, so you're going to have to do this for me. Is Flick there?'

Suki breathlessly said, 'She's right here, right with Biscuit.'

'Good, because it's going to take two of you. There's a bottle of hydrogen peroxide in the water closet out back. The outdoor facility. I keep it just in case. You're going to feed it to her.'

Suki stopped. 'But Mr Lowell—'

'It's going to make her throw up. It's not going to be pleasant, but it's the only thing that will purge her. Go! Go and get the bottle. I'll stay on the line.'

Suki and Flick crashed through the back door. Lowell's back yard was just as cluttered as the front, and in its centre smouldered the remains of some other bonfire he'd been burning. Sweet, charred smells – almost like the smells of a barbecue – enveloped Suki as she followed Flick around the yard towards the outhouse sitting up against the back fence.

The outhouse had once been an outside bathroom, and in its centre a dry, cracked toilet bowl still sat. In the intervening years, Lowell had built shelves up its every side, cramming them full of all the odds and ends he had acquired across a long life of tending to the estate. Consequently, it took some time – and not a little panic – before Flick, bracing one foot in the cup of Suki's hands, had unearthed the bottle of hydrogen peroxide from one of the uppermost shelves.

'Is that it?' asked Suki, as Flick came crashing back to earth.

'Come on, Mr Lowell's still on the line.'

'I'm five minutes out,' barked Lowell, when Suki picked up the receiver again. 'How is she?'

Suki cast a look at Flick, who only shrugged.

'Breathing,' was all Suki could say.

'OK – you're going to take a teaspoon, just one mark you, and put it to the back of her throat. Can you manage it?'

At that moment, another phone started trilling in the room. Suki recognised it, at once, as the sound of her own iPhone – and knew, by the ringtone (a particularly noisome piece of black metal she had adopted purely because it enraged her mother), who the caller was. Numbers. Chances were he'd been trying to get hold of her all morning; it was only here, where her iPhone fleetingly had reception, that he'd been able to get through.

But all that could wait. 'Yes, yes,' she said, 'we can manage it. Mr Lowell, we're doing it right now.'

Suki put the receiver gently on to the stack of magazines and rushed to where Flick was crouching, the beleaguered Biscuit at her side. 'One teaspoon, to start with,' said Suki. 'It's going to make her throw up whatever's left inside her, whatever she's eaten. Biscuit,' she said, 'you're going to be OK. We're going to make you . . .'

Suki's words faltered, for she had already seen the look on Flick's face. Her eyes, dark and harrowed, looked from Suki to the ailing dog. And it was then that Suki recognised what she had not seen before. While she'd been scrambling from the phone to the hearthside, while she'd been juggling the bottle of hydrogen peroxide and

168

the teaspoon in her hands, rallying her courage for the task to come, Biscuit had breathed her very last breath. Her muzzle lay, at peace now, in Flick Garrick's lap. No longer did her breast move raggedly up and down. No more tremors worked up and down her legs. There was a deep, meaty scent as some remnant leaked out from underneath her tail to soil the blankets on which she was lying.

She was dead, and all was empty in the room.

Suki and Flick must have been sitting in shell-shocked silence for two minutes when the tranquillity outside the cottage was torn apart by the guttering complaint of an engine as Hubert Lowell's Land Rover slewed to a stop on the forested pathway outside. Startled from her silence, Suki picked herself up, meaning to meet Mr Lowell in the doorway – but, in that same moment, her iPhone started tolling again, the same heavy guitar riff that announced it was Numbers calling. She was reaching for it, fumbling to disconnect the call, when the cottage door opened – and there stood Hubert Lowell, his aged face lined in expectation and exasperation, his expression poised somewhere between petition and prayer.

'Did it work?' he gasped, eyes scouring the room and landing on where Biscuit lay, her muzzle still in Flick Garrick's lap. 'Did you administer it?'

Suki had managed to fumble her iPhone into silent mode when Lowell's eyes took in the brutal reality of the scene. She watched, the phone vibrating in her hand, as he reeled across the room, dropped to his knees by the hearth, and hoisted Biscuit's inert form on to his lap. 'I'm sorry,' he was breathing. 'Oh Biscuit, what happened to you?' – and Suki, suddenly desperate for fresh air, burst out of the cottage door, out into the smouldering front yard and the remnants of the bonfires scattered around.

The iPhone was still vibrating; Numbers was either being particularly persistent or he was particularly bored and desperate for somebody to speak with.

Her heart was racing. She wanted to run – run away from the cottage, away from Lowell's sobbing, away from insinuations of poison and murder. But she could not run – and Numbers had always been the one to talk her down from the brink in the past. She was still breathless as she answered the call. She fancied she could still smell the last of Biscuit in the air around her.

'You like to keep a boy waiting, DARLING,' crooned Numbers down the phone.

'Numbers,' she stammered, 'you won't believe what—'

'No, *darling*, you won't believe what *I've* found. Well, my treasure, I've been doing the digging – just like you asked. Trawling the internet mostly, of course. Well, it happens to be my specialty. And, by God, Suki, this Deirdre Shaw – national treasure, they call her? Well, they can't be digging too deeply. There's no shortage of people happy to gripe about her in their interviews and memoirs. No shortage of industry gossip either – people she screwed over on her way to the top. I'll wager your own dear grandmama might have a thing or two to say about that.'

Suki's heart had stopped its relentless, discordant beating. Perhaps it was the fresh air, or perhaps it really was

Numbers's voice, but she found herself taking deep and steady, calming breaths.

'Numbers, what did you find?'

'Well, I set out like you told me to – plotting Deirdre Shaw's movements on the run-up to her attending Farleigh Manor. Now, as far as I can see – and it wasn't too difficult to get into her agent's computer, their security must be dated something like 1994! – she kept a full calendar. Various demonstrations across the last couple of months – a private event for Netflix, and one showing off her baking skills for L'Oréal. Well, at least she moves with the times. She did a three-day stint at the Women's Institute Land Fair at the start of September, a demo on the South Bank for Harvest Festival only last Wednesday, and it seems she had to cancel an appearance on *Good Morning Britain* so she could cook at this weekend of yours. Now, *that* might be something worth digging into – what's so special about Rupert Prendergast and party that she'd bump an appearance on national TV? All you need to do is look at her emails with her agent (I've had a good nosy through *those*) to know she was still a glory hog after forty years in the business. A bit of attention is like catnip to these celebrity types. But the *real* thing you'll want to know, the thing that might cast this whole sorry business in a new light for you Sherlock Holmes wannabes, is what she did at the end of August . . .'

'What's that?' asked Suki. She had flashed a look back at the cottage, where a single primeval howl from Lowell was the last, sudden and violent expunging of his grief.

'Seems Mrs Shaw got hired to cater a private dinner at a law firm out in Holborn, Chancery Lane. Podcock and Blake. You heard of them yet, Suki *darling*?'

'Podcock and . . . Numbers, I have absolutely no idea what you're talking about.'

'They're a small firm, highbrow solicitors – intellectual property, creative disputes, media mismanagement. The whole *shebang*. Well, it seems Mrs Shaw was hired to cater a dinner they were hosting for a raft of special clients. These law firms, Suki, they're as dirty as the rest of them – treat your clients to a slap-up dinner, take them for a jolly down to Spearmint Rhino, and you've won your firm a nice fee for the future. And guess who works – or, I should say, *worked* – there, Suki? Guess whose name cropped up in the emails, the very person who organised and enlisted Deirdre Shaw to cater the event?'

'You're killing me, Numbers. Who?'

'A little man by the name of Prendergast.'

Suki blanched, '*Rupert* Prendergast . . .'

'Strike one, Suki. There's more than one Prendergast. This one goes by the name of Richard.'

Suki's eyes widened. 'It's his son. He's here too.'

'Well, you'll want to go digging around him, Suki, because Richard Prendergast was the one who hired Deirdre to cater the event at his firm. And it seems the evening was more "miss" than "hit" – young Mr Prendergast got his marching orders from the firm one week later. It seems he let some important clients slip through the firm's fingers. Didn't pull out all the stops. Deirdre Shaw didn't cut it for them – so off they went to

172

somewhere more glamorous, somewhere younger and hipper and . . .'

Suki's mind was reeling. 'When did you say?'

'August.'

Scarcely two months had flown by since then. Two months until Deirdre Shaw was lying dead in the rhubarb. 'She was a family favourite. Rupert used to use her as a private chef – that is, until his wife Georgette put an end to it . . .'

'And well she might,' said Numbers, 'because that's the other thing you ought to know about Deirdre Shaw. Deirdre wasn't one who believed in the sanctity of marriage. Well, she liked marriage well enough – she did it three times over – but they never seemed to last. Infidelity, every time. It seems she just couldn't say no. Her second husband, James, published a poisonous memoir about her three years ago. Made a pretty penny out of it, by all accounts – and it's still going on. The *Daily Mail*'s serialising it again next weekend – and all on the back of the obituary he's just written about her. I'll ping it over to you right now. It seems there wasn't much love lost between them. He'd been her manager, once upon a time, so, when she shacked up with the next in line, he lost everything. His wife, his career, his house . . . He kept the kids, of course – well, Deirdre was off filming all over the world, so somebody had to. James had been a high-flying agent to the stars. Then he was a stay-at-home father to three motherless girls. You can imagine his anger.'

Suki really could. She said, 'This obituary, what does it say?'

'Just about the most waspish things you can imagine. Read it for yourself. There,' said Numbers, 'it's flying through the ether on its way to your inbox right now. But here's the kicker, Suki darling – James had rocked up to her demonstration at the South Bank last week. Two days before she landed at Farleigh. It seems it was something he liked to do on occasion, just to rile her. Deirdre had a good mouth-off at her management about it, over email the next day.'

'Numbers, you don't think . . .' A terrible thought had occurred to Suki. But what if they were looking in entirely the wrong place? What if Farleigh Manor, and everything that had happened here, was just a terrible conflation of coincidences? Was it really possible that Deirdre Shaw had been murdered by somebody who wasn't here at the manor at all?

The door to the cottage opened, and out into the light staggered Lowell, bearing Biscuit in his arms. Behind him, Flick Garrick's face was blotched and red where her tears had cascaded down.

'Numbers,' she said, 'you've been a superstar, as ever. I owe you. But I've got to go.'

As she hung up, she looked back at Lowell, who had lain poor Biscuit down on the earth. Moments later, a shovel was in his hand and he was breaking the earth on the other side of the bonfire's remnants, preparing the grave into which his beloved life's companion would be laid.

Poison, thought Suki. It was all over the manor. It had turned all of Rupert Prendergast's guests – save for Rupert himself – to ruin on the night she and Prudence had arrived. And now it had robbed the life of a sprightly English setter, choked the breath out of her, extinguished the light in her eyes.

There was a heat haze coming off the remains of the bonfire. Suki found herself staring into it, and remembering, starkly, the scorched clearing in the heart of the woodland.

Her iPhone buzzed, as Numbers's email appeared on her home screen marked 'Deirdre Shaw Obituary, James Wright'. She crammed it into her pocket, determined to honour the moment unfolding in front of her now.

Something terrible had happened here. Something terrible still was.

The only question was whether they could figure it out before it happened again.

Chapter Ten

'There's been another killing.'

Prudence had her head in the oven, manhandling the roasting pan from one shelf to another while testing the plumpness of the pheasant breast with the tip of her finger (hardened, across the years, so that it hardly ever felt the heat). Upon hearing the words, she lifted herself gracefully from the oven, removed her spectacles to defog them on the cuff of her sleeve, and finally located Suki, standing in the kitchen-garden door.

'It's Biscuit,' said Suki, before her grandmother could go on. 'The gamekeeper's dog. Poisoned, by something she ate in the woodland. She just limped down to the river, Grandma – but, by the time we could find Mr Lowell, she was gone. Mr Lowell's burying her right now.'

Prudence took a deep breath and reclined against the sink unit. There were six hours until the banquet began. Six hours until Rupert Prendergast and his party gathered for their triumphant, valedictory feast. The clock was ticking – but, somehow, it felt as if it was counting down the seconds to something else as well.

'Well,' said Prudence, 'at least that proves one thing, beyond any reasonable doubt.'

'Grandma?'

Prudence led her out of the door again, into the low October sunshine spilling down over the kitchen garden. There they stood together, looming over the rhubarb patch where Hubert Lowell's makeshift cross still punctured the earth. 'There's a poisoner here at Farleigh Manor, Suki. A foolish one, if I'm any judge. One who never really understood the terror of what they've been doing, or how easily it might go wrong. You see, Suki, they've lost control of their own plot. The poison slipped through their fingers. Deirdre Shaw didn't die of a heart attack at all. It was here, staring us in the face all along.' Prudence reached into her apron pocket and produced a roll of crumpled paper. 'It's the menu she left behind, my dear. Take a look – see if you can spot it.'

Suki took the crumpled paper in her hand. On it, four days of recipes were written up in an elaborate, cursive hand – but only the first day's menu had been ticked off, like a good schoolgirl marking off her chores.

Suki read, 'Wild venison ragu. Soup of butternut squash . . .' She stopped. 'But what's this got to do with what happened, Grandma?'

'Stop reading what's there, Suki, and start reading what's missing.'

Suki didn't follow. 'Missing, Grandma?'

'Pheasant, Suki. Deirdre didn't serve pheasant that first night she was here. So why was there a pheasant carcass, sitting in the Frigidaire, just begging some new cook to come along and make a consommé with it?'

177

Suki strained at the paper. There was something here, something her grandmother was seeing, something just beyond Suki's grasp.

'Deirdre ate it herself, Suki. She never could resist indulging herself. But somebody had got to the pheasant first. Laced it with the poison that killed her. Then, of course, we came along and used its leftovers. Seems there was just enough poison left in that carcass, after I'd boiled the goodness out of its bones, to put Gray Williams in hospital and to send the rest of Mr Prendergast's party staggering to their toilet bowls that night. Mr Prendergast was right, Suki – we *did* poison the shooting party. We just had no idea that was what we were doing.'

Suki stammered, 'And the robbery . . .'

'Poisoning the whole party spooked our killer. They knew what had happened. Knew it wasn't food poisoning. Knew it wasn't a bad bottle of wine. Well, Alice Pendlebury doesn't touch a drop, does she? So they waited until their first opportunity, came down here and ransacked the place, emptying the larder. That simpleton constable might have thought they were just opportunists, coming after kitchen iPads and KitchenAids and all manner of other gadgetry. But he was wrong. They came in a blind panic because they knew there was still poison in this kitchen. Their murder was done, but the poison was left behind. They'd lost control of their own plot.'

'Then what happened to Biscuit, out in the woods?'

Prudence shook her head wearily. 'Our killer isn't very good at cleaning up after himself.'

'Or *herself*,' whispered Suki.

'Indeed,' said Prudence, and tramped back inside.

'Grandma,' Suki said, hurrying after her and watching her take the first pheasant out of the oven. 'Is it possible – the poison, it might have been administered elsewhere? Numbers got back in touch. He told me about Deirdre's ex-husband, James. He's just published an obituary of her. You won't believe the things he says . . .' Suki reached for her iPhone and opened the attachment Numbers had sent through. She'd scanned it as she cantered down from Lowell's cottage, desperate to be away from that place of death. ' "Deirdre Shaw might have fooled the world, but she couldn't fool those closest to her. They knew that, for as much charm and good humour as she had, there was an equal weight of waspishness and manipulation. Like any good cook, Deirdre knew when to add sugar – and when to add spice." Numbers said she was demo-ing down on the South Bank, in London, only last week. James rocked up and made a scene.'

'James Wright lost a livelihood when his marriage collapsed. He had cause to be disgruntled.'

'But Grandma, what if *he* orchestrated it? There's motive coming out of his ears. Isn't it possible that he—'

'You're forgetting, Suki, that the poisoning happened right here, right in this kitchen. It was pot-roast pheasant that put Deirdre Shaw in her grave.'

'Then James might be in league with somebody here. They plotted it together.'

179

Prudence mused on the idea, even as she started carving the pheasant, setting aside its juicy meats for the bonbons she needed to make.

'I met James Wright on more than one occasion. I never took him for a killer. A coward and a craven, perhaps; the man has just about enough guts to write a nasty memoir about someone he once loved. Killing, Suki, is quite a different matter. No, our killer's here – right here in the manor – I'm sure of it. The question is motive.'

'There's motive enough, floating around,' said Suki. She too had returned to the kitchen countertop, where she started furiously dicing a string of red onions, just as Prudence had shown her. 'That's the other thing Numbers dug up. Richard Prendergast – he used Deirdre Shaw for a client event at his firm, Podcock and Blake, at the end of the summer. Only, the event didn't go well – Richard made a hash of it. The clients slipped through his fingers, and Podcock and Blake fired him soon afterwards.' Suki faltered. 'What if . . . what if he blamed Deirdre? He lost everything. You've seen the way his father speaks of him – it's like there's no respect at all. What if Richard hit a low, couldn't cope with his career being dashed, couldn't stand the way his father looked at him? He might think it was Deirdre's fault. She's the one who didn't pull out all the stops for their dinner. She's the one who wasn't modern and glamorous enough to bowl over the clients. So his mind starts turning to murder and . . .'

Prudence had scraped the last shred of meat from the pheasant's skeleton. Pointedly, she put the carcass in a pot, with half-a-dozen peeled shallots and chunks of parsnip. 'Call that bookshop at Nutwood St Knowle. If they have a copy of James Wright's memoir, tell them to set it aside. I believe it was called *Bitchin' in the Kitchen*. We'll have just about enough time to go and pick it up when I get back, before we have to be chained, lock and key, to this kitchen.'

Suki wheeled around. Prudence was already wringing her hands dry on a tea towel, and then heading for the boarded-up kitchen-garden door.

'Back?' Suki asked. 'Back from where, Grandma?'

'Well, dear, if there's one good thing your escapade with that sorry English setter has done, it's set the mind to whirring. And it seems to me that a murder has three vital ingredients: the victim, we already know; the motive, we're no closer to finding out; but the *method* – well, we're on the brink of knowing exactly how it was done.'

'But Grandma, you said . . . poison.'

'Ah yes, Suki, but there are as many poisons in this world as there are ingredients. It's Biscuit's unfortunate encounter that might be the key to the whole mystery.'

At least the sun was shining. There was a peculiar beauty about the cold October sun. The truth was, Prudence was cutting it fine to leave the kitchen at all – there was far too much to be done to entrust it to Suki alone (though she was loath to admit it, the girl – like all untrained assistants – was as much a hindrance as she was a help in the kitchen), and, in spite of the unusual

181

circumstances of this job, Prudence's professional pride meant that, even now, she didn't intend to serve anyone a below-par supper. One way or another, murder or not, this weekend was going to figure in these people's memories for many years to come – the rest of their lives, if Prudence was any judge – and, whenever they spoke about it, she would not have them denigrating the supper they were served.

But she could spare herself an hour. An hour to try and decipher that had happened to poor Biscuit – and, by consequence, what manner of murder had befallen Deirdre Shaw herself.

Prudence followed Suki's directions until at last she reached the same bank of Hill Beck where Biscuit had staggered out of the woodland; the very same place, she reflected now, where Jane Sutcliffe had fallen and, cracking her head on one of those stones being washed clean in the river, breathed her last breath. Halfway here, she had heard the grumble of engines somewhere behind – no doubt the shooting party was returning, disgruntled, to the manor house, another day ruined by an unfortunate demise. Prudence supposed Rupert Prendergast would be none too happy with that – if Deirdre Shaw's death had seemed a mere inconvenience to him, what would he think of the death of a creature so lowly as a gamekeeper's dog? – but that was a problem for later in the day. Right now, she had but one question on her mind: what was it Biscuit had eaten that took away the poor dog's life? And was the source of it the very same thing that had felled Deirdre Shaw?

She started looking at the beck, but all around was only clover and grass, a picnicker's emerald idyll. On the bank itself there were the tell-tale signs of water voles, the openings to their burrows just above the water, old dandelion clocks and cow parsley – but nothing, she thought, that might endanger a life. Not unless you were Jane Sutcliffe and tripped on those slippery rocks, of course.

She lifted her eyes. There, above her, hung the woods out of which Biscuit had stumbled. Yes, she thought, the edges of the forest – where the air was close and the shadows propagated all kinds of different growth – were an altogether better place to start looking.

So she went into the trees.

Prudence had always loved woodlands and wild places. It stemmed back to the days before she was part of the cookery circuit at all, those long childhood summers when her father – a Yorkshireman by birth and by heart, who had run the family greengrocer's until the calamity of not one, but two out-of-town shopping centres had signalled its doom – would take her on long camping holidays, and show her how, if you were prepared to invest a little imagination, there was food almost everywhere you looked. It was her father who had taught her that the real value of stinging nettles was in the luscious, smooth – and not at all stingy – soup they made. It was her father who taught her about elderflower fritters, and how spinach was nothing compared to fat hen; and how even a common cattail had a bulbous root you could depend upon for starch. It was her father, too, who taught her the rules of wild mushroom picking. The signs of their gills and caps, their stems and skirts.

And it was mushrooms she went looking for now.

They were everywhere, if you knew where to find them – gathered around the exposed roots of trees or growing in long channels up the dead timbers that always pockmarked a forest. As she went, Prudence sifted the edible from the inedible, taking samples of the very worst she could find and slipping them inside the clear plastic sandwich bags she'd brought up from the kitchen. There was enough poison in here to kill Biscuit – enough poison, she felt certain, to wipe out the entire Prendergast party, if Prudence so desired – but the thing that kept plaguing her was that *dogs are not stupid*. A human being could easily stumble into this woodland and decide to sauté whatever toadstools they found with a little garlic and butter – human beings blustered their way through lives, thinking they were impervious to the cruelties of nature – but a dog would never be so careless. A dog would smell danger. And, what was more, a dog would *never* just wander over and gobble up a stand of fungi, poisonous or not. It just wasn't in their instincts.

Which meant it had to be something else that killed Biscuit.

Which, in turn, meant it had to be something else that killed Deirdre Shaw.

The thought was vexing Prudence as she pottered further into the woodland. By now, she'd already filled her plastic bags with wild mushrooms – just to be certain

– and, by the time she stumbled upon the clearing with the scorched earth and ring of stones, she was beginning to dream up wilder, more outlandish ideas. She was quite certain Prudence wouldn't have stuffed the pheasant she'd eaten with poisonous fungi herself – apart from everything else she was, she was a competent, knowledgeable chef – and, certainly, nobody else could have done such a thing; at least, not without Prudence discovering it and wondering which guest had sneaked into her kitchen, surreptitiously stuffed the pheasant she ought not to have been eating, and sneaked off again. Logic dictated that it had happened some other way. But what?

She was scouring the clearing – no doubt the work of Lowell, looking after the woodland – when her eyes landed on some tiny fragments of white, glinting in the bed of dry leaves at the roots of an ash tree, just beyond the edge of scorched earth. As she tramped there, she could not ignore the remains of some rabbit – feasted on by carrion birds, or perhaps a fox – that sprawled at the clearing's edge. The place smelt of charcoal and ash, but there had been death here too.

Crouching down, she was surprised to see that the white was not natural; perhaps it had blown off whatever had been burning here – though, by the look of it, it had only been the undergrowth Lowell had been burning back. Reaching down, she fingered the white fragments – and found them, at last, to be scraps of card, laminated by tape. She turned the first one over. In small block capitals were written the words RUPERT/GEORGETTE. On the second was written GRAY/TERENCE'.

Prudence felt a sudden chill. Somewhere, in the woodland, there was a crackling – as of some branch being split underfoot – but, when she looked around, it was only shadows that she saw.

Then, beyond the edge of the clearing – in a little pocket of open earth, where sunlight cascaded through the canopy above – something else caught her eye.

She had not often seen this plant before. If it was what she thought it was, there was good reason for that. It stood a little under head height, with a smooth hollow stem, changing from dark purple to green as the plant reached its height. At its crown, the last of its small clusters of white flowers were dying away as autumn tightened its grip on the forest. It almost looked, she thought, like Queen Anne's lace – wild carrot, as her father used to call it. Queen Anne's lace belonged in a meadowland, though, or the edge of some farmer's field – not a forest clearing. Very carefully, she stroked its leaves, finding them smooth and hairless. Then, when curiosity got the better of her, she snipped away a length of stem and cluster of flowers from its top and slipped it inside the last of her sandwich bags.

Time was ticking on so, with her samples securely stowed away, Prudence hurried back the way she had come, dropping out of the woodland, just as Biscuit had done, until she found herself back at Hill Beck. It was good to step back into the sunlight, even if she was standing on the site of some century-old murder.

She was almost back at the manor – a whole hour had passed, the Prendergasts' banquet one step closer to being served – when she first heard the voices. They were far away and indistinct – but, even so, there was little doubt they were coming from the manor. Prudence didn't have to make out the words to understand these were voices raised in anger – yet, the closer she came to the sweeping driveway that circled Farleigh Manor like some medieval moat, the more she began to hear.

It was when she rounded the edge of the manor itself, reaching the lower orchard wall, that she saw the figure bursting out of the open door. The argument, it seemed, had been raging in the entrance hall, with the doors flung open to the world – and now, out of it, Richard Prendergast erupted, almost as if he'd been thrown out by the scruff of his neck.

He was marching, however, of his own volition – and, stalling at a distance, Prudence was quite certain that it was the gravelly, throaty voice of Maxwell Pendlebury flurrying after him. Though she did not see the old man, she heard his final, vehement cry – 'You're the same as your father, you dog!' – and the sudden slamming of the manor door.

Richard Prendergast stopped in the middle of the driveway and Prudence, only half-obscured by the protection of her camper van, could see the way he was shaking. Whether it was in rage or humiliation, she was not quite sure. He craned a look back at the manor's facade – placid, now that Maxwell was gone – and stood, rooted to the spot, until the shakes had left him. If she was not mistaken, his eyes were brimming with tears

– and surely that spoke more to humiliation than it did to anger.

He looked back, turned around – and now there was no hiding; his eyes locked with Prudence's, and she stepped out of the semi-shelter of the camper van.

'I didn't want to come here anyway,' Richard said, when it was clear he could say nothing. 'A shooting weekend? With my father's old crowd? I can think of a thousand things I'd rather be doing. Chemotherapy, for instance. Having a rectal exam.'

Prudence's eyes opened in astonishment.

'But no,' Richard went on, 'I just *had* to come. Pretend to be a chip off the old block, as always. Take your gun, Richard. Put a bullet between its eyes. And then glory in it – eat what you've killed! You'd think he was the Great White Hunter. There's a picture of him, somewhere, standing over the lion he killed. Just never tell him those guides of his had drugged it first. By God, it's the twenty-first century – do we still have to pretend? Heaven forbid he should eat a little tofu. A Portobello mushroom burger . . .'

'Richard,' Prudence ventured, incredulously, 'are you a . . . vegetarian?'

'Vegan,' he said, 'except, of course, when I'm with my father. I'm sure he'd rather I was homosexual – and you only have to look at the way he's constantly smirking at Mr Williams and Mr Knight to know what he really thinks of *that*. Yes, Mrs Bulstrode, I'm vegan three-hundred-and-fifty days of the year. And then my father summons me as his bloody squire and I have to fall into line. They all think I'm cut from the same cloth as him. That's why Mr Pendlebury's got his knickers in a twist too. They think I'm Rupert Prendergast reincarnate. My father expects me to start bringing my own parties here sometime soon – he fancies it's all a family tradition, all the backstabbing and philandering that's gone on here over the years. What none of them understand is I'm my own man. Or . . .' he faltered, 'I'm going to be.'

Richard was about to stalk off, somewhere over the estate, when Prudence said, 'What was Mr Pendlebury so angry about?'

'Oh, it's all on account of that afternoon I stayed behind with Alice. I suppose Mrs Pendlebury was using it to taunt him. Me, the younger man. But all she did was show me some dancing. She said Maxwell's too old for the ballroom – and, besides, he never really did like it anyway. I hardly even *wanted* to do it. I was only being polite. And we were out on the shoot just now, and she kept dropping silly little hints – you know the kind of thing, that she might swap him for a younger model, somebody who was still up to it, if you know what I mean. Well, Maxwell took offence at that. I can only thank my lucky stars that Mr Lowell had to call off the shoot. I'm quite sure it would have ended with some terrible accident.'

Prudence said, 'Well, Richard, it sounds like you've been served a raw deal. Mr Pendlebury will calm down, won't he? In time for tonight?'

'Oh, *tonight*,' said Richard, with a scornful shake of the head. 'Yes, I daresay he'll forget about it by then. He's put me in my place, and that's quite good enough for him. Well, it always has been before. I'm not the first "other man" Mr Pendlebury's taken offence to. Alice can hardly look at another fellow without him flipping his lid.'

Prudence knew that sort of man well enough. 'He thinks he owns her.'

'He thinks she ought to just toe the line. He's not so very different from my father in that respect. They're the centre of the universe. There's not a thing on Earth as important as their own egos. But Maxwell made a bad choice if he ever thought he could tame Alice Pendlebury.'

'Frith,' said Prudence, remembering the guest register. 'Her name was Alice Frith.'

'Maxwell only wanted her for a child – and he never got one, so he's always been bitter. Good God, she's twice my age. I'm not remotely interested in her – for dancing, or anything else. I'm *especially* not interested in women my father used to sleep with!'

Prudence blanched – though, by now, she had expected nothing less. Parties like this might not have been so louche as to call themselves 'wife-swappers', but there was always an air about them that suggested a certain *sharing* had taken place over the years.

'Your father – and Alice Pendlebury?'

'Well, it's hardly breaking confidences to say it. It was a long time ago, before my time, that's for sure. My father had an eye for the ladies. He's the sort who thinks taking a mistress is practically obliged. A generation ago, he'd have kept a little flat nearby for his *liaisons*. The worst thing is my mother – she knows all about it. It's just an accepted part of life. But if *she* ever dared to dream about . . .'

'Taking a lover?' Prudence ventured.

Richard shuddered. 'Well, it would never happen. She has too much self-respect. Carrying on like that, at their age – it's intolerable.'

Prudence saw her opening and said, 'Your mother threw Deirdre out, though, didn't she?'

'What?'

'Deirdre Shaw. Your father was using her for private catering but your mother thought there was a little more to it, didn't she? Well, perhaps she could bear somebody taking her husband to their bed at night – as you say, it's practically *obligatory* for some sorts of people – but to have another woman constantly popping up in her *kitchen*? That must have been another matter.'

Richard shuddered, folding his arms around her body. 'Deirdre Shaw. I wish I'd never heard the name.'

'Of course, you used her too, didn't you?'

Richard's eyes flared with a look of such anger that Prudence was quite certain the name had invoked strong feelings. Indeed, Richard Prendergast looked more furious now than he had done when chased out of Farleigh Manor by Maxwell Pendlebury's bitter invective.

'What do you know about that?' he whispered.

'Deirdre was my friend,' Prudence shrugged, making a show of ignoring his frustration.

'Yes, well, it was my father's idea. Like *everything*. Show them some showbiz clout, he said. Show them

191

you know how to pull strings. Well, maybe – but Deirdre Shaw was about twenty-five years out of date for the evening I ought to have thrown. And did she take instructions? Did she even *care* that one of our prospective clients had a serious shellfish allergy? By God, she nearly killed the man. It's no wonder I found my head in a noose at that firm. Of course, she *told* them I hadn't passed on the information. But she was nothing more than a disgruntled old cook who thought she knew better. Put *me* on disciplinary for that, would they? Hurry me out of the building? And all because of Deirdre Shaw?' Richard grunted, inaudibly. 'I'll put a bet on it, Mrs Bulstrode. Deirdre Shaw didn't die of a heart attack, but she wasn't murdered either – no matter what's ticking away in that head of yours. I'll wager she did for herself. Slipped some caustic soda into her supper, or choked on a chicken bone. She was past it, I'm telling you – losing her marbles, I shouldn't wonder. If her death was suspicious at all, it was all down to *her*.' Richard took two strides away. 'Well, Mrs Bulstrode, I suppose I should make myself scarce before this evening – give old Maxwell an opportunity to sort his head out. Let's just hope Alice stays out of his warpath this afternoon. That lot in there, without even any shooting to be done? Well, you never know what's about to kick off. They got that extra wine delivery as well. They'll be sozzled by six o'clock. You could serve them ham sandwiches and they wouldn't know the difference between that and whatever it is you've got planned.'

Ham sandwiches, thought Prudence as she left Richard, marching out across the estate, and hurried toward the kitchen-garden door. There were times in life when what you really wanted – perhaps even *needed* – was something as simple and unexciting as a humble ham sandwich. She could have used that ballast in her belly right now.

As she returned to the kitchen, Suki looked up; her face had been buried, not in *The Body in the Beck*, but in her iPhone.

'Oh, Suki, really,' Prudence said, bustling to the countertop – where she proceeded to empty her pocket of all the sandwich bags filled with mushrooms and cuttings from the woodland. 'Put the silly thing away. We've got some work to do – *investigative* work, before we have to start chopping onions.'

'It's investigative work I'm doing, Grandma. Look – there's no need for us to head back to the bookshop in Nutwood St Knowle. I've got James Wright's memoir right here. *Bitchin' in the Kitchen*, just like you said. Grandma, he's a spiteful, spiteful man. This book – it's nothing more than a hatchet job.'

'A book?' Prudence said, almost aghast at the very suggestion. 'On a *telephone*?'

'Yes, Grandma. It's the twenty-first century . . .'

Prudence rolled her eyes, in exasperation. 'Books are things of paper and binding, Suki. What you've got there is just words on a screen. And not very good words either. James Wright is many things, but a writer he is not.' She sighed. 'I've already told you – you're casting the net too wide to think about James at all. How could a man, more than a hundred miles away, have put some taint on that pheasant she ate? And, more to the point, how could it have been dumpy James Wright who broke through that door and ransacked this kitchen?'

That got Suki's attention. At last, she lifted her eyes from the iPhone.

'What have you got there, Grandma?'

'Poisons,' she said. She lifted one of the bags. 'Funeral bell,' she said, marvelling at the rich, chocolatey skin of the fungi inside. 'Deathcap and destroying angel. It's the angels you have to look out for. It looks innocuous enough, doesn't it?' It did, thought Suki – just a scrawny, white mushroom, at least to her untrained eye; she'd have thought nothing of chopping it up and sprinkling it into an omelette. 'Well, it's not. A scrap of this in your soup and you'll be dead within twenty-four hours. Oh, you'll probably feel well enough for most of that – but, once it's in you, it won't be stopped. Your liver, your kidneys – all of it, ruined beyond repair.'

'Then that's it,' said Suki, suddenly alert. 'Could it – could it have been an *accident*, Grandma?'

'I can't see how. Deirdre Shaw knew as much about foraging as I do. No, whatever happened here was more subtle than that. It had to be something she couldn't detect. Our poisoner might have lost control of the plot after the fact – but they knew what they were doing, at least at the outset.' Prudence produced the last sandwich bag, in which there lay a sprig of the plant she'd taken, at first, for Queen Anne's lace. 'I don't know,' she whispered, 'but there's something about this, something I'm not seeing.'

'What is it, Grandma?'

'I'm not sure. But there must be a book in the manor library, some way I can identify it. Suki, I need you to start with the onions, and I need you to get a stock simmering away. No poison in our stock this time – let's be sure of that.' She made certain the poisonous fungi from the woodland were safely back in her pockets and picked her way across the kitchen. 'I'll be back, just as soon as I've identified this.'

'Oh, *Grandma*,' said Suki, with righteous indignation. 'You really have got to move with the times, you know. You don't need books and glossaries and taxonomies. Bring it here.'

Against her better judgement, Prudence returned to the counter and lay the sprig, still safely concealed in its sandwich bag, down. Before she had stepped aside, Suki swept in with her iPhone, took a snapshot image of the plant and quickly appended it to a message.

'Let me guess,' said Prudence, with only very mild disapproval. 'Numbers?'

'There'll be an app for this, Grandma.'

'A . . . what?'

'An app. An *application*. Numbers will have this identified in half the time it would take you to even reach the library . . .'

Suki sent off the message, then slumped back into her seat with a triumphant smile.

'Well,' said Prudence, 'let's wait and see. But it doesn't get you out of the onions, young lady, and it doesn't get you out of the stock.' She glanced at the clock, hanging on the kitchen wall. 'Four and a half hours, Suki. We're cutting things rather fine.'

Chapter Eleven

Richard Prendergast left the shelter of the woodland path and heard the waters of Hill Beck babbling somewhere below him. How long had it been since he left the manor? One hour? Two? The sun might still have been shining in the sky, but there was no doubt about the season; the autumnal chill had more bite to it the later the day grew. Richard was beginning to wish he'd brought a coat. He was beginning, in fact, to wonder if the whole escapade was pointless. As soon as his father got back to the manor, to reconvene with the other guests, Maxwell would back off. That was the problem with his father's group of friends – they weren't friends, not really, not in the way Richard would have recognised. Old associates was a better way of putting it, each with their own slights and personal grievances against the others. Maxwell wouldn't have had the balls to go after Richard, not if Rupert were there; it would risk all the old enmities coming up, the old stories about Rupert and Alice – all from a time before Maxwell, of course, but damaging nonetheless. Richard didn't know what a confident, brassy woman like Alice was doing with a tedious old baboon like Maxwell anyway. Or rather, he *did* know, and thoroughly disap-proved. At the age of twenty-five, Richard Prendergast still believed that his match, when it came, would be made for love. He didn't yet understand that people make all sorts of pacts in their romantic lives. He still had youth on his side.

The brook was below him. There were stories about this place, weren't there? Some old nursemaid who'd met her end, tripping and bashing her head on the rocks in these waters. He remembered his father talking about it once when he was only small – the ghoulish history of the country house where he liked to spend his summers. But it seemed to Richard that a place as tranquil and beautiful as this had not been marred by murder – not really.

There was movement somewhere above him. His head whipped round. No figure approached him along the track – but that could only mean that, whoever it was, was under the branches of the trees that clung to the escarpment.

'Hello?' he called out. 'Is there anybody there?' Then, after a time, when only silence prevailed, he shouted, 'Mr Pendlebury, is that you?'

He reached the water's edge and, bowing down, took a rock in his hand. If there was somebody up there, he'd show them.

A figure materialised – not from the border of the woodland but along the bank of the brook itself.

'Oh,' he said, 'Mrs Pendlebury, it's you.'

At least Alice had her coat; evidently, she'd planned on leaving the manor again, instead of being driven out. It occurred to Richard, as she approached, that she really had been a beautiful woman, once upon a time. It occurred to him, shortly after that sentiment had entered his mind, that she was *still* a beautiful woman. It wasn't just her petite frame that made her seem so young, he thought. It was something in the sparkle of her eyes, bewitching and green – like those Farleigh Fairies people sometimes spoke about, some story from time long ago, the true heyday of the manor. There was a playfulness to her that, though he had protested the very idea when he was speaking to Mrs Bulstrode, really did excite him. He looked at her now, picking her way long the water's edge, and he wanted nothing more than to hurry to her side, perhaps thread his arm through hers – on the pretext of helping her along, of course, but in truth just so that he might breathe in the scent of her perfume.

No sooner had the idea entered his head, he tried to rid himself of it. He was being ridiculous. He was being a fool. He was being everything Maxwell told him he was being. He had to remind himself that Alice and his father had, once upon a time, had their fling. If that couldn't dampen whatever eruption of emotions was bubbling away inside him, nothing could.

'Richard,' she said, 'I'm so glad I found you here. I real-ise Maxwell . . . confronted you. I wanted to make sure you weren't too thrown.'

She had reached him on the water's edge and together they sat down, their feet only inches from the water where Jane Sutcliffe had died.

Fleetingly, clouds obscured the late October sun. It was funny how quickly the estate could be thrown into shadow by a few scudding clouds.

'He's a bully, Richard. He's always been a bully. He looks for the weakest target and he goes after it with everything he has. I suppose he thinks he's a lion, picking off the lame wildebeest. Well, these men and their hunting! But you mustn't take anything he says to heart. Lord knows, I don't – and I've been married to the man for twenty long years.'

Richard hardly dared say what he said next, but the words came to his lips all the same, 'Why *did* you marry him, Mrs Pendlebury?'

She moved closer. 'You can call me Alice.'

'It doesn't make sense. You . . . and *him*. You and any of them. You and . . .' He would have said 'my father', and no doubt ruined the delicate beauty of the moment – but, at that moment, he sensed movement again. This time, he was quite certain it was coming from the woodland above them. It hadn't just been Mrs Pendlebury's approach he'd become aware of before; something was moving, up there, something in the darkness.

They were being watched.

Alice seemed to have sensed it too. 'Maxwell,' she uttered, and by instinct drew her fur coat around her. 'I told you, Richard – a bully, through and through. All he wanted out of me was a child. An heir, he used to call it, like he belonged in some princely court, like he has titles and lands to hand down, not just a pot of gold festering in an account at Coutts.' A shudder ran through her. 'It would be better if he just dropped dead. Better if somebody . . . Well, I've thought of it often enough.'

They turned, together, to face the shadows on the fringe of the woodland.

Movement – movement up there, between the branches . . .

Alice shuffled closer to him. Richard, damning himself, tried to resist putting an arm around her shoulders.

Then, out of nowhere, a single gunshot split open the skies above Farleigh Manor; a single gunshot, scything through the silence at the bank of Hill Beck; a single gunshot that came from just above them.

Richard couldn't resist the instinct then; it all happened too quickly. He threw his arms around Alice, and – just as a second shot rang out – dragged her to the ground.

The mix to make the bonbons was almost finished by the time the iPhone buzzed with Numbers's response. So much for the speed and efficiency of the twenty-first century. Prudence had already shredded the pheasant meat, blitzing it up in a mixing bowl with plenty of cold butter, and was preparing to shape them before depositing them in the chiller until the service was almost nigh, when the blasted thing started shrieking – and Suki, who was doing sterling work with the stock, scrambled across the kitchen to pick it up.

'Well?' said Prudence, deftly turning the bonbons in more breadcrumbs and patting them into shape. 'Has technology come to the rescue?'

Suki looked up. 'Hemlock,' she whispered.

Prudence steeled herself, cleaned her hands of the bonbon mix at the sink and, wringing them dry, crossed the kitchen to where Suki stood.

She'd placed the iPhone on the counter, and on its screen there flickered the images Numbers had sent through. Prudence didn't need to look closely to know that he was right; she would have liked nothing more than to suspect he was wrong, then bustle up to the library to prove it – but the confirmation was all that she needed. She ought to have known it all along; it was only the frisson of horror that came with it that had stopped her from saying it out loud the moment she stepped back into this kitchen. Poison hemlock – it didn't take much to kill a person.

'He's right, isn't he, Grandma? So does that mean . . .'

Prudence stepped into the kitchen-garden door, hoping that the blast of fresh October air might give her a chance to think. Above the gardens, out on the drive, she could see Maxwell Pendlebury tottering forward to meet a Land Rover advancing along the track. Lowell, perhaps – or one of the party who hadn't yet returned from the shoot? It was surely not Richard Prendergast because the young man had sworn to stay away until it was nearly nightfall.

She turned over her shoulder. 'It's what killed her,' she said. 'It has to be. So now we have two of our main ingredients: the victim, and the method.'

'How do you think they did it?'

Prudence said, 'Keep it simple, Suki, just like all the best recipes. There is elegance in simplicity. The hemlock was in the pheasant she ate. It wouldn't take much, and it would be near undetectable. The question is – who was here, in this kitchen, to administer it? Who came to visit

Deirdre on the evening that she ate that pheasant? Yes, method we have, Suki dear – but it's motive we're still missing.'

'Richard Prendergast, who blamed her for losing his job,' mused Suki.

'Georgette Prendergast, who'd been cuckolded one time too many in her life.'

'Rupert Prendergast, who knew she'd got too close.'

Prudence returned, with a flourish, to the kitchen counter, opening the Frigidaire and proceeding to line up all the ingredients she'd need to make both the dragon-fruit sorbet she'd had in mind since Nutwood, and the spiced bread-and-butter pudding she'd thought about since. Let them have the choice, she thought; at least they wouldn't be able to say they'd been short-changed.

Then, into the silence, Suki said, 'Or James Wright, Grandma. Staging the whole thing from a distance. Directing it, somehow . . .'

'Oh, Suki!' Prudence exploded. There had been a thousand thoughts tumbling through her mind, but every mention of Deirdre's ex-husband just clouded it. So what if they knew Deirdre was poisoned by hemlock? What did it matter to know the means by which it had been done unless it opened the door to the murderer themselves? She'd have to ask Mrs Mathers. Find out who might have come down to the kitchens to instruct Deirdre that evening.

Was it so very wrong that, every time, her mind wheeled back to Rupert Prendergast? He was the one who'd orchestrated the whole thing. It was only by Rupert's design that Deirdre had been here at all.

'Put the phone down, Suki. Stop thinking about James.'

'But it's fascinating stuff, Grandma. Just look.'

Prudence marched across the kitchen, meaning to manhandle the iPhone out of the girl's hands and lock it in a drawer until supper was served. But, as she reached out to pick it up, Suki whirled it away and read, ' "Deirdre could be the most delectably delightful person at a party, but it only took a few moments out of the limelight for all of that positive energy to turn to despair and defeat. Was it a kind of depression that assailed her? I rather think not. Spitefulness is not a mental illness, and we must not treat it as such. Deirdre loved nothing more than taking out her frustrations on those who adored her. It was as if she was constantly weighing up the scales, trying to balance the joy and light she'd given to others with the darkness and lack of love she showed those closest to her. Only by balancing the scales could she truly be at peace." '

At last, Prudence snatched the phone away. 'Just a disgruntled ex-husband who wasn't satisfied that he couldn't have what he wanted. That story's the same the whole world over. We've one or two of them in this manor house right now.'

Except Prudence's eyes were, against her wishes, being drawn down to the flickering iPhone screen. There was no doubt, she thought, why *Bitchin' in the Kitchen* had been such a success. People always liked a little

204

titillation. Being permitted to step through the door and spy on a marital breakdown and all the acrimony that followed held a certain ghoulish appeal. Not even Prudence, weathered as she was, was immune to that. Probably, she thought, it had all contributed to Deirdre's lasting appeal to the television broadcasters; when you got Prudence Bulstrode, you got creativity and culinary ambition in spades – but, when you got Deirdre Shaw, you got all of that, plus the sordid tabloid headlines as well. It was all just another part of what they'd started to call the 'attention economy'.

Prudence hated herself for it, but as she marched across the kitchen, meaning to deposit the iPhone in a drawer, her eyes still flickered over the words lighting up the screen. And perhaps she could have ignored it, even then, if one particular word hadn't leapt out at her. Perhaps she would have tossed the phone in a drawer and returned to her task, blitzing up dragon fruit for the sorbet to come. But one word leapt out at her, and she had to read on.

Rhubarb.

Prudence looked up. Suki had returned dejectedly to her prep – good Lord, taking away her iPhone practically constituted taking away her soul! – so at least she did not see it as Prudence started feverishly scrolling through the text.

It was like fireworks going off in the space behind her eyes. It was the feeling of having mixed together some insane ingredients, plucked from the four different corners of the world, and, having done so, stumbled across a flavour so delectably unique that it was going to revolutionise cooking. It was the kind of moment that made one want to shout out 'Eureka!' and leap out of the bathtub, trailing bubbles into the street where you screamed (stark naked) about your discovery.

'Suki,' Prudence whispered, after some time, 'Suki, come here. Deirdre – she *knew* she'd been poisoned . . .'

Suki had just looked up from the chopping board, where she'd been generously slathering thick slices of challah with butter and brown sugar – but, before she could quiz her grandmother further, the kitchen door flew open and standing in the doorway stood a breathless Mrs Mathers.

'Oh, Mrs Bulstrode, I'm sorry – you've already got so much on – but he's asked for you personally. Says it's the least you could do, after all the fuss you've been causing.'

Prudence bristled, but said only, 'Mr Prendergast Senior, I presume?'

'He's outside the manor now. I told him you wouldn't want it bringing down to the kitchen, not while you're in the middle of all your prep. Apart from anything else, it's the hygiene! And there's been enough bad hygiene in this kitchen—' Mrs Mathers slapped a hand to her mouth as if only just realising what she'd said. 'I didn't mean it like that, Mrs Bulstrode. I only meant to repeat what they've all been saying. Not that I believe a word of it, of course. Not that I believe *one jot*.'

Prudence, who was quite past caring whether these guests blamed the cleanliness of her kitchen for their stomach upsets or not – especially when, at some point soon, she'd have to divulge *exactly* how they'd been poisoned and, with any luck, which one of them had done it – said, 'What's happened, Mrs Mathers?'

But Mrs Mathers, still wringing her hands, could only say, 'I think you'd better come.'

Three and a half hours, thought Prudence wearily as she followed Mrs Mathers up through the manor. Three and a half hours and this rabble would want to be sitting around their table, toasting their own greatness with a prize banquet laid out before them. At this rate, they might be able to have a few pheasant bonbons – but the main course really would be beans on toast.

At least her fury was enough to side-line all thoughts of rhubarb from her mind. Soon, she had followed Mrs Mathers past the open dining-room doors – where the table was already half laid and the candles stood unlit in their candelabras – and into the manor's entrance hall. The front doors had been thrown open to the October winds. Prudence could already see Terence Knight and Gray Williams standing on the drive – and, beyond them, Rupert Prendergast, hanging from the door of the Land Rover with his rifle, broken open, at his side.

In a pool of blood on the gravel there lay a dead roe deer.

It was a small specimen, perhaps only foaled at the start of the summer, and, by its look, it was evidently a doe. She was freshly dead and, by the satisfied look on Rupert Prendergast's face, Prudence knew exactly how.

With his pheasant shoot abandoned, he had set out on a little private hunt of his own. And what a prize it was: the deer had taken two bullets, one to the shoulder and the other to its rump. It wouldn't have been enough to kill it straight away, thought Prudence, so Rupert had presumably done the decent thing and, having caught up with it, wrung the poor beast's neck.

Prudence was no moral vegetarian. She'd dealt with all kinds of carcasses in her time on the circuit. But there was something about the superiority of Rupert Prendergast standing above his kill – as if he was some gallant prehistoric hunter, who'd just taken down a mammoth armed only with a sling and a spear – that turned her stomach. Even so, she approached and stood at a respectful distance, while Rupert told the story of his daring kill to Mr Williams and Mr Knight. She was still standing there when Georgette bustled out of the manor, fresh from the shower.

'Oh, Rupert, really!' she said. 'Haven't we had enough blood for one weekend?'

'A short few generations ago, you'd have thrown yourself at me for less,' laughed Rupert. Then his eyes found Prudence. 'Mrs Bulstrode, just the woman I wanted. Well, what do you make of it? Have you ever seen a finer specimen?'

Dozens of times, thought Prudence, but she knew better than to say it. 'Am I to understand—'

'I've just brought you dinner,' he announced.

There was so much wrong with this that Prudence didn't know where to start. A man who enjoyed shooting as much as Rupert Prendergast ought to have understood it well – but even a young deer needed hanging before it was butchered and served. Three and a half hours from bloody corpse to dinner plate wasn't just ridiculous – it was a waste of good meat, a dishonour to the deer whose life had just been taken. Hanging a deer allowed its enzymes to get to work. Tough meat could be tenderised, purely by the processes of nature – and, the longer it hung, the better that deer would taste. Three and a half hours? With a little bit of care, three and a half days would be better.

'Mr Prendergast, I know you're proud of the kill – but, sir, rigor mortis hasn't even set in yet. If I was to butcher this deer and serve it today, well, all of its muscles would contract. It would tighten. You wouldn't be eating a delicacy tonight. You'd be giving your jaw a workout. It's a young deer, sir, but if you want the best out of it, well—'

'Nonsense!' announced Rupert. 'This is our final night. Our weekend's been ruined already. This could be its crowning achievement.'

Nonsense? thought Prudence, struggling to contain her horror. What was nonsense was the idea that she should butcher the deer now. It wasn't even ready to prepare it for hanging. By evening, she'd be able to prepare it but, if they wanted anything better than old shoe leather for dinner, they ought to be waiting for anything from three days to a week.

There were footsteps behind her. She turned to see Maxwell Pendlebury approaching from the manor.

'Good Lord, Rupert – the marksman scores again! She's a fine-looking little thing, isn't she?' Maxwell pottered over, using his walking cane, and prodded the deer's rump. 'Venison for taking home with us then, is it? Something to send us off with.'

'There's plenty to go round, but we'll be having a taste of her tonight. Mrs Bulstrode here's quite the *expert*. I'm sure, whatever challenges there are in fresh meat, she'll be able to surpass them. Won't you, Mrs Bulstrode?'

Prudence stiffened. Every fibre of her being – everything she'd ever been taught, everything she'd ever experienced in a kitchen – told her she ought to refuse the ridiculous request. But if tough, flavourless venison was what Rupert Prendergast wanted, tough, flavourless venison was what he could have. He would learn this weekend, if never again, that he didn't know more and better than everyone else in the world. She'd just make certain that the dishes she'd already planned were perfect; at least the other guests wouldn't have to suffer.

'Then it's decided,' said Rupert. 'Where's that boy of mine? I'll have him help you take her down to the kitchen. Richard?' he called. 'Richard?'

There was an awkward silence, as Maxwell Pendlebury's cheeks purpled and he refused to look Rupert in the eye.

'There he is!' exclaimed Georgette. She was looking beyond Rupert, along the track leading away from the manor, down through the copses and toward Hill Beck. 'And . . .' she hesitated, trying to process it, 'Alice too?'

All eyes turned that way. Richard Prendergast and Alice Pendlebury were walking, side by side, back toward

Farleigh Manor. When they got close, Maxwell's purple cheeks became so flushed with colour that, it seemed, all the blood had been drained from everywhere else in his body. He turned, back to the manor house doors, refusing to acknowledge what he'd seen. 'Well, Rupert,' he said, if only to change the subject, 'good to keep traditions alive, in any case, after this hell of a weekend. Eat what you kill – that's the Farleigh way, old boy. That's what we've always done. And with all this business in the kitchen, whichever reprobates upset the apple cart, it will be good to do one thing right. I, for one, have every faith that Mrs Bulstrode can work some magic and serve venison tonight.'

Prudence watched him go. *Magic*, she thought. It would take more than magic. Sorcery of the highest order. Hollywood stuff. The best chef in the world couldn't control the processes of putrefaction. What they asked of her was almost sacrilegious. The deer would be ruined. A life spent in vain. It made her blood boil.

Then something else occurred to her, and at once her blood ran cold.

It was what Maxwell Pendlebury had said that stirred it in her. *Good to keep traditions alive. Eat what you kill – that's the Farleigh way.*

They'd said that at the beginning, hadn't they? That's what the pheasants hanging in the larder had been – the kills from the first day's shoot, hanging there until the meat was rested, relaxed and ready to be served. Served tonight.

Prudence hardly heard as Rupert Prendergast, seemingly oblivious to the oddity of Richard and Alice walking

211

back across the estate together, ordered his son to ferry the deer through the kitchen-garden door. She hardly acknowledged Richard's look of squirming distaste that he – the secret, closeted vegan – might get the deer's tacky blood all over him as he bore it away. Because, standing in the manor house doors, she was reaching into her pockets, ferreting through the sandwich bags filled with poisonous mushrooms that were still crammed in there, and producing the little scraps of laminated white she'd found in the woodland clearing. She looked at them now: RUPERT/GEORGETTE, the first one read. GRAY/TERENCE.

She drew a breath inward. 'Oh,' she whispered, and 'Oh' again.

How stupid had she been? How stupid, from the very beginning? It had all been like putting sugar in a salt cellar all along. Looking at one thing, but tasting another.

She took off through the main manor house doors, and weaved her way down to the kitchen by the service stairs – just in time to see Richard labouring through the boarded-up back door, cradling the young doe in his arms. Suki, who had been at the counter – she'd dug out that iPhone again to scroll through James Wright's poisonous words – was looking up with horror, but it hardly matched the horror that was lining Richard's face.

'Into the larder with it, Richard.' There was a second larder, empty but for small sacks of seedling potatoes; at least, in there, she could forget about it for half an hour, figure out what she could do. It occurred to her, there and then, that the very best course of action was to send Suki out to the butcher's at Nutwood St Knowle for a prime piece of venison already fit to be cooked; by the time the Prendergast party knew of her deception, it would already be done – and, with a little luck, one of them would be behind bars.

If that simpleton constable could be trusted to make an arrest . . .

She saw Richard, still frozen with horror, and said, 'To me then, lad, and go and get washed up.'

She took the deer out of his arms and bore it into the second, empty larder. It would need hanging – but, for the moment, she lay the cadaver down on a pile of sacking in the corner.

When she returned to the kitchen floor, Richard was at one of the sinks, feverishly scrubbing at his fingers, his hands, his forearms – every square inch of exposed flesh.

'He's a monster,' Richard said, soap suds foaming up and down his arms. 'It's all for vanity. It's all for pride.'

'To eat what you kill,' said Prudence.

'As if that makes it any better. Honouring the hunters of old!' he scoffed. 'I tried not to hit anything, that first day, but he knew what I was up to. I'd have been eating a life I snuffed out tonight if this kitchen hadn't been broken into! And I'm supposed to feel *good* about it. Mark my words, Mrs Bulstrode – in fifty years' time, we'll look back on eating meat like we do on slavery. It's prehistoric! It's positively barbaric!'

Richard stormed out of the kitchen.

There was a silence as Suki watched him leave. Then she turned to Prudence and said, 'What's happened? What is it?'

'Change of menu,' said Prudence, with fire, 'and a change of approach. Suki, darling, we've been looking at it all wrong. I can't believe how stupid we've been. It's all so clear now.' She opened her hands and spilled the little laminated scraps on to the kitchen counter, where all the ingredients for her original starter – leeks and hazelnuts, and a salty anchovy dressing – had been lined up. 'I found them in the woodland, Suki, where that big pyre had been built. But it wasn't until now that I realised what they are – how they change everything we've seen. They're the name tags from the pheasants in the larder. The pheasants the party shot on the first day, when Deirdre was still alive.'

Suki wasn't sure she understood. 'What does it mean?'

'It means we've had it wrong, all along. Whoever laced the poison in that pheasant, they didn't do it for Deirdre Shaw. They knew which member of the party would be eating each bird, so they sneaked in here and laced the pheasant with hemlock – not so that Deirdre would die, but so that somebody else would.'

Suki faltered for a moment before she said, 'Who?'

'Not Rupert or Georgette,' said Prudence, looking at the name tags. 'Not Gray Williams or Terence Knight. The pheasants they were due to eat were still hanging in the larder when our killer came back to clean up after himself. He – or she – panicked, you see. They didn't real- ise Deirdre was greedy enough to spot a nice pheasant hanging in the larder and take it for her own. So, when Deirdre dropped dead, they knew something had gone wrong. They needed to cover up after themselves. What if they'd done something wrong? What if the taint they'd introduced to this kitchen had somehow spread? Well, of course it did, didn't it? Every last person in Farleigh Manor fell sick with it after we served its remainders up to them. That spooked our killer. They'd already killed one person they didn't mean to. They didn't want to wipe out the whole party.' Prudence paused. 'We've been looking at it backwards, Suki, my dear. We oughtn't to have been looking for a murderer at Farleigh Manor. Not *just* a murderer, in any case. We ought to have been looking for a murder victim.'

Suki whispered, 'Deirdre Shaw was just caught in the cross-fire . . .'

'I'm afraid you're right, Suki.' Prudence took a long, deep breath and tried to steady her mind. 'But there can no longer be any doubt. Somebody at Farleigh Manor wanted somebody else at Farleigh Manor dead. They were supposed to die tonight, at the banquet. And *we* were supposed to serve the dish that killed them.'

Chapter Twelve

Suki hurried across the kitchen. Was it just her imagination, or was the air really ripe with the rich, metallic scent of blood? The faint, iron tang of the butcher's shop? She tried to set it out of her mind as she looked at the scraps of laminate card Prudence had sprinkled on the surface.

'But Grandma,' she whispered, suddenly afraid that she might be overheard, 'that only leaves Richard, and Alice and Maxwell Pendlebury. You're not saying one of them is meant to die tonight?'

Prudence cast a look at the kitchen-garden door, mindful that nobody had come in to eavesdrop upon them. Then, solemnly, she nodded. 'Somebody in this manor wants one of them dead. God knows, there's enough enmity here for it to be any of them. But somebody planned it, down to its finest detail. They knew the Prendergast tradition – to eat what you kill. So, at some point, just after these pheasants were hung in the larder, they stole in here and laced one with hemlock. Its leaves, its seeds, its stem – it doesn't matter what. The whole plant's a poison. Our killer would have got away with it as well, if it hadn't been for Deirdre Shaw's infamous greed. A nice, juicy pheasant, she'd have thought. Well, she could stretch the rest out across the party. One pheasant wouldn't matter . . .'

'Then it has to be one of the others,' said Suki. 'Our killer – Rupert or Georgette. Mr Williams or Mr Knight . . .'

Prudence shook her head. 'Think a little deeper, Suki dear. Just because these are our potential victims, it doesn't exonerate them. And one of them could be our killer as well. Richard Prendergast . . .'

She fell silent. Richard was a young man, simmering with resentments – but those resentments were primarily reserved for his father; and, right now, looking at the name tags, Prudence was quite certain that, if any of them harboured murderous thoughts toward Rupert, they had not decided to act on them this weekend. That Rupert's pheasant had still been hanging in the larder proved that it had not been the one harbouring the hemlock.

Unless . . .

A terrible thought entered her head; that the banquet tonight was supposed to have been a bloodbath, that the whole Prendergast party had been condemned to die. But she could not believe it. That she would be the tool of murder – it was almost impossible to fathom. That she would, unwittingly, have become the murderer's hand. That somebody had meant for Deirdre to be the same . . .

'Grandma,' Suki ventured, after the silence had lingered too long, 'if they didn't get it right the first time – if Deirdre ruined their plans and paid the ultimate price for it – well, what if they haven't given up? If somebody was set on murder this weekend, do you really think they'd just shy away from it just because it went wrong?'

Prudence was quiet, thoughtful, reflective. Her eyes roamed around the kitchen, taking in all the ingredients they'd lined up – all the things they'd prepared to serve this evening. What Suki had said seemed preposterous, but only at first. Georgette Prendergast had insisted they scour the kitchen clean, replace everything Deirdre had used – and, with a little bit of help from their burglar, they'd done exactly that.

But how was she to know that, sometime in the night, one of them hadn't stolen into the kitchen to spread their taint again? How was she to know that the bonbons she'd just mixed up and rolled in breadcrumbs, ready for the deep fat fryer, didn't contain within them some touch of the deadly hemlock? How was she to know, for certain, that the sprigs of herbs she'd used hadn't been threaded through with the poison leaf, or the hanging pheasants massaged with the deathly flower?

'No,' she said, 'not unless they intended a bloodbath. Nothing here is named any more. They couldn't direct the killing.'

'So what now?' asked Suki.

Prudence looked at the clock on the wall. If the killer's plan had gone right, that clock would have been counting down the hours to murder. Only three hours, now, separated them from the supper service. Time, thought Prudence – it was the only resource she needed, and it was slipping through her fingers, even now. Three hours to put before them a three-course dinner of roast pheasant and celeriac rosti, parsnip puree and winter greens, rich indulgent mushroom sauce; desserts of dragon fruit and bread-and-butter; a starter which, only two hours before, had been cantering across the Farleigh Estate, with hardly a care in the world.

'I need you to go into Nutwood St Knowle,' Prudence said – and thought back, fleetingly, to the last time Suki had sat behind the wheel of the camper van. Had that really only been a few days ago? It felt like a different world. 'To the butcher's, if he's open . . .'

'On a Sunday, Grandma?'

'I'll put in a call. I'm loath to do it, Suki, but sometimes a little sprinkling of celebrity can open doors – quite literally, in this case. I need you to bring back a cut of venison loin. I'll carpaccio it for our starter.' As she was speaking, she gravitated to the second larder, where the dead doe still lay in the sacking. Was it unimaginable, she thought, that it was itself laced with some poison? That Rupert Prendergast was the killer, and that he'd found his second way of committing the deed? But no – he'd have had, somehow, to have corrupted the entire animal; he'd be set on a course of massacring everyone in the manor.

Trying to unknot this thing was close to impossible – not without knowing who the intended victim was.

As she stood at the kitchen-garden door and watched Suki leave, iPhone in one hand and roll of cash in the other, a hundred different thoughts tumbled through Prudence's mind. She was sure the girl could be trusted;

she wasted no more time worrying about her camper van ending up in the bottom of some ditch with a sozzled Suki behind the wheel. If nothing else, the events of this weekend had sobered her up. No, her thoughts turned to Richard and the Pendleburys. They spooled back to Maxwell chasing Richard out of the house; they turned to the way Rupert sought to control and hem in his son; they turned to Richard and Alice, returning from their private moment out on the estate.

One of them was meant to be dead tonight.

It ought to have been the apex of the weekend.

A sudden thought occurred to her, and she bustled out of the kitchen-garden door, past that rhubarb patch and up to where Suki was already choking the camper van to life. That poor camper – already it was putting up a guttering complaint against the inexperienced driver manhandling its gearstick.

'Suki!' she called out. 'Suki, stop!'

Suki hung out of the driver's window. 'What is it, Grandma? I'm being gentle – but this thing's *ancient*.'

'It's not that, dear. It's that iPhone of yours.' She paused. 'I wondered if you might give me one of its numbers.'

'Where's she off to?' said Maxwell Pendlebury in the drawing room of Farleigh Manor, where the guests had gathered for afternoon cocktails in anticipation of the evening to come. Mrs Mathers, in attendance, was steadfastly ignoring the muttered complaints of the party at her drink-mixing skills, and the not-so-subtle inferences

220

from Georgette Prendergast that she ought to leave them to do it alone. One more night and the Prendergast party would be gone; after that, if she found the courage, Mrs Mathers would write to the consortium who owned the manor and discuss the possibility of banning them from ever coming again.

Maxwell Pendlebury stood at the drawing-room window, watching through the rippling curtains as the camper van weaved its way from the manor.

'I'm sure Mrs Bulstrode has her reasons, sir,' said Mrs Mathers. 'I'm quite sure it won't affect this evening's festivities.'

'Well, she'll have Rupert to answer to if it does. The way she's upset the weekend already. All this talk of *murder*.'

A chill ran through Mrs Mathers at the very sound of the word. Whatever the truth of it, she would be happy when it was finished. Prove there'd been a murder or not, she thought – she just wanted it finished.

Her hand was trembling as she served the last drink, an old-fashioned gin rickey meant for Georgette Prendergast. Then, thinking that her job description really didn't involve being a cocktail waitress as well as a housekeeper, she scuttled out of the room.

As she was leaving, Richard Prendergast appeared in the door.

The rest of the party had already assembled. The only one missing was Rupert Prendergast, who was upstairs, freshening himself up after his successful hunt. Richard looked around the room, pointedly trying to ignore the empty seat at Alice Pendlebury's side. He did not mean to catch Maxwell's eye, but moments later the old man was scathing him with a look. Richard marched straight to the drinks trolley, poured himself a bourbon – he'd be glad when this weekend was over, and he could get back to his teetotal ways – and winced as he drank it.

'No son of mine would wrinkle his nose at the finest bourbon like that, Georgette,' snorted Maxwell.

Georgette Prendergast, who had been sashaying around the room with her Manhattan in her hand, rolled her eyes at the attempted slight. 'Well, Maxwell, perhaps if you'd *had* a son, you'd have learnt one of the golden principles of becoming a parent: we *discover* what our children are like, Maxwell; we don't control it.' Georgette had reached Richard's side, and slipped a motherly hand around his waist. It made him feel about eight years old.

There was something in what Georgette had said that seemed to truly irk Maxwell. Richard could see it in the way the lines deepened across his face; he'd looked just the same when he'd discovered Richard and Alice in their little tête-à-tête and deemed them uncomfortably, unnaturally close.

'If I *did* have a son, I wouldn't mollycoddle him like you do this one,' said Maxwell. 'How a lion raised a mouse, I'll never know.'

At that moment, all the other eyes in the room – Gray Williams and Terence Knight in particular – turned to the doorway, where the very lion of whom Maxwell had been speaking had just appeared.

222

Rupert Prendergast was already dressed in his dinner jacket; his hair was swept back and still shimmering from the shower he'd taken.

'I've told you about that tongue of yours, Maxwell. Mouse or not, Richard's still my son.'

Richard Prendergast had not been expecting as much; he felt his mother's arm tighten around him. Half of him wanted to shake her off, but the other half wanted to melt into the embrace, just as he'd done when he was a young boy.

'Yes, well, you've got some work to do on him, Rupert, I'll warrant you that.'

'Shut your mouth.'

Richard did not know he was going to say it until he did. He'd been content to let the elders indulge their passive-aggressive battle, just survive the evening and get out of here in the morning. Perhaps it was his mother's closeness that had emboldened him. Or perhaps he'd been goaded into it – all this talk of him not being 'man' enough, all this talk of him being cowardly and a 'mouse'. He saw, by the look – half outrage, half amusement – on Maxwell Pendlebury's face that he truly had been baited. But it didn't stop the old man rounding on him.

'Now, look here—'

'No, *you* look here!' Richard exploded, shaking off his mother's conciliatory touch. 'It's not my fault you didn't have a child. Not my fault you never got your heir! Not my fault you ended up a hobbling old goat, without even an ounce of happiness in his life.'

'Richard!' Rupert roared.

223

'No!' Richard roared in return – and his voice carried through the house, out into the hall where, even now, Prudence Bulstrode was hurrying past.

In the hallway, Prudence stopped. She crept, by degrees, closer to the drawing-room door, now hanging ajar as Rupert Prendergast left it and marched, stalwartly, deeper into the room.

She could hear all their voices at once. Voices raised in anger. Voices raised in attempts at pacification. There wasn't a single one of them not shouting now. Goodness, she thought, what a rabble of 'friends' this lot were. What a riot of resentments were alive in that room.

'Richard,' Rupert Prendergast seethed, 'this has gone too far. You're going to apologise to Maxwell, right now. He's one of our oldest friends.'

'Maybe to *you*, father,' Richard seethed, 'but he's no friend of mine. He's done nothing but belittle me this weekend. Nothing but attack – and why? Because he's old and spent. Because he's waking up to the fact that his whole life was about money – money and ambition. And what got lost along the way? Well, love, that's what. He's angry and he's twisted and he's taking it all out on me, just because he's—'

'DYING!' roared Maxwell, and suddenly everything in the room was silent.

In the hallway outside, Prudence shrank from the door.

'Yes,' snorted Maxwell, 'that cheered you all up, didn't it? None of you knew, did you, that that's the reason dear Rupert sprang this weekend on us, after so long? Don't

224

tell them all, I told him. Don't make a fuss. But, yes, I should like to see old Farleigh Manor again, just one time before I die. The fun we had here. The laughter. The . . .' his voice choked off, 'romance. Well, now you know it. Dead by Christmas, if my surgeon's right. An aneurysm, right here in my heart – and none of this, none of this battling and being spoken to like I'm filth by some jumped-up little cissy over here, will be helping. By God, Richard, the way my heart rate's spiking, you've probably shaved a week off what's left of my life.' He stopped. 'Well, go on then, say something!'

Richard stammered, 'I . . . I didn't know.'

'Of course you didn't,' Rupert Prendergast seethed, into the silence. 'None of you were meant to. It was my friend Maxwell's wish.'

Prudence could see, through the sliver left open between the doors, that Rupert had gone to Maxwell's side. For the first time, she thought she understood the frailty of the old man. She'd had an uncle who perished from a heart aneurysm as well, though his came without warning. She looked at Maxwell, now, and marvelled at how bitterness could intensify as a man grew older; how, at the end of each life, came a reckoning, a moment when you held yourself to account – for better or worse.

'We *are* going to celebrate tonight,' Rupert began, his voice rising authoritatively as he spoke. Not for the first time, Prudence could truly imagine him holding court in some boardroom in the City of London. 'We're going to toast this man's life. We're going to toast the fine times we've had here across the decades. We're going to remember the good times that *all of us* had, and what Farleigh Manor has meant to us. Our dear friend Maxwell won't be with us the next time we gather here. Let's honour that tonight – in drink, in song, and, hell, in the deer I shot today. There are to be no more arguments. There are to be no more misdemeanours. This weekend has suffered enough. There is to be no more talk of murder and death, for there's quite enough of that in the air – quite enough, without having to imagine even more.' Rupert paused, and Prudence heard, through the doors, an audible intake of breath from across the party. 'Come on then, you sorry lot, let's get the celebration started. Everyone – your glasses in the air! Richard, you too!' There was a pause, before finally Rupert said, 'To our dear friend Maxwell Pendlebury – not long for this Earth, but never to be forgotten!'

Nutwood St Knowle was bustling with Sunday daytrippers as Suki – in guttering fits and starts (she really was not a natural driver) – found a parking spot on the edge of the village green. Stepping out into the afternoon sunshine, she reflected that it was good to be away from Farleigh Manor, if only for a short time. Not that toiling away in the kitchen bothered her any longer; it was the whole oppressive nature of the place, the knowledge of what one of them had planned, the idea that she and her grandmother might easily have been the ones to serve up the poison. Only two short days ago, scurrying into the village bookshop just across the green and emerging with

226

the copy of *The Body in the Beck* now sitting on the passenger seat of the camper van, she'd been titillated by the whole idea of murder at the mansion. Now, the reality of it felt so much worse.

The butcher's shop sat on the corner of the village green, but its awning was very definitely rolled up and a handcrafted sign in the window said that it would not reopen until 9 a.m. the following morning. Suki looked through the glass at the fat sausage whirls sitting in their refrigerated unit, and the brace of unskinned bunnies hanging from a hook at the back of the counter, and was bewildered to discover that there was a separate counter set aside for 'Vegan Fayre'. Well, she supposed, even the old village butcher's had to move with the times – though quite what vegans would be happy chowing down on a Portobello mushroom sausage that had been bathing in the air of a real butcher's she wasn't sure. Even so, the idea of taking a soya sausage swirl back to Farleigh and serving it up for Richard Prendergast rather appealed to her. The look on his father's face would certainly be worth it.

But then she remembered that there was every chance somebody had planned to end Richard's life tonight, and suddenly there wasn't a single little victory in the world that could make her smile any more.

Prudence had promised she'd put in a call – but either that call had been met with silence or the butcher hadn't yet roused himself from his Sunday afternoon snooze to make it down to his shop. After pottering on the pavement for a little while, Suki made her way back to the camper van. Better to wait there, she thought, than to be seen loitering outside the shopfront.

In the front seat, if only to pass the time, she picked up her copy of *The Body in the Beck* and started perusing its pages. Something about it didn't tantalise her this time, though. Murder seemed so fascinating when seen at a distance; up close and personal it was quite a different matter. There were a lot of things in life that were like that, Suki reflected. Boys, for instance . . .

Idly, she flicked through the pages. Katie Winterdale was slowly building up her thesis that, pushed to breaking point by their nanny's behaviour – and terrified of what it might mean for them if the affair she was conducting with their father was ever exposed – they tricked her into paddling in the waters of Hill Beck, then pushed her bodily into the rocks. Tantalising stuff, Suki thought, if you were a true-crime aficionado. The worst aspects of human nature became kind of thrilling when you were sitting in your armchair at home with a nice cup of cocoa, thumbing through the pages of a beloved book; when you didn't have to live it.

The words were blurring in front of her, so she went back to the picture section instead. But even this reminded her of the last time, when she'd followed that map – and ended up carrying a dying dog back through the woodland, then watching as his weeping owner buried him in a hole in the ground. The stink of it was still all over her.

She flicked through the pictures, barely paying any attention at all – until, finally, she came to the second plate section in the book, and the very final picture of all. There, according to the caption, stood Jack and Mary Farleigh, only a few short months before their deaths. In the picture it was the summer of 1971, and they stood in what Suki realised was the kitchen garden, above the very same rhubarb patch that was, this very moment, commemorated with a cross for Deirdre Shaw. Another figure stood with them, a much younger man, probably barely Suki's own age – and it washed over Suki, then, how their lives must have been. Nearly ninety years of suspicion and stories. Ninety years of seclusion from the turning of the world. Ninety years with only each other for company. The longest prison sentence in the world didn't last that long – but at least they had each other. It was bewildering, now, to see them standing with anybody else . . .

Her eyes returned to the caption under the photograph: 'Jack and Mary Farleigh, on the eve of their deaths, share a happy moment in their beloved kitchen garden with—'

There came a hammering at the window.

Startled out of her skin, Suki flurried up in the driver's seat, spilling her copy of *The Body in the Beck* back on to the passenger's side. When she looked around, a round, ruddy face was peering at her through the window, fingers as plump as sausages lifted up to rap on the glass. The big, piggy face made a gesture that suggested she should wind the window down – and Suki, heart still beating wildly, opened it a crack.

'You're the lass Mrs Bulstrode sent, are you?'

Suki stammered, 'Y-yes.'

'Aye, well, follow me, girl. I'll get you sorted. Just make sure Mrs Bulstrode keeps her part of the bargain – come through Nutwood on your way home tomorrow and take some pictures with us outside the store.'

The butcher, thought Suki. He was only the butcher. It was only the fact that she'd been reading that book, and the caption her eyes had landed on, that made the word seem as suddenly sinister as it did. *Butcher*, she thought. *Butchery. Just another word for murder.*

As she stepped out of the car, the butcher was already knuckling his way across the green, bound for his shop-front. 'Venison she's after, is it? A lovely piece of loin. If it's carpaccio she's making, tell her to think about oranges too. Not that I'd dream of telling somebody as esteemed as Prudence Bulstrode how to treat her meat, of course.'

Suki hurried after him, leaving the camper van behind.

And leaving behind the copy of *The Body in the Beck*, which had landed, open at the photographic plate section, on the passenger side; open at the picture of Jack and Mary Farleigh standing in the kitchen garden, the much younger man standing between them and smiling – as if he, alone in all the world, was their friend; as if he might even have been their confidant.

Prudence's heart was racing as she reached the door of the housekeeping office and, finding it ajar, popped her head around the corner, just to make sure that nobody was inside. Relieved to find it empty, she slipped within, hurried to Mrs Mathers's desk and, picking up the telephone receiver, unfurled the scrap of paper on which she'd written the number from Suki's iPhone.

She couldn't believe she was doing this. It went against everything she stood for: honesty and openness, and a good old-fashioned work ethic.

She dialled the number, listening to the telephone exchange click in; then, as the telephone at the other end rang on and endlessly on.

She was beginning to think it was all in vain, that it had been a stupid idea anyway, when the ringing abruptly stopped and a suspicious voice on the other end of the line said, 'Yes?'

Yes, thought Prudence. *Yes.* Was there a more dismissive way of answering a telephone than an ordinary, mumbled, 'Yes?'

She coughed to clear her throat. She couldn't quite believe she was about to say this. 'I'm looking for a young man who likes to call himself "Numbers". Now, that isn't his name, or so I'm led to believe – but it's what he likes to call himself. *Numbers*. Might I—'

'Who is this?' came the voice, squeakier now. 'Where did you get this number?'

'Numbers?'

There was a silence.

'Numbers, my name is Prudence Dorothea Bulstrode, but you probably know me better as Suki's grandmother. It was Suki who gave me this number, dear. She's off on a little jaunt for me and—'

'Did you find him yet?' Numbers interrupted; then, when Prudence did not instantly reply, he added, 'Your

231

murderer, Mrs Bulstrode! Have you strung him up on a gibbet?'

'A *giblet*?'

'A gibbet, Mrs Bulstrode! The gallows! Or . . . is he under lock and key?'

'Just how much has Suki told you?'

'Enough to know your poor Mrs Shaw was taken out by hemlock poisoning. Enough to know somebody had it in for her from the start. Enough to know—'

Prudence said, not unkindly, 'Well, my dear, things have moved on a little since then. That's rather why I thought it would be useful to be in touch. Now, Numbers, dear, time is ticking. I've a three-course dinner to serve in' – she glanced at the clock – 'two and a half hours, and I can't waste time chitchatting with you. But I know you're a dab hand at computers, dear. I know you go poking around where you're not wanted. And I rather hoped you might be keen to do it again.'

Numbers said, with a lingering curiosity, 'Do go on, Mrs Bulstrode.'

'Two words, young man. Maxwell Pendlebury. I'm sure you'll locate him without too much trouble on that internet of yours. He's the founding director of' – Prudence tried to cast her mind back to what Mrs Mathers had said, upon their first meeting – 'Countrywide Finance Systems. I dread to think what it does. Stockpiles money, I shouldn't wonder. He's that sort. I want you to do some digging.'

'He's your killer, is he?'

Prudence thought: *there's every chance he might be our victim – but what good would it do killing a man already condemned to die?*

'He has a younger wife, Alice Pendlebury. I daresay she hasn't lifted a finger in her life, not unless it was wrapped around a champagne flute – but I need you doing some background on her as well. And . . .'

Numbers said, 'Anything else, DARLING?'

Prudence ignored the jocular tone in Numbers's voice. 'A young man, by the name of Richard Prendergast.'

'Oh, *him*. I've already dug the dirt on him for darling Suki. Unemployed, at his age?' Numbers scoffed. 'Well, I'm sure if he wanted to come and work for me, I could show him a thing or two. There's money to be made without even getting out of bed on a morning.' He hesitated. 'Speaking of which, Mrs Bulstrode, I do assume there's a nice little *per diem* coming my way? Time is money, after all.'

'Well,' said Prudence, with her sweetest smile and intonation, 'I was rather thinking you might give me a few hours of your time in return for not telling the local constable in Chelwood Ghyll who told my granddaughter that she really ought to sneak into my camper van while under the influence of a considerable amount of alcohol.'

On the other end of the line, Numbers froze. 'Mrs Bulstrode, I assure you, I meant Suki to sleep it off in there, not to—'

'You may call me back on this number, young man,' said Prudence, the smile still playing in the corners of her

233

lips. 'Oh, and *Numbers*, might I give you one piece of advice? If you're looking to, one day, be a real suitor to my grand-daughter, perhaps a *real* job – perhaps even a *real* name? – might work wonders.'

'Oh, Mrs Bulstrode,' said Numbers, this time with the hint of a smile of his own. 'I think you might have me completely wrong.'

'Be sharp about it, Mr Numbers. The clock is ticking.'

Prudence meant to dash down to the kitchen, make sure the celeriac was grated and the rostis ready for the pan, but the moment she slipped out of the office door, Mrs Mathers reappeared. Prudence sighed; it was as if the anxious, fretting housekeeper had a sixth sense telling her whenever somebody had slipped inside her office.

'Oh, it's all going off, Mrs Bulstrode, it's all going off! I tell you, I've aged a decade in this day alone.' She took a deep breath. 'Guests fighting, then making up, dead deer being hauled in – and the way they speak to you, Mrs Bulstrode, as if *you're* the one spoiling all the fun, when, really, there's no fun to be had in the first place. These people just oughtn't to be friends. They should be flung to the far corners of the Earth and told that's it, they're done, they can't be within a hundred-mile radius of each other any more!'

The effort it had taken to explode with such emotion seemed to have quite exhausted Mrs Mathers. She dropped against the office wall, disrupting a corkboard and a plethora of Post-it Notes, and panted heavily, all the while wringing her hands. If somebody had acted like this in the theatre, thought Prudence, they'd have been called an old ham – but Prudence was under no doubts that the woman was genuine.

'And Mr Pendlebury, dying! That's what it's all been about, you know. Him roaring at Richard like that. Yes, he's always been quite jealous of his old friend Rupert on that account.'

'That account, Mrs Mathers?'

'Well, I've heard them sniping about it before – what Maxwell would have done if he'd had a son, how he'd have raised him properly, how Rupert's raised a cissy. It's like they're living in the nineteenth century, of course, the way they speak about it. Heirs and legacies! Maxwell's just envious that he never got his. And there he is, dying, without a child to pass it all on to.' She paused. 'You've got children, Mrs Bulstrode. I have my Marjorie. She's a teacher down in Nutwood St Knowle, with a little one of her own cooking in the oven. Well, it's what life's all about, isn't it? Can you imagine the feeling – knowing you're about to die, and no matter how hard you worked, no matter what money you piled up, none of it's worth anything because there's no one to carry it on?'

Mrs Mathers continued to talk but, whatever she was saying, it all just seemed to fade away for Prudence. All of this talk of children, of heirs and legacies – there was something wrong with it. Something that did not fit.

Prudence began to pace up and down. She closed her eyes, trying to imagine it back into being. It was something she'd overheard, or some snippet of conversation in which she'd partaken, something that no longer made any sense. *Children*, she thought. *Heirs to inherit.*

And suddenly, she was back on the darkened corridor, that first night at Farleigh. In her mind's eye, she was palming her way along the corridor, listening to the sounds of retching in the bathroom up ahead. Then she was there, right there at Alice Pendlebury's side, telling her that everything was going to be OK.

'I'm not sick because of alcohol, Mrs Bulstrode. You poisoned me, you stupid woman. I know what bloody food poisoning feels like. By God, it's ten times as intense as the worst morning sickness ever was.'

There it was. Those words had been lodged in her head from the very beginning, just waiting until the moment they could bubble to the surface. And here they were.

There was a secret in this. She was certain of it.

Because if Maxwell Pendlebury had no heir, and yet his wife had once been pregnant . . .

Prudence hurried to the desk, almost barging Mrs Mathers (who let out a terrified squeal) out of the way as she did so. She was still floundering out her apologies as she hit the 'redial' button on the telephone and waited for Numbers to pick up.

'Now, really, Mrs Bulstrode, DARLING!' Numbers announced (and Prudence thought it wise that he should stop calling everybody 'darling' if he really wanted to impress Suki – nobody liked a man who spread himself far and wide; just look at Rupert Prendergast). 'It's hardly been ten minutes! I can work wonders, Mrs Bulstrode, but I do need a little time.'

'My commission has changed, young man.'

'Changed?'

'Or, rather, it's expanded.'

Numbers said, 'And I suppose the small matter of my fee hasn't changed in line?'

Prudence considered this. 'I'll cook for you, Numbers, if you do this for me and call me back in the next hour. It will be the finest meal you've ever eaten, I should think – finer than all of the kebabs and super-noodle sandwiches and energy drinks I'm sure you've been eating. But this is urgent. Alice Pendlebury, née Frith, may have had a child sometime before she was married. I need you to find out when that was. If they exist out there, I need you to find out who's listed on the birth certificate as the father.'

'A doddle, Mrs Bulstrode.'

'Then it's a deal, Mr Numbers.'

Prudence hung up the phone.

The camper van was halfway back to Farleigh Manor, three miles out of Nutwood St Knowle, when Suki – who had been harrying at the accelerator and wrestling, fiercely, with the gears – started hearing its complaint. She was used to the camper complaining – it just didn't like her driving – so, for the next few minutes, she ignored the grumbles and groans coming from under the bumper. She ignored, too, the smell of something burning that seemed to be coming from somewhere deep inside the contraption. Cars and vans and all kinds of engines smelt, thought Suki. It was just what they did. If she wound the windows down, she could hardly even smell it.

It wasn't until she started seeing the smoke, billowing in thick grey plumes from the dashboard grille, that she brought the camper van to a halt. This she did so inexpertly that, moments later, half the camper van was buried in a hedgerow, while the other half poked out dangerously into the road.

Suki groaned and got out of the cab – first having made sure that the venison was hidden away, out of the direct sunlight. Not that there was much sunlight left any more. She checked her iPhone – its battery was almost gone – and saw that it had already inched past 5 p.m. Less than two hours separated her from the dinner service now. Her grandmother would surely need a half hour of that at least to prepare her carpaccio with the venison in the glove compartment. Whichever way she looked at it, this situation was not ideal.

It was even less ideal half an hour later when she was still waiting at the side of the road, trying to flag down any driver who passed. It was even less ideal fifteen minutes later still when the only driver who'd cared to stop had given her the name of the AA roadside assistance service – and she'd used the last flurry of power in her iPhone to call them, only to be told that there might be a three-hour wait before they could attend. So much for customer service; now she sat, glumly, in the open camper-van door, considering how long she should wait before setting off at a run. Three miles at pace was beyond her. She fancied she could walk it – and turn up, no doubt, just as supper was about to be served.

She had returned to the pages of *The Body in the Beck*, and that picture of the elderly Farleighs that drew her eye so much, when a voice called out for her.

'Hey there, you're Mrs Bulstrode's assistant! And this, here, isn't it Mrs Bulstrode's van?'

She looked up. On the opposite side of the road, perched on a BMX bike surely meant for a teenager, was a young man she remembered as being Constable Littleton from Nutwood St Knowle. Out of uniform – and wearing what Suki could only think of as a ridiculous lilac spandex bodysuit – he hardly looked like police material; but, then again, Suki could recall him pottering around the manor house kitchen after the break-in, and he'd hardly seemed like police material back then either.

'Constable Littleton!' she exclaimed, tumbling out of the camper. 'You've got to help. I've got to be back at the manor, about an hour ago, and . . .'

Tutting at her, he started shaking his head. 'You've run this thing off the road.'

'I haven't,' said Suki. 'Something started smoking, right there in the engine. I did the best I could.'

Constable Littleton dismounted, about as gracefully as a man in lilac pink spandex can, and ambled across the road. After much fumbling, he had popped open the hood on the camper van and was now peering inside with the inquisitiveness of an expert detective.

At last, he looked up. 'I always expect there'll be a big switch,' he said, shaking his head ruefully. '"On" or "Off". "Broken" or "Not Broken". Like a fuse box, you know. You can just flip it and everything will be all right.' He paused. 'Alas, it's never true. It'll be a fan belt. Or an injection thingy. Fuel transition module.'

Suki was quite certain this last item didn't even exist.

Then her eyes landed on his bicycle.

'I need to get to the manor. It's urgent. It's the last night of the party and . . .' She faltered, her words petering away. This was about so much more than delivering the venison on time. It was about so much more than making sure she was there to spread out the parsnip puree and make sure her grandmother's plates looked professional as they left the kitchen doors. 'Constable Littleton, I'm going to need your bike.'

The constable's eyes flared wide open. 'But that's my treasured possession! I've been riding it ever since I was a boy. No, no, no – I couldn't possibly permit you to—'

But Suki was already scrambling towards it.

'I'll bring it back, Constable. You know where I'm going. But I need to—'

'Not on your life!' the constable cried out, and then he too was tumbling towards the BMX, wrestling hold of the handlebars. 'If you need to get to the manor on time, well, you can jump up on my handlebars, or scooch up behind me. This bike's been my loyal companion since I was ten years old. She'll get you there on time, I promise – but only with these feet on the pedals!'

Suki looked down. Constable Littleton might have been a slight, gangly kind of fellow – but the one thing he did have was a set of powerful-looking calves.

'OK,' she told him. 'You're on. Just get me there in one piece. I believe a life may depend upon it.'

The moment Prudence opened the ovens to lift the pheasants out, so that they could rest before being carved, steam billowed out in great clouds, completely fogging up Prudence's glasses. She was just done wiping them clean when she looked up and saw, through the windows, the most unusual sight. Suki was sailing back to Farleigh Manor – not at the wheel of her beloved camper van, but balanced on the handlebars of a man in lilac spandex.

For a moment, Prudence was quite sure she was seeing things. Perhaps she herself had been poisoned; perhaps some taint still remained in this kitchen, and she was breathing it in along with the scent that came off her thick, creamy mushroom sauce.

She was sharpening the carving knife when the kitchen-garden door burst open – and there, standing beside a man resplendent in lilac cycling shorts and bib, was Suki. It took Prudence a little longer to acknowledge the man as Constable Littleton, from Nutwood St Knowle – but, once she'd recognised him as such, it all started to make a little more sense.

'Suki!' she exclaimed, and bustled over, through the reefs of parting steam, to the girl.

'I brought it, Grandma,' Suki declared, and produced a bundle of wax paper in which the venison loin had been carefully wrapped. 'But, look, I brought something else.'

Prudence looked Constable Littleton up and down.

'Pleased to be of service,' the constable saluted.

But it hadn't been the constable Suki meant. She was producing her second object, the copy of *The Body in the Beck*, when Prudence declared, 'It was Numbers who confirmed it. Suki, twenty-five years ago – five years before she married Maxwell Pendlebury – Alice Frith had a child.'

Suki said, 'Oh . . .'

'It's the one thing Maxwell Pendlebury always wanted. An heir, to carry his fortune. And what a fortune he has, Suki – Numbers dug it out. He pored through the records for Countrywide Finance, up at Companies House. Maxwell Pendlebury, one of only three shareholding directors in that company. He's worth seven million pounds.'

'But that would mean that there's a seven million pound inheritance?' Suki whispered.

'And, without an heir, Alice is due to inherit. But put yourself in Maxwell's shoes, Suki. Remember what we know about Alice Pendlebury – or, rather, what we know about the woman Alice Frith used to be. She has a child out there, Suki. His name is Matthew Stapledon. She gave him up for adoption, twenty-five years ago this summer, and he was raised in a humble little family on the Norfolk Fens. Now imagine this: Maxwell Pendlebury, who has guarded his fortune like a dragon to his hoard all of his life, has no heir to bequeath his life's treasures to. He knows it will go to his wife, who has always had a wandering eye. And he knows, one day, that – if the circumstances are right – it might find its way to her bastard son, given up all those years ago. The son Alice Frith bore for another man; the son she could never give him, no matter how much he craved it.' Prudence paused. 'Numbers found the birth certificate in the county records office. It's all been digitised, he tells me. Well, I suppose technology marches on. She refused to name a father on the paperwork, Suki, but we've been in this manor long enough to hazard a guess as to who that father might be. The man, perhaps, that we know Alice was drawn to all those years ago. The man whose secret offspring Maxwell Pendlebury would hate inheriting his money more than anyone else. The man who's been his closest friend, and closest rival, for all of their lives.' Prudence paused. 'Rupert Prendergast,' she whispered.

In a second, Suki had produced her copy of *The Body in the Beck* and opened it up to the photographic plate section. Slapping it down on the counter, she directed Prudence's eye to the page. Even Constable Littleton, bewildered beyond measure by the conversation going on in this kitchen, crowded in to see.

'What am I looking at?' Prudence whispered, adjusting her spectacles.

'Maybe you're right, Grandma. Maybe there's motive in Maxwell Pendlebury and this story of his wife's secret son. Or maybe – just maybe – it's a little more complicated than that. Take a look at that picture. Read the caption.' She paused, waited until the wild, outlandish idea had sunk in. 'Grandma, I think it's been here all along. I think it explains everything that's happened here in the manor since the moment Deirdre Shaw arrived. And I think it might finally explain what happened here on the twenty-eighth of August 1886.' Suki paused. 'Grandma, I think we can solve two murders tonight.'

'Serve up supper,' said Prudence, marvelling at the picture she'd just seen and all its manifold ramifications.

'Yes, Grandma. And serve up some justice as well.'

Chapter Thirteen

Mrs Mathers had appeared in the kitchen doorway, her face flushed red with anticipation. 'They're all seated, Mrs Bulstrode. All drinking their aperitifs. You're not going to be much longer, are you? You haven't got much more to—'

Prudence, who had been steadfastly ignoring Mrs Mathers fretting about in the doorway, looked up from the counter where she'd been arranging the slices of thin venison loin with warm shallots, horseradish crème fraiche and segments of peeled, charred orange. Without the time to marinade the venison and let it mature, she'd seared it on a hot griddle pan – and now it sat, rich and vibrant, as the star of the dish. Rupert Prendergast might guess, she supposed, that it hadn't come from the deer he'd killed this afternoon – but that wouldn't matter, not by the time dinner was through.

'Are you ready, Mrs Bulstrode?'

Prudence cast her eyes around the kitchen. For half an hour now, she'd been the only one here. This was when she liked working in kitchens the best – when, left to her own devices, she could simply *create*. Well, some joy had been sucked out of the creation tonight but it had, at least, been replaced by a different feeling; a feeling that some terrible wrong was about to be put right; the feeling that, by the time the pheasant was being served up, a murderer would be unmasked. Deirdre Shaw might not have been her true friend in life – indeed, they might have snubbed each other at parties, avoided each other on the demo circuit, steadfastly refused to attend village fetes where the other was due to make a guest appearance – but, in death, she would be grateful for what Prudence would do this evening.

'I'm as ready as I'll ever be, Mrs Mathers,' she declared. 'Service, please.'

Flick Garrick had been waiting at the bottom of the service stairs, just beyond the kitchen door, and soon she joined Mrs Mathers to ferry the starters to the trolley waiting above. For her own part, Prudence remained behind. At a private dinner like this, only twenty minutes would separate the appearance of the starters and the appearance of the main course. The pheasants were already well-rested, but she would need to work in a blitz to get them carved and the plates looking perfect before Mrs Mathers and Flick Garrick returned.

Before she set to work, she went to the windows over the sink and, scouring them clean of condensation with the sleeve of her blouse, looked out over the kitchen garden and the moonlit estate beyond. There were no headlights approaching the manor from the woodland trail, no silhouettes tramping along the orchard wall to enter by the kitchen-garden door. Inwardly, she cursed. It wouldn't be long, she told herself. They'd be here soon.

Nearly twenty minutes later, when the pheasant breasts were perched atop their celeriac rostis, themselves perched atop luxuriant swirls of parsnip puree, with ramekins filled with buttery winter greens and little porcelain jugs brimming with creamy mushroom sauce, Mrs Mathers and Flick returned to the kitchen doors. Though they seemed hesitant to come in – like penitents, thought Prudence, turning up at a temple, caps in hand! – she did not encourage them. It was better this way. 'I'll help,' she declared – and soon, though the whole thing seemed frightfully peculiar to Mrs Mathers, Prudence herself was bustling the plates up the service stairs, arranging them on the trolley waiting in the reception hall above.

'We'll take it from here, Mrs Bulstrode,' Mrs Mathers said, wrestling the trolley from Prudence to wheel it away.

But the time had come, thought Prudence. Suki and Constable Littleton might not have returned, not quite yet, but she would have to get the party started. They would simply have to join it when they arrived. With a little good fortune – and, God knows, they deserved some this weekend – they might even arrive at the most opportune moment.

'I wouldn't hear of it, Mrs Mathers. It's the main course. I should like to see it served myself.'

Mrs Mathers froze. 'It's rather ... irregular, Mrs Bulstrode. We sometimes have our private chefs take a bow after dinner is served. You know, when the dessert has been cleared away and everyone's enjoying a little dessert wine. But to appear in the middle of ...'

Prudence knew Mrs Mathers was right. The very idea of the chef waltzing in there while dinner was being served – it broke the spell, it diminished the sorcery, it put everyone on edge; it was like a writer who sits on the arm of their reader's chair, listening out for every 'ooh' and 'aah' as they turn the pages. Nobody wants to be scrutinised like that, thought Prudence, but the time for petty worries was long gone. Tonight's dinner was going to taste perfect – but, one way or another, it was going to be ruined. So Prudence simply shrugged and, letting Mrs Mathers take control of the trolley, walked abreast of her as they approached the dining-room doors.

As she followed Mrs Mathers through, she saw the shooting party as if for the very first time. Rupert Prendergast was sitting, in a midnight-blue evening jacket, at the head of the table, with Georgette – dressed in satin – at his left-hand side, and Richard (dressed, as if for a family portrait, in the exact same colour and cut as his father) at his right. On one side of the long table, Terence Knight and Gray Williams sat, more casually dressed but still with a formal air, while Maxwell Pendlebury dominated the opposite end to Rupert, with Alice sitting on his right, and in his shadow.

As Prudence followed Mrs Mathers through, Rupert Prendergast considered her sourly. Then, remembering the occasion, he said, 'You worked wonders with my deer, Mrs Bulstrode. If that's what you call tough shoe leather, well, I should like to see what wonders you can work with a doe that's been left to hang.'

'It's the taste of the kill,' smiled Maxwell, from the opposite end of the table. Then, as Flick slid his main course into place in front of him, he said, 'It's just a shame we aren't eating our own birds tonight. For old times' sake.'

There seemed to be no better opening than this. Prudence steeled herself, as Flick Garrick slid the final plate in front of Rupert Prendergast, and said, 'Be thankful you're not eating your own birds this evening. I'm afraid there's no doubt about it any more – your very lives depended on it.'

Rupert Prendergast, who had already started forking at the pheasant on his plate, gaped as he let his knife clatter on to the tabletop. Apart from that ringing sound, there was silence in the dining room.

'Mrs Bulstrode,' Rupert began, 'I wondered why you'd shown your face so early, but now I'm instructing you, as your employer, to scurry back to your kitchen and set about our desserts. In short, madam, to *do what you are paid for*. I'll have no more interruptions this evening. This is a joyous occasion.'

'A joyous occasion that, if everything had gone to plan this weekend, would have ended up with a corpse.' Prudence paused while every eye in the room opened fractionally wider and focused upon her. 'I'm sorry, Mr Prendergast, but there can be no doubt. Deirdre Shaw did not perish of a heart attack, out there in the rhubarb. But nor was she murdered. She was an innocent victim of a scheme that would have seen one of you dead tonight. She was killed by a pheasant, poisoned with hemlock

– but the pheasant wasn't meant to be eaten by her. It was Deirdre's rotten luck that she lifted that particular pheasant down from the hook in the larder and roasted it for herself.' She paused. 'And it was your good luck, Alice, that she did exactly that – because, if she didn't, the pheasant you would have been served tonight, the pheasant that's on the plate in front of you, right now, would have been the last meal you ever ate. This would have been your last supper.'

There was uproar at the table. In an instant, Rupert Prendergast was on his feet, remonstrating with Prudence, a single, meaty finger extended and wagging at her like he was telling off a particularly truculent hound. 'Mrs Bulstrode, this is quite enough! You don't know your place, woman! By the sounds of you, you don't know your own mind! What happened to Mrs Shaw is regrettable, but you can't sashay in here to tell us that one of our number ought to be dead – and, worse still, that somebody at this table had planned it!'

Prudence steadied herself. It was easy to feel intimidated under a barrage from Rupert Prendergast, but somehow his words sloughed off her tonight. 'Oh, Mr Prendergast,' she ventured – and was relieved, at that moment, to hear a door latch clicking somewhere beyond the dining-room doors, and the unmistakeable sound of Suki and Constable Littleton talking as they came along the hall, 'I didn't say it was somebody around this table. Oh, you've all got reason enough to stab each other in the back. Old friends, eh? But no, none of you schemed to turn this valedictory return to

Farleigh Manor into the perfect moment for murder. None of *you* did – but, Mr Prendergast, you're not the only ones at the manor.'

Prudence turned around. As her eyes gravitated to the dining-room doors, they landed first on Mrs Mathers – who recoiled, as if under some terrible accusation herself – and Flick Garrick, who backed bodily away, barely able to comprehend what was happening.

Then the dining-room doors opened. In walked Suki, side by side with Constable Littleton – still in his lilac spandex, but now draped in an old fur coat he'd borrowed to ward off the nocturnal chill.

Standing behind them, his own face creased up in confusion, was Hubert Lowell.

'Mr Lowell,' said Prudence. 'I'm glad you could join us. Come in, come in.'

Even Rupert Prendergast was silenced now. Around the table, partners took each other's hands; even Alice, despite the depth of her animosity toward her husband, reached out for her husband's touch – and, no matter what the cocktail of emotions coursing through him, he allowed her that little comfort. She was shaking, thought Prudence – and shaking more perceptibly still ever since Hubert Lowell had walked into the room. That was the exact moment when any shred of doubt she'd been harbouring vanished into thin air. The way Alice looked at Lowell; the way he refused to look at her. The truth was exploding in the air all around them.

Lowell looked around, intense suspicion deepening the creases on his face.

He hardly looked the same as the man Prudence and Suki had seen in the pages of *The Body in the Beck*, standing cheerily between the Farleigh twins that summer before they died.

He hardly looked the same, but half a century had passed since then – and it was undoubtedly the same man.

'I'm told you wanted me, Mr Prendergast,' Lowell ventured, warily – though, even now, he must have known that Suki and Constable Littleton had lied.

Rupert Prendergast turned his withering eye on Prudence. 'You'd better explain yourself this instant, Mrs Bulstrode – and it better be good. I'll ruin you if it isn't. If you've come here just to destroy my friend's final weekend among his loved ones, I'll—'

'There'll be no need for that, Mr Prendergast,' piped up Constable Littleton. 'Mrs Bulstrode's explained everything to me, and I'm quite sure she has the truth uncovered.'

Every eye in the room considered the man, standing at the door in a fur coat and lilac spandex, and goggled.

'Who's this lump?' Maxwell Pendlebury began.

'Constable Alfie Littleton, sir. I'm here to make an arrest.'

There would have been some spluttered guffaws around the table – a man dressed like that could hardly arrest his own sense of shame, let alone a fully grown human being – but Prudence immediately weighed in, 'I didn't come here, this weekend, thinking it would end like this. But then again, I'm sure none of you came here this weekend expecting that one of you might have been murdered. Deirdre saved you from that, by giving her own life in your stead, Alice. I believe she even knew it, by the end. But perhaps that's getting ahead of ourselves. If you want the truth of the matter, we have to go back twenty-three years – to that last summer of the old millennium. A bygone age.

'That, of course, was the Prendergast heyday. You'd been coming here for fourteen years already, ever since that glorious summer in 1985. A tradition is a fine thing, isn't it? Those youthful, perfect summer days. An age when new romances could blossom. Where new loves could bloom. Those weekends you came here were always hotbeds of romance, weren't they? Well, weekends outside of normal life very often are. And you, Alice, you always enjoyed yourself, didn't you? There was always some romance in the air for the Alice Frith of old.'

Maxwell Pendlebury was burning vermilion at Prudence's impudence, and in particular these mentions of his wife's impropriety of yesteryear – but it was Rupert himself who weighed in. 'I don't see what Alice's love life has got to do with anything. She's been happily married for nearly twenty years, damn it.'

'Yes,' said Prudence, 'you tied the knot with Maxwell and remained devoted ever since then – well, it had always been your plan to marry rich and be taken care of, hadn't it, Alice? To have your fun, break a few hearts, perhaps have yours broken along the way – but then to find a man of not inconsiderable means, someone who could both adore you and keep you, long into the ever after. And why not? Plenty of people marry for much less, and – going by the comments in the manor's guest-book – I don't think there's any doubt about the sincerity of your feelings for Maxwell.' She paused. 'But that isn't where this thing starts. This thing starts before Maxwell, when you were interested in other things. Other passions, Alice. Other men. Men like . . .' She turned over her shoulder to where Suki and Constable Littleton stood with Lowell, who was nervously sipping from a hip flask from his belt. 'Men like the estate gamekeeper, Hubert Lowell.'

At the table, voices were raised in disapproval. 'Slander,' Maxwell was saying, 'absolute slander!' while Georgette rose from her seat to try and calm her husband down, and Terence Knight and Gray Williams bowed their heads together to whisper privately among themselves. Alone at the table, Richard Prendergast kept his head down low, desperate for this to be over.

'I'm afraid it's true,' Prudence resumed. 'You see, there's a moment in the visitors' log, Alice, in the summer of 1999, when you quite clearly state that you've met the love of your life. Your future husband, here, chips in with a comment of his own – and to any passing reader, it probably seems that this was the moment when the two of you truly clicked. But it isn't the case, is it? You didn't marry until four years later. The man you'd fallen in love with that weekend wasn't Maxwell. It was Mr Lowell. It must have been an intense feeling – a highborn lady like you, and the cheap and cheerful gamekeeper on the estate. The stuff out of a bestselling bonkbuster, perhaps.

But it kept drawing you back to Farleigh Manor, across the next years, didn't it? It's clear in the visitors' log – you spent the next years here whenever you could. Oh, yes, you still came for Mr Prendergast's parties but, between times, almost every excuse you had, you came to Farleigh. With family and other friends. Alone, even, if I'm reading the guestbook correctly. But it wasn't love for Farleigh Manor itself that drew you here. It was love for Hubert Lowell.'

Lowell's voice erupted from the corner, the hip flask dropping from his lips and back to his pocket, 'Alice, it's not what she's saying. She's stark raving—'

'Oh, shut up, Hube!' Alice snapped. Then she turned, doe-eyed, to her husband. 'It was nothing, Max, and it was before you. One summer, that's all, and an age before we—'

'One summer?' Lowell breathed, aghast in the corner. '*One* summer? By God, Alice, it was my life.'

'But not yours, Alice,' Prudence said, her voice heavy with the sadness of the revelation, the hearts that were being exposed and broken, right now, in this room. 'You always knew that, sooner or later, you were going to make a better match. Whatever was drawing you to Mr Lowell here, it wasn't enough to sustain you for a lifetime. You could never imagine a life like that, could you? Just the *gamekeeper's* wife? So, when Maxwell Pendlebury – older and wiser, richer and with so much more to offer a lady with your kind of aspirations – declared his hand, you willingly walked away from the love you felt for Mr Lowell and embraced a different life instead.' Prudence

255

hesitated, just long enough to let the idea settle – like the most bitter kind of snowfall – across the room, but not long enough for any of the party to interrupt. Then she went on, 'You forgot about Hubert, didn't you, Alice? Oh, he was here when you came back to the estate – and for a time he was able to pretend. But you never truly forgot about her, did you, Hubert?' Prudence turned to him now.

'It festered in you, didn't it?' asked Suki. 'Those summers she came here, flaunting Maxwell on her arm – that big diamond ring on her finger . . .'

'And then?' said Prudence. 'Then you found out.'

There was silence in the dining room – until, at last, Maxwell Pendlebury breathed, 'Found out what?'

Prudence looked at Alice, who was visibly shaking in her seat. One of her hands was still entwined in her husband's; the other gripped the edge of the table, its knuckles turning white. 'Alice,' said Prudence, 'would you like to do this part?'

But Alice didn't look at Prudence. She looked at Lowell instead. 'Hubert, you fool – it's the ancient past. The past! It's done and dusted and—'

'Oh, it's never quite done,' said Prudence, 'not something like this. Alice, you might remember that night when you were sick and I came to the bathroom, thinking I ought to help. You told me I'd poisoned you – and, of course, you were quite right, not that we knew it at the time. But you said something else, something that didn't occur to me as significant until much later. You spoke of morning sickness from a time long ago. But, of course, you and Mr Pendlebury never did have a child – as much as you both might have wanted it. The child you had came before that, and you didn't raise him for your own. You had Hubert Lowell's child, and you gave him up for adoption. Well, we've already established, haven't we, that you could never accept that lowly kind of life, that you were always focused on a much bigger prize. It seems nothing was going to stand in your way – not love for Mr Lowell, not even love for your own flesh and blood.'

Maxwell ripped his hand away from Alice – and it was only then that Prudence knew, for certain, that her original theory had not an iota of truth in it; Maxwell Pendlebury hadn't known about his wife's child, and the knowledge was like a dagger in his side.

'I should have known something was strange when I saw that book in your cottage, Mr Lowell,' Suki said. 'Not Deirdre Shaw's *Game Night*. The other, dog-eared one, hidden in the alcove. *So You're Going to Be a Parent . . .*'

'She told me she was pregnant,' Lowell trembled. 'I thought we'd start a life together. A proper life, not just stolen weekends. I got that book and I read it every night, picturing you both at my cottage, picturing the life we might have led. But then . . .' Lowell's voice started fraying, his words splintering apart. 'She called me one day and told me she'd miscarried. That our child was gone – and that was the end of that. That was the end of *us*.'

'You never got over it,' said Prudence.

'I thought I had. But then . . .'

Prudence looked at Alice, whose face was now streaked with tears. Maxwell had kicked his way back from the table, each hand clutching the arm of his chair like he needed to hold on to something or else fall clean away.

'Can't you stop this?' Rupert Prendergast asked – and, for the first time, Prudence detected not arrogance and conceit in his voice, but genuine concern. 'Maxwell's heart, it can't take this kind of—'

'I'm sorry,' said Alice, and she was saying it to both Maxwell and Lowell. 'How did you find out?'

Lowell whispered, 'A fluke. Just rotten luck. I saw his face on the television news. Some race he'd won at college. Some award he'd been given. He looked just like you, Alice. Or – he looked just like me. The perfect mixture of the two of us. It got my mind whirring. It wasn't hard, after that. I found a birth certificate in the county records – but, of course, there was no father's name given. You'd eliminated me from your life, and you'd eliminated me from his. I never even got a chance. But you hadn't been back to Farleigh in years by then. I hoped, to hell, I'd never set eyes on you again.'

'So imagine how it felt when, several months ago, you realised that the Prendergasts were returning for a reunion weekend,' said Prudence. 'That Alice Pendlebury would be here too. Something exploded in you, didn't it, Mr Lowell? And you decided, there and then, that you would settle old scores.'

Hubert Lowell's face had been creasing all this time, but now it turned as livid purple as a bruise. 'You're barking mad, woman! She's sitting there – right there, as alive as anybody else! A man can't be convicted of murder

258

when his victim's sitting there, about to tuck into a nice plate of dinner!'

'But you already know, Mr Lowell, that your poison found its way into somebody else. Deirdre Shaw didn't die of a heart attack, and she knew it, even in those final moments of her life. You see' – and here Prudence sashayed across the room to take Suki's iPhone, on which she'd been recording the revelations on her camera, straight out of her hand – 'I always knew there was something meaningful about that rhubarb patch. Rhubarb wasn't on the menu Deirdre had devised. Why, I kept wondering, had Deirdre gone out there and started ferreting around in the patch for whatever rhubarb stalks had survived past summer's end? It didn't make sense. Well, not to me – not then. Not until I remembered Deirdre's lifelong hatred of the fruit. And not until, thanks to her husband James's waspish memoir here, I remembered why. Deirdre's hatred of rhubarb started early in life. Her mother used to stew it, and stew it badly – it made Deirdre so sick, and her mother was so insistent on her polishing it off that it rather became a trigger for her. Mr Lowell, to put it plainly: rhubarb always made Deirdre vomit. It had ever since she was a girl. So when she realised she'd been poisoned, when the tell-tale signs of it started tremoring up and down her body, she did the only thing she could think of – she went to make herself sick, in the hope that it might save her. She was too late, of course.'

'Just like it was too late for Biscuit, when we tried to feed her the hydrogen peroxide from your store,' said Suki.

'Ah, Biscuit,' said Prudence, 'another innocent in all of this. Because you lost control of your poison, didn't you, Mr Lowell? Along came Suki and I to pick up where Deirdre had left off – and the very first thing we did was use the carcass from the pheasant you'd poisoned, the pheasant you swapped for the one Alice had shot on that first day's hunt, to make a soup for our guests. There was enough poison in the bones of that bird to put one of this party in hospital, and to send everybody else to their toilet bowls in the dead of night – everybody except Rupert, who hadn't touched a drop.'

'Consommé,' Rupert scoffed. 'I need some real meat in my broth.'

'When you found out what I'd done, you knew straight away what had happened – you realised, somehow, that the poison had got further than you intended. And you knew you needed to stop it before more innocent people died. That's why, while Suki and I were out shopping in Nutwood St Knowle and most of the guests here were out taking in the fresh air, recovering from the privations of that night, you staged a robbery right here, in the manor house kitchens, and took the pheasants from the larder. Everything else was cover. You feared you'd made a dreadful mistake, switched out the wrong birds, or that the taint had somehow spread while they were hanging in the larder. So you took them and you burnt them on one of your pyres in the woodland. We can only guess, after that, how the poison found its way to Biscuit. Personally, I don't believe it came from those pheasants. But, by the sight of those scorched patches in the woodland, those controlled fires you've been setting, there was more than enough hemlock out there for it to have found its way into Biscuit's food chain somehow. I'm right, aren't I, Mr Lowell? You'd been cultivating the hemlock since summer.'

Lowell just stared at her.

'Which brings us,' Prudence declared, 'to Jack and Mary Farleigh – and the last time there was a murder at Farleigh Manor.'

Lowell's eyes flared. 'How do you know about that?' he snapped, and took another swig, long and deep, from his hip flask.

At his side, Suki produced the copy of *The Body in the Beck*.

'It was right here,' she said, 'here all along.' She opened the book to the photographic section and held it up so that everyone in the room had the chance to see the elderly Jack and Mary Farleigh standing with the youthful Hubert Lowell, that glorious summer in 1971. 'As soon as I saw it, something clicked at the back of my mind. Mr Lowell, it's where you got the idea, isn't it? The hemlock . . .'

Lowell backed away, only to find Constable Littleton standing – steadfast, in fur coat and lilac spandex – in the doorway. Behind him, the door had been quietly locked.

'Mr Lowell, I believe only you can tell this part of it.'

Lowell stammered before he said, 'Jack and Mary were good to me. I was only a lad. My father had served them half of their lives, and I was going to take over. The beautiful, far-ranging Farleigh estate. I didn't know them for long. The last year or two of their lives.'

'But they liked you, didn't they, Mr Lowell?'

'I was a good boy. I didn't judge them. I didn't hold truck with all the whispers and rumours down at Nutwood St Knowle. I didn't much like the company of other people either. I think they liked that about me. A couple of recluses, who'd found one of their own.'

'Figuring this out means going back even further in time,' said Prudence, 'and finally solving the riddle of what happened to Jane Sutcliffe. I can hazard a guess, Mr Lowell. If you won't give voice to it yourself, perhaps you might tell me if I'm going far wrong?' She waited for Lowell to reply, but when there was only stony silence, she began, 'I think it's fair to say, by all the reports, that Jane Sutcliffe was a cruel woman – hired more for her good looks than for her child-caring capacities. The children could see it, even if their father – quickly besotted by the young woman – could not. We can imagine how that felt for the Farleigh twins, and we can imagine, too, how they might have started plotting ways to get rid of their cruel mistress. It wouldn't be beyond the imagination of children. And we know, of course, how imaginative they were . . .'

It was at this point that Suki cut in. Still brandishing *The Body in the Beck*, she flicked through its pages and said, 'Mary Farleigh spent all her waking hours inventing stories about the fairies who lived here at the estate. The Farleigh Fairies, she called them. If you browse the library carefully, you can still see the way she decorated the margins of all her father's old books.' She paused. 'But it's Jack Farleigh where the secret lies – and, if we're right, Mr

Lowell, it was Jack Farleigh who had the idea. Jack, you see, had always been fascinated by the flowers and trees and plants of the estate. It's not beyond the realm of comprehension to think he knew about poisonous mushrooms, and belladonna, and poison hemlock. It's not beyond the realm of comprehension to think that, between them, they—'

At once, Lowell exploded, 'What do you know of them, to put words in their mouths? What do you know, just from some tittle-tattle book you've picked up, spouting off its gibberish, like all of the others? You didn't know them,' he snapped, '*I* knew them.'

'Then perhaps you might tell it, Mr Lowell,' said Prudence. 'Because we're right, aren't we? Something about the easy smiles and carefree manner in that photograph – it doesn't speak to two haughty landowners and the gamekeeper's lad jobbing on their estate. It speaks to . . . friendship, of a kind.'

'Aye, that's right, they were my friends.'

'And they told you, didn't they? They confided in you. They . . . confessed?'

Lowell's eyes darted around the room. He lifted his hip flask, took another deep swig, as if to give him courage.

'They didn't mean it to be murder. There wasn't an ounce of badness in Jack and Mary Farleigh – I don't care how many books have painted them as the devil's children over the years. They only meant it as a childhood game. A prank, perhaps you'd call it now. Something to stop her hectoring. Something to stop her from bullying them whenever their mother wasn't looking. The thought of a picnic, down on Hill Beck, used to fill them with glee. But Jane Sutcliffe had a way about her, a way of turning everything to ruin. All they wanted was to be left alone. A picnic, down by the beck, without her needling at them and barking and controlling everything they did. They weren't to know it would kill her. They'd read about it, right there in the library, in one of their father's books – how hemlock tea would put you to sleep for a hundred years. Well, to a couple of bairns with their heads filled with fairy stories, that seemed simple enough. How were they to know what it really meant? How were they to know that, in the real world, folks don't go to sleep for a hundred years? They die.' He stopped, panting heavily, as if the exertion of summoning the memory had worn him out. 'When they realised she was dead, they tried to revive her. Dragged her down to the beck, as if the water might bring her back. But it never did – and, nearly ninety years later, they were still carrying that day around them, like a shroud.'

'Until they confessed to you,' said Prudence.

'Aye, and passed on not five months later.'

'They needed to unburden themselves,' said Prudence. 'To release themselves from the secret, so that they could pass on in peace. But what if they'd known, Hubert, that that deed of theirs would one day give rise to a second, altogether nastier, planned murder? What might they have thought if they'd known they were *your* inspiration? Because it's where you got the idea, isn't it, Mr Lowell? When murder came to your mind, and you wondered how it might be done, it was only natural that you'd turn to their story. Because they got away with it. And so could you. You would make sure that Alice ingested hemlock, just as Jane Sutcliffe did; you'd make sure she dropped dead, right here in this dining table, while you were somewhere far away. So you set about raising your pheasants for the autumn shoot – and, somewhere along the way, you took one from your pens and fed it on hemlock seeds, until the poison that killed it imbued every piece of sinew and flesh in its body.'

'We can guess you did it more than once, Mr Lowell,' interjected Suki. 'A stunt like this, you'd need to practise. The bonfires around your home, they're filled with the leftover bones and bits of carcass from things you've had to get rid of. What's the bet that, among all that, are the carcasses of your early test birds? And what's the bet that it's one of those carcasses that Biscuit pulled off a fire and ate, so that the poison was suddenly in her body too?'

Lowell's face had creased, and his eyes shimmered with tears. 'Biscuit,' he whispered, agonised, to himself – and it struck Prudence as tragic, then, that the man wept more for his beloved English setter than he did for the human life he had taken.

Then she remembered the cross on the rhubarb patch and thought: in the end, when he realised what he'd done, the man did have a heart. It had itself been poisoned and withered across the years, but it was still there, beating inside him.

Suddenly, the windows of the dining room at Farleigh Manor were strobed with blue lights. Alice Pendlebury didn't notice; she was on her knees, at Maxwell's side,

265

scrabbling to take his hand – even as he remained rigid, refusing to take it. All other eyes turned to the sweeping windows along one side of the room. Mrs Mathers hurried there, her eyes agog, to watch the lights approaching.

'Aha!' announced Constable Littleton, his fur coat swishing around him as he crossed the room to stand at Mrs Mathers's side. 'The cavalry is here. But I suppose it should be the lead officer who makes this arrest.' He turned, accidentally flamboyant, to Hubert Lowell, still propped in the corner, and said, 'Hubert Lowell, I am hereby arresting you for the manslaughter of—'

'Don't bother, boy,' said Lowell, and took the very last swig from his hip flask. After he was done, he cast it down and let it crash across the floor. 'I won't be going anywhere – not tonight, and not ever. Farleigh's been my home, man and boy. It's Farleigh where I'll stay. Farleigh where I'll—'

'Now, look here!' declared Constable Littleton, and flashed across the room, a vision of lilac. 'I am a man of the law, and you, sir, have committed one of the gravest offences on the statute books. Whether you come to the station in Nutwood St Knowle with us or not isn't a matter of personal choice. It isn't like you're sitting here, at this fine table, deciding whether you'd like red wine or white wine, gravy or redcurrant jelly. You're under arrest, in the name of the law, and that's the end of—'

'Constable,' said Prudence. 'Constable?'

Constable Littleton looked around. While he had been pontificating at Lowell, Prudence had bowed down to

266

pick up the hip flask from the dining-room floor. Now she held it to her nose, breathing in its fumes deeply.

'Oh, Mr Lowell,' she said, with a terrible sadness. Because the scent she was breathing in wasn't the tang of some alcoholic spirit; it was grassy and earthy, wild and of the woodland. The hip flask itself had retained some of the warmth of the mixture he'd been drinking all evening. 'Hemlock tea?' she whispered.

Suki's eyes opened in fright.

'The same mixture Jack and Mary gave Jane Sutcliffe,' Lowell said. Then, taking out a handkerchief, he dabbed at the sweat now beading on his brow. 'Let them in, Constable, but there'll be no taking me away.' His hand was already clutching his stomach. Prudence fancied she could see a distant, faraway look in his eyes. 'Let me end it like the Farleighs did – right here, in their home, just where they belonged.'

Prudence could hear the constabulary hammering at the manor door. She rushed to Lowell's side, waving Constable Littleton and Suki past, out into the hall.

Prudence did not know why, but she called out for Mrs Mathers to bring her a stool. When it arrived, Lowell simply waved it away. 'I should like to stand for this last bit.' The poison was working its effect on him now; Prudence fancied it had been the same for Deirdre, and pictured her feebly staggering out into the kitchen garden, scrabbling in the rhubarb with what fleeting moments she had left. 'Alice,' Hubert Lowell said, and, though she was still trying to cajole Maxwell into taking her hand, she looked up to meet his gaze. 'I'm sorry.'

267

She might have mouthed the words too; Prudence wasn't sure – because, at that moment, Constable Littleton returned, leading a phalanx of officers dressed rather more appropriately for an arrest.

It didn't matter. Though Hubert Lowell was still alive, by the time the officers had hustled through the doors, he was sliding out of all reason, clutching his belly and crashing back against the dining-room wall. How long did hemlock take to kill? What was it Numbers had said? Half an hour, an hour, depending on the concentration of the tea you'd imbibed. Lowell had known the game was up ever since Suki came for him at his cottage; he was ending it on his terms, in the only way he knew how.

'Time to end the secrets at Farleigh Manor,' he uttered – and those were his last lucid words.

They didn't have time to get the handcuffs on Hubert Lowell.

He was already gone.

Chapter Fourteen

Farleigh Manor sat under an azure sky the following morning. The late autumn sun sparkled on the waters of Hill Beck. It lit up the ancient chimneystacks on top of the manor house roof. It dazzled the eyes of Rupert Prendergast, Maxwell Pendlebury, Terence Knight and all the rest as they drove, in convoy, down the long, snaking drive – never to return to Farleigh Manor, and all of its memories, for as long as they lived.

And, in the secluded orchard behind the kitchen garden, it dappled the earth upon which Prudence Bulstrode and her grand-daughter Suki stood, quietly considering the graves of Jack and Mary Farleigh.

'Perhaps that's it,' said Suki. 'Ghosts laid to rest, Grandma.'

Prudence nodded. She'd spent the morning carefully clipping away the thistles and nettles that had flourished, unchecked, across the Farleigh twins' graves. Apart from anything else, it was a good reason not to be doing her ordinary duty, standing on the gravel drive with Mrs Mathers and Flick Garrick, wishing the guests a fond farewell. Not one of them, it seemed, had wanted to speak to her anyway; Rupert Prendergast had been up before dawn, harrying Georgette and Richard until they were packed and ready to be on their way. She did not feel sad for Rupert – but, in the end, she had felt wretched for Maxwell Pendlebury, and threaded through that was some modicum of shame that, at one point, she had thought him the mastermind behind the murder. As controlling a bully as he might have been, the secrets of last night would blight what remained of his life.

The graves were tidied, and on to each of the long-flattened burial mounds, Suki and Prudence placed small bouquets, taken from the manor. The gesture was small – but, Prudence thought, significant. The Farleighs had been buried unattended, their lives uncelebrated. An eternity of condemnation for a childhood mistake seemed the saddest miscarriage of justice, to Prudence.

But as for Hubert Lowell . . .

'Do you think they might bury him there?' asked Suki, as they drifted away through the plum and apple trees, under the brick arch and into the kitchen garden – where Mrs Mathers was quietly tidying away the cross that had been so hastily erected on the rhubarb patch, a symbol of Hubert Lowell's regret. 'I think it's what he would have wanted. He didn't have any other family, did he? But the Farleighs had liked him – and, well, it feels like they're tied together somehow, doesn't it? Bound up for eternity?'

Prudence wasn't sure she held much truck with eternity, but if there was anything that could bind people together, she supposed it was a secret like murder. 'But I like to think the secrets are done with now, Suki. I like to think that Farleigh could have a different life, perhaps even build a different reputation.'

Mrs Mathers looked up as they approached. 'All gone,' she said, and dusted her hands as if just finishing up some horrendous household task. 'Mr Knight and Mr Williams were the last to leave. The kindest among that lot, if you ask me, but I somehow doubt we'll see a soul among them again.'

And perhaps that was for the best, thought Prudence. It was like when her Nicholas had died: sometimes you needed to draw a line and tell yourself 'that was the past, but out here is the future'.

'Can I help you with your cases, Mrs Bulstrode?' said Mrs Mathers, as she danced after them, through the kitchen-garden door, up the service stairs and into the manor house entrance hall. 'I've given Flick a few days off. I'm afraid she's terribly thrown by the whole business. She was so fond of Mr Lowell, you see – Mr Lowell and that dog of his. I wonder if she'll come back at all.'

'And you, Mrs Mathers?'

The manor was empty, and it echoed with their voices. 'Well, I rather think things might feel different here from now on. There'll be a new gamekeeper on the estate, I'm sure. And perhaps – well, once the dust's settled and the journalists have come, and everyone's written their pieces on the final unravelling of Jane Sutcliffe's death, well, perhaps it might be a kinder sort of a place.' She paused. 'It's been my life, Mrs Bulstrode. I suppose I'm like Jack and Mary Farleigh, and even Hubert Lowell, in that. I don't suppose I'm ever going to leave.'

Once their cases were ready, Mrs Mathers led them out on to the driveway – where Prudence's camper van was sitting, sparkling in the low autumn sun.

'Constable Littleton says it was the fanbelt,' Mrs Mathers explained, 'but the lads at the station were more than happy to have a new one fitted, and at short notice, in gratitude for all you did. They polished her up as well.'

She was gleaming, thought Prudence. They'd hung an air freshener above the dashboard, and cleaned all the upholstery. They'd even packed sandwiches and a flask of tea as well – something to sustain them for the long journey ahead. 'Not quite necessary,' said Prudence to Suki as they settled in and started the engine. 'I was imagining we'd stop along the way for the nation's finest service-station breakfast.'

'Grandma!' said Suki, with horror.

'I'm not a snob, Suki dear. Sometimes there's nothing better than slap-up bacon, eggs and hash browns. I shall buy you the dirtiest of burgers for lunch, if you want it. I'm sure you've had quite enough of game cooking for a lifetime.'

Suki grinned.

With the windows wound down, and the solitary figure of Mrs Mathers waving to them animatedly from the driveway, Prudence drove the camper van down the long, winding road. Soon, Farleigh Manor was receding in the distance behind them. Soon, even the beautiful, autumnal streets of Nutwood St Knowle had faded away.

It was as soon as they hit the motorways that Suki knew she was, finally, on the way home.

'Do you think they ever forgave themselves, Grandma? Jack and Mary Farleigh?'

Prudence dwelt on the question for a long time. 'Does the idea upset you, Suki?'

'A whole lifetime punished for it,' Suki said. 'Yes, I suppose it does.'

'I like to think they found their way, in the end,' said Prudence. Then, sadly, she added, 'Which is more than Hubert Lowell could ever have done, after what he did. Suki, lives are long, long things. Few of us live them perfectly. Even fewer resort to murder. But I do believe there's compassion in all of us. I like to think that Jack and Mary Farleigh found compassion for themselves, in the end.'

'At least they had each other.'

They drove on – until, sometime later, the signs for a service station started flashing by. Suki could feel her stomach grumbling, even now. It was like it *knew*.

'I don't suppose you'll get paid for this weekend, will you, Grandma?'

'I rather think not,' Prudence replied. Then, with a wry smile, she added, 'But let's not forget, of course, that *you* were never getting paid, Suki. You being here was *my* payment for all the fuss you caused with this camper.'

Suki groaned and flattened her face against the window. 'I've paid you back, Grandma – haven't I?' she asked, in plaintive fashion.

Prudence took the slip road for the service station ahead. Then she said, 'Oh, in *spades*, Suki. In absolute *spades*.'

There were only a few cars parked in the services. Prudence was guiding the camper into a parking space meant for lorries when she added, 'Do you know, it occurs to me that Mrs Mathers is right. Come the end of this week, when this news has been all over the news-papers – and, I should think, this internet of yours – there'll be a clamour of writers looking to tell the story in full. No doubt your Ms Katie Winterdale will be up at Farleigh again by Friday night. But she's not the only one who could tell this story, Suki. She wasn't there when it happened.'

Suki's face creased. 'What do you mean, Grandma?'

'Well, you're going to need something to stop you from going back to Netley Pike and Chelwood Ghyll and sliding back into your old ways. I daresay our old friend Constable Hardman is still hot on the trail of my dastardly camper-van thief. It would do you some good, I think, to keep your head down – and perhaps not attend quite as many of these late-night "raves" with your friend Numbers.'

'You've got Numbers all wrong you know, Grandma, he's really not . . .' Suki had more to say, but only now did she truly start quizzing her grandmother's words. 'You mean *me*, Grandma? Write an article?'

'Or a book, Suki. On the ground at Farleigh Manor. Well, it *was* you, my dear, who put the last piece of the jigsaw in place. If it hadn't been for you, I'd have stood up at dinner and accused Maxwell Pendlebury of orches-trating the whole thing. That photograph of Mr Lowell turned the story completely on its head.' She paused and turned off the ignition. 'Think about it, Suki. You could use something to focus you. To get those gears in that head of yours whirring, so you don't slide back to mischief.'

Prudence had already clambered out of the camper when Suki said, quietly, 'I was rather hoping I might be able to help you a little more, Grandma. You know, only if you need it. And only if you, well, might *want* me to.'

Inwardly, Prudence's heart soared. She couldn't stop a pleasure like this from bubbling up to her lips. 'Well, Suki,' she said, 'I'm sure we can think about that. You might have to work on those knife skills – and you might have to learn the difference between basil and oregano, but, yes, I daresay there'll be lots you could help with . . . if you wanted.' She paused. 'I'd hate for you to be disappointed, though. There won't always be a murder to solve.'

Suki climbed out of the camper and followed Prudence across the asphalt, bound for the service station – and the promise of the dirtiest burger within.

'Oh, murder or not, Grandma, I think I'd like to tag along. You never know what might happen.'

'No,' grinned Prudence, marvelling at Suki's newfound enthusiasm for the kitchen as they stepped inside. 'No, you never do.'

Acknowledgements

This has been a tremendously exciting journey – and to write a novel after so long in the kitchen has been a dream come true. I'd like to give my heartfelt thanks to my literary agent, Heather Holden-Brown, who has accompanied me on this adventure, and for going along with all my enthusiasm over the years. Thanks, too, to my editor Krystyna Green, who gave Prudence the chance to reach readers, and the wider team at Constable for believing in me – no book is written in isolation and Prudence couldn't have a better team around her. Lastly, I'd like to thank you, dear readers, for giving Prudence the opportunity to sit on your bookshelves! I hope, one day, that these Prudence Bulstrode mysteries are as loved in your family as the Golden Age greats have been in mine.

Read on for a sneak preview of the next
Prudence Bulstrode mystery,
The Proof in the Pudding . . .

Chapter One

'Well, Mrs Bulstrode, there you have it, just like you left them – one hundred of your finest figgy puddings, all in a row.'

One hundred and ten, thought Prudence as she perambulated up and down the shelves in the walk-in larder. A good cook always knew to make ten per cent more than she'd actually need. Well, you can always count on there being a waiter who'll trip over his own shoelaces, or somebody else who'll 'accidentally' drop one on the kitchen floor, just so he'll have something to sneak home after shift. In a lifetime of working in kitchens, Prudence had seen it all.

She'd rarely seen a walk-in larder as palatial as this one though. This was the sort of larder that suggested there might be a new world hidden at its end. She'd worked in grand kitchens smaller than this larder, which – she reflected now – felt more like a wine cellar, with different crannies for spices and condiments, an alcove dedicated to baking ingredients, a shelf full of glass jars where various starters bubbled and frothed, and corners where strings of onions, parsnips and game birds were hanging. Prudence loved larders like these. There was a real sense of exploration that came with poring through their shelves. Her figgy puddings, no matter how many of them there were, were the least remarkable thing of the lot.

'How are they looking, Mrs Bulstrode?'

Each figgy pudding was wrapped in muslin cloth, tied off with Prudence's signature crimson ribbon. They'd been maturing here for six weeks, ever since that Halloween weekend when Prudence had first driven her camper van up to the tiny Yorkshire village of Scrafton Busk and entered these hallowed kitchens. She prodded one with a finger now, then lifted it to test its weight – and, peeling back the muslin cloth just a whisper, drew in its heady scent, of nutmeg, cinnamon and sultanas. The scent of the rum was enough to get a woman sozzled, thought Prudence – and that was precisely as it should have been.

'Oh,' Prudence smiled, with some satisfaction, 'I think they'll do.' There was a twinkle in her eye as she turned around. In the larder doors, the steadfast figure of Marianne Thomas was standing as statuesque as a soldier. Marianne the Magnificent, they called her on the 'events management' circuit. (In Prudence's heyday, 'events management' hadn't been nearly as grand as it was nowadays – there'd been a time when anyone with a healthy dose of common sense and commitment could organise an event; now you had to hire a *professional*.) Marianne was willowy and blonde, but had the focus, precision and attitude of a Roman legate leading his legion to conquer an untamed land. She had a clipboard and everything. 'Have the rest of my ingredients arrived?' Prudence asked.

Marianne checked her wristwatch and Prudence heard her counting the seconds, from one to ten, beneath her breath. Then, on her waist, a little pager started buzzing. 'That will be them now, Mrs Bulstrode. But your kitchen assistant is attending – so perhaps we ought to take a tour of the dining hall?'

Kitchen assistant, thought Prudence. Well, that was what she was. But she also happened to be Prudence's grand-daughter. There was a time when the thought of Suki taking charge of a delivery would have frightened Prudence to her very soul; the words 'wayward', 'errant', 'short-sighted' and 'contrary' had been invented for girls like Suki. But she'd aided and abetted Prudence on five jobs now and, with each one, she was growing a little more skilled. Yes, Prudence thought, Suki could easily handle a delivery. 'Lead on!' she said to Marianne, and marched out of the larder, leaving the figgy puddings behind.

A barrel load of turnips cascaded over Suki's head.

'Ouch!' she cried, hopping from foot to foot. 'Ouch! Get – these – ouch!'

Suki's actual words were much more fragrant than these. The word that exploded out of her mouth when the last turnip – a brute of a vegetable, surely fit to be used as the weapon in a very bloody murder – cracked her on the side of the head was so fragrant it sent one of the Grange's front-of-house staff scuttling away in horror. Evidently, they didn't have the very worst kinds of swear words in the remote Yorkshire dales.

'I'm sorry, Miss,' said the lorry driver, standing on the platform at the back of his vehicle. He'd been angling one of the pallets onto the elevator platform when the barrel slipped free. 'I normally deliver furniture, you see. It's difficult to spill a four-poster bed, or a garden bench. We're not trained in turnips and winter greens.' Scratching his head (and finding some not inconsiderable flakes of dandruff,which he proceeded to flick away), he looked back at the crammed interior of his lorry and said, 'What are you doing, battening down for winter? There's enough food in here to feed an army.'

'The whole village,' Suki replied, rubbing the bump on her head where the turnip had tried to end her short life.

'What?'

'I said the *whole village*. We're cooking for them all.'

'The whole village? What, expecting to be cut off, are you? I'll tell you – I've had a devil getting this lorry up those snaking roads. A bit more snowfall and I'll have to spend the winter here myself.' It must have been here that the lorry driver, as dashingly handsome as a naked mole-rat, decided to chance his arm. 'Hey, you could keep me warm with some turnip soup!'

Ice cold, Suki said, 'No thank you. Just help me get this lot into the Grange, would you? Time's ticking on.'

The Grange: it sat in the heart of Scrafton Busk like an imposing castle – which, in a sense, it was. Constructed five hundred years ago, at the behest of some minor pretender to the throne – whose family had decimated itself in the War of the Roses, a big barney designed to prove whether Lancashire or Yorkshire was best – it even retained the turrets of its former fortifications. It had, the history books said (Suki's friend Numbers had been only too eager to do the research), been a singularly useless castle – positioned badly, protecting a dale which few people knew about and over which even fewer cared, it had been more vanity project than impregnable fortress. In all its days it had seen not one siege; no armies had met in glorious battle on the pastures of Scrafton Busk, no king had lost his head in its courtyard and no runaway princess taken into its tower for protection.

Just as well, then, that the National Trust had turned it into one of the most glorious visitor attractions in the whole of the county. A building that had proven pointless as a seat of power was, hundreds of years later, very much in demand as an arena for concerts, festivals, one or two party political conferences

– and tonight, a feast, the like of which Scrafton Busk had never known.

'Here,' said the lorry driver, 'I've got five sacks of King Edwards, a barrel of marmalade – I didn't know the stuff comes in barrels! – and a case of malt whisky. Hey, you don't think I could have a bottle, do you? A tip, for all this hard graft?'

Suki barely listened. She was gazing out over the snowy pastures of Scrafton Busk. In front of the Grange, the village green was an expanse of pristine white. At its heart stood the snowman the village children had made – somebody had evidently offloaded an unwanted scarf, because the poor creature was wearing a knitted monstrosity of the most lurid pink – and, arrayed around the green's edges, were all the picture-postcard houses and shops of the village, every one of them strung up in twinkling Christmas lights. By the time evening came around, Scrafton Busk would be lit up in glorious reds, greens and blues. There'd be wassailing on the green, no doubt, and sleigh bells jangling in anticipation of Christmas.

Suki's eyes did not deceive her: a red-breasted robin had landed on the snowman's top hat, and there he stood, trilling a merry tune.

Was ever a sight as perfect as this? she thought. It might as well have been taken directly from a chocolate box.

She didn't suppose anything terrible ever happened in a place as picture perfect as Scrafton Busk.

Somebody was calling her name. She turned around – just in time to get slapped in the face by a crate of iced scallops as the driver lifted it from the lorry – and saw her grandmother halloing her from the doors of the Grange.

'Just bring it all through,' said Suki, wiping a scallop from her cheek. 'If we're not in the kitchens and prepping in an hour, the evening's already lost.'

'I'll have burger and fries!' the lorry driver cackled. 'I say – burger and fries for me!' he repeated, but Suki was already gone.

Prudence was waiting for her in the doors of the Grange. 'I want to show you something,' she began, and soon Suki was following her into the heart of the building.

'This place used to be the Great Hall,' said Prudence at last. They had come to the doors of the Grange's most palatial room, a hall ten times as big as the village hall back home in Chelwood

Ghyll. It was, Suki thought, a quarter the size of a football field. Ostentatious chandeliers hung from the rafters. Christmas lights and wreaths garlanded every window in every wall. And, across its length and breadth, grand oak tables were currently being expertly laid by the Grange's very own silver service staff.

Suki was quite taken aback. She'd been on various assignments with her grandmother, but nothing quite like this.

'Well, Suki, dear,' Prudence smiled; the twinkle in her eyes told Suki that her grandmother was relishing the challenge. 'Do you think you're ready for this? One hundred villagers, all invited to the Midwinter Feast. Every man, woman and child from Scrafton Busk will be here under this roof, tonight. They'll be eating our muffin-topped winter stew. Our winter root crumble. Our lamb shank hotpot and Scarborough woof. Squidgy chocolate pears.'

'Your figgy pudding, Grandma.'

'My figgy pudding indeed. Suki, this isn't going to be easy. It's you and me against a hundred ravenous stomachs. They've been waiting all year for this. And our bosses are counting on us to give them exactly what they need. You know what's at stake . . .'

Actually, Suki wasn't quite sure. The Forward Reach Energy Corporation, who were sponsoring the event, seemed to have some vague idea about winning over the villagers by romancing their stomachs. Suki didn't quite know what for and, right now, she didn't care to ask. All that she cared about was that the clock was ticking, the lorry driver was still out there cracking jokes to himself while he spilled and bruised all their prize ingredients, and that she was still – despite her grandmother's best efforts – a novice with her knife skills.

'To the kitchens, Suki!' Prudence declared, with a flourishing smile. 'We've got quite a battle ahead!'